The Angels Will Not Care

Books by John Straley

The Angels Will Not Care

JOHN STRALEY

Grateful acknowledgment is made for:
"In Praise of Limestone" from *W.H. Auden Collected Poems* by
W.H. Auden, edited by Edward Mendelson.
Copyright © 1951 by W.H. Auden. Reprinted by permission
of Random House, Inc.

This edition first published by Soho Press in 2018
Soho Press, Inc.
853 Broadway
New York, NY 10003

Straley, John, 1953–
The angels will not care / John Straley.
Series: A Cecil Younger investigation ; 5

ISBN 978-1-61695-919-7
eISBN 978-1-61695-920-3

1. Younger, Cecil (Fictitious character)—Fiction.
2. Private investigators—Fiction. 3. Cruise ships—Fiction. 4.
Alaska—Fiction. I. Title
PS3569.T687 A82 2018 813'.54—dc23 2017055376

Printed in the United States

10 9 8 7 6 5 4 3 2 1

The blessed will not care what angle they are regarded from,
Having nothing to hide. Dear, I know nothing of
Either, but when I try to imagine a faultless love
Or the life to come, what I hear is the murmur
Of underground streams, what I see is a limestone landscape.

IN PRAISE OF LIMESTONE—W. H. Auden

The Angels Will Not Care

1

Home

It was coming down to the last months of the twentieth century and I couldn't wait for the parties to end, particularly since it didn't seem I had been invited to any of them.

It had been two months since the shooting and I still hadn't shaken off my bad mood. Whether I was to blame or not had never really been decided but when I saw my friends downtown in the bookstore or in the coffee shop they would pat the outside of their pockets, then look at their watches and mumble excuses as quickly as they could.

This is only partially to explain why I was crouched in a wet salmonberry bush watching a chicken coop through my foggy binoculars. My feet were wet and my legs were cramping. The rain dribbled down on me like warm beer. I had thought of giving private investigations up before but never with as much seriousness as this.

It was the middle of August and we had had now only

three sunny days all summer long. Those days had been emeralds of sparkling green water and blue sky. Gray rock, white snow and the lush blanket of trees running down the steep sided mountains to the tidelands. Those sunny days were actually cruel, because the rest of the summer had been so wet: warm and mild, no dramatic storms, only low clouds closing off the mountains and pebbling the surface of the shallow puddles with rain.

It had been on one of the only clear emerald days that Grant McGowan had taken a gun and held it to his fiancée's head out on the back deck of his derelict boat moored in Thomsen Harbor. He told the first policeman on scene that he wanted to talk to me.

Grant had been a mill worker before the pulp mill closed down. He had made a decent living working as a shill for the company's public relations crew after the shutdown. They would trot him out at hearings or in set-up articles about the impact of the mill's closeout on the community. Grant made a good unemployed blue-collar victim for the congressional committees that were convened to bail out the timber business. Grant was smart and hard-working and he was living in appalling conditions on a forty-foot wooden boat that was sinking, very slowly.

But the truth was Grant never lived any better when he was working. He had always been a drinker and a fuck-up. That was how we had become close.

Grant had a florid imagination that embellished every story with a kind of heartfelt drama. He wanted his tales to be more than barroom talk, more than the drama that fills every heavy-metal rant and cowboy ballad. Grant wanted to be bigger than life, in real life, and as a result he lied about almost everything. It was the world, he claimed, that had kept him from realizing his true potential, the demands of making a shitty living that kept him from following his true nature. And this true nature changed with almost every sitting at the bar.

Once he had grabbed me by the elbow at the bar and blared into my ear: "Canada, Younger! They've got workingclass poets in Canada!"

"No shit?" I said and kept looking at my wobbly reflection in the bar mirror. "Hell of a health care plan too," I added.

"Younger . . ." He wheeled around, stepping on the foot of a bald-headed cannery worker with five earrings in one ear. I couldn't tell if it was a man or a woman. "Younger. God dammit, there's no reason I can't be a poet of the working class too." The person with the earrings limped toward the bathrooms. I strained my neck around to check out which room this creature was headed for.

"Other than the fact that you're no longer a worker," I offered.

We laughed and Grant bought a round and we toasted to working poets of Canada.

The police had given me a radio hidden in a flack vest that I wore over an extra-large black raincoat. So as I walked down the dock to where Grant was holding his fiancée at gunpoint I looked like a badly dressed umpire who was hearing voices.

Grant had his arm around Vicky loosely. I would have mistaken it for a casual embrace, until I saw the Ruger Blackhawk .44 with rust blotching the blueing. Grant had to cock his elbow out at an odd angle to get the long barrel to rest on her ear. Vicky's head was shaking. Her mouse-brown hair hung limply to her shoulders. She had a cigarette in her right hand but I never saw her take a draw on it. The ash fell on the painted deck.

The police had briefed me. They would listen on the radio. They just wanted me to talk. Keep him busy. Don't argue. Don't make deals or negotiate. Try and emotionally free up the situation; avoid hard choices. They were getting their people in place. Standing in front of Grant and Vicky I felt stupid in the clothes and the vest. I started to take the flack jacket off and Grant became tense.

"What is this shit?" I asked him. "You want to be in *Newsweek* or something? This is crazy."

"I know you've got a gun in there, man." Grant tightened his grip on his own pistol and stood up straighter. Vicky grimaced, her breath escaped in short whining bursts. She dropped her cigarette.

"Oh for Christ's sakes, Grant!" I said and slipped back into the vest. "Like I'm going to come down here to kill you? What do I need a fucking gun for?"

"She says she's leaving me, Younger."

Vicky shook her head and shoulders but did not speak.

"Well, I can't see why. I mean, you're such great company, Grant." I smiled and tried to step over the gunwale of the boat. Behind me more police cars were rolling up into the parking lot of the Forest Service building. It was about a seventy-five-yard shot. Doable, I thought, but not preferable.

"Let's get out of here, man," I said, and my voice cracked. "This is more trouble than either of us need. Especially on such a beautiful day. I'll tell them it was a gag. Vicky, I'm sure, will back me up on this. Come on, man—we can work this out and I bet we can watch baseball on TV. What do ya say?"

The radio in the vest squawked. I fished for it and Grant pulled the hammer back on the Blackhawk. Behind me I heard police car doors slam. I heard footsteps on the gravel.

"I'm a fuck-up, Cecil," Grant said and he was crying. "I'm not fooling anyone. Vicky's all that matters."

"Oh you're not a fuck-up," I said. "If you are, what does that make me? I've been right there with you and I'm not about to kill anybody."

"Oh, you got everything, man. You got a rich family. You got a sister and a girlfriend with a good business. I ain't got shit. All I got is Vicky." Grant was crying hard now. Snot rolled down his lip into the stubble of his three-day beard.

"Then kill yourself, asshole, and let Vicky go!"

He took a deep breath and the muscles on his arm relaxed. He smiled at me sweetly and, as I think back on it now, with some pity, then lifted the gun to his temple and fired.

Vicky's hair was covered with bone and brain matter. She held her sparkling red hands out in front of her and started screaming at me: unformed words, curses, hysterical animal sounds. Then I heard the pounding of police boots running from both ends of the dock.

The radio on the vest crackled and I heard the sarcastic voice of a police lieutenant cut through the din.

"Thank you, Sigmund Freud."

But now I was crouched in the wet salmonberry bushes with a small flashlight in my mouth and fogged-up binoculars in my pocket. The salmonberries sparkled in the rain and lights from the cars on the roadway made thin lines of light breaking across the dark brush like straight pins snapping to a magnet's attention. A fat drop of water landed on the back of my collar and I hunched my shoulders as it slid down my back.

A lawyer in town had taken pity on me and offered me a job to find out who had been killing her chickens. This was the third night of the surveillance and I was having no success in solving the problem. This was causing me to rethink my career.

The chickens were safe and quiet behind the wire. I turned off the flashlight and squatted on the stump I'd covered with an old boat cushion. On my left, waves broke softly on the black granite beach and on my right, a van with a broken muffler drove past dolloping out the thumping chords of amplified dance music. I thought I recognized a song by Weapons of Choice. I emptied out my sealed jug of tea and stretched. I'd give it another hour.

I walked down the path to the beach and looked out over the bay. Sitka sits on the outer coast of the southern Alaska panhandle. From where I stood I could see three islands in the dark. Their forms were like the profiles of fallen animals. It was late but the horizon still held daylight: broad streaks of silver drawn from black clouds. There was no red, only the even grays of water, stone and unobstructed air over the ocean. I took a deep breath. The wind carried the faint smell of salt water and a hint of the cedar trees on one of those distant islands. Rain and gray light off gray water. In the distance a passenger ship powered off out to the northwest. She was lit up like a birthday cake, moving easily on to her next port. I thought of the passengers curled down in their bunks digesting the last of their surf-and-turf. I thought of having one last champagne and orange juice before falling asleep reading an overlong spy novel I had probably already read before.

I cannot see ghosts. I envy those people who can and I wish I could talk to the dead or at least hear their thoughts. Maybe then I could shake this mood. I don't know.

I've done a little time in jail and an old guy I met there told me the Indians could see more than was in the world but white people cannot see the things that are right in front of their face. That's the way I had been feeling all summer long. As if there must be something around me. Something important that I just couldn't see. But of course I'm a white man and that must account for my irritability. An Indian friend of mine said nothing pisses off white men like not being invited to the party. And I guess that was how I felt. All over the world—all over the island, in fact—there were parties going on and I couldn't get into any of them.

I thought of Jane Marie. She had been living in my house for three years now. In the past she had thrown wonderful parties that were fun and calamitous even if no one got drunk. But after the shooting, understandably, she stopped inviting people over as much. Now she was going out to picnics and potlucks on her own. She always asked me to come along and I think she meant it but I didn't go.

This summer we did our own chores and read our own books. I was reading books about the early arctic expeditions and Jane Marie was only looking at travel brochures. We had bought an extra reading light for the bed just so we didn't have to discuss when to turn off the light.

All islanders, no matter what their ethnicity, live with a certain kind of longing. It's a type of travel lust that is kept in check by fear of the unknown world. Tlingits have it. White people just make an aesthetic out of it. Living on an island is its own excuse to stay home and dream. I have lived here nearly fifteen years. I was born in Juneau, which is a landlocked town on the mainland, and even if it is prone to a kind of small-town megalomania that being the capital city creates, Juneau didn't really prepare me for life in Sitka. The smaller the city in Alaska, the more tolerance is required. Gossip stings, friends get on your nerves, simple things cost more and everything you hear on the news seems distant and slightly strange, as if the news was being badly translated from another language. Sitka has eight thousand people, hardly a village, and it requires about as much tolerance as I can muster.

If you want to live on an island, you need either a government job or at least a couple of crummy jobs. I was a private investigator, which seemed to me to account for several crummy jobs at once. I had been working three cases lately and none of them was paying much. A woman from the east coast called and wanted me to find her old boyfriend and the father of her ten-year-old daughter. Apparently the boyfriend was exactly ten years behind in his child support payments. I told her I could find him and this was true, because, in fact, I had just had a cup of coffee with him two days before at the airport. He was off to work up on the slope for an outfit that worked with some sort of geological mapping system. I told the old girlfriend this and she thanked me but never sent me the fifty dollars I had suggested as my fee.

I was reviewing the file on a child abuser who was begging his lawyer for post-conviction relief. I made a couple of thousand dollars reading the file and re-interviewing some of the witnesses and the investigating officers. But that was the end of it. The only new trial this guy was ever going to get was in fourteen years after he was released and re-offended.

And then there was this dead chicken case. A handout, I knew, but still a job. In fact my client thought one of her former clients was harassing her by breaking into the chicken coop, taking the chickens, and depositing them around the neighborhood. One morning there had been a dead chicken on her doorstep. The lawyer had brought it in to me to see what sense I could make of it. She flopped it on my desk, a white Cornish Cross with a broken neck. A bird as dead as a chunk of coal, feathers swirled in a confused rumpled pattern. Dead eyes like sequins. I'm not big on the physical evidence of death. Death all looks the same to me but that's probably because I don't like looking at it.

Jane Marie has a higher tolerance concerning the subject of death. She lost a brother and a father in her childhood. She knew about spilled blood and mourning. Her mother and her sister both had gone off on the twisted path that grief sometimes presents. The mother down sadness and the sister toward anger. Jane Marie was very brave, which was both lucky and unlucky for me, I guess.

I have reviewed the files of hundreds of murder cases. I've been in rooms with blood smeared down the wall and vomit in the corner. I've talked to survivors shocked and made stupid with grief, and I never really made any sense of them. In the center of each murder was a dark and sometimes casual craziness. Each death investigation was about extending the curve and getting that last glimpse of the sensible life: imagining the final moments, the last uttered words, the concussion and the salty taste in the mouth.

So I know the details of death but not even the slightest truth of it. I did see my father die of a heart attack on the floor of a casino, but it happened so far away from home that his death is only a weird memory, like a movie I saw once and don't care to think of again.

Grant's death was different. It happened in my own hometown, on the sunny dock where I had cleaned fish and drunk a beer at the end of a day out on the water. As I stood on the beach behind the chicken coop I was thinking of Grant but for some reason I thought of something I wanted to tell my father. I wanted to tell him that this wasn't my life here tangled up like half a mile of snarled fishing line in the trees. That this was just the story of my life. The story I was telling myself, and the story my friends told about me. But my life, my actual life, had to be somewhere else. Surely, my life had to be somewhere else. Maybe with him. I don't know.

I felt some warm pressure against my knees. I looked down and there was a big goofy-looking dog. He was white and had a slobbery kind of face that seemed to be smiling up at me. He curled into me and then I could see what he was trying to give me. It was a dead chicken in his mouth, as limp as phlegm but still warm. The dog looked proud and kept trying to hand the bird to me.

I let out a long sigh and patted his big blocky head.

"Professor Moriarty, I assume," I said to no one in particular.

2

Embarkation

It was dark on my street. The fish plant was busy with freezer trucks backing up to the loading docks. The wind from the west was blowing the smell from the channel back up onto the streets. Music was coming from the native meeting hall and a couple of fishermen were walking side by side down the sidewalk. They wore dirty float coats and they had their red rubber boots rolled down. One was smoking a cigarette and he nodded to me as I shouldered past him. I was carrying the dead chicken under my arm and as I walked past the two men I heard the smoker mutter something and they both laughed. A truck with a rusted-out back bed and a bad muffler rolled by.

I've lived in this particular house for seven years. It is built out on pilings over the steep rocky beach. I grew up in an old hunting lodge in Juneau. The home of my childhood was sold years ago. My mother lives in Santa Fe. Our family house is now a bed-and-breakfast. I stayed there some years ago and even slept in my old room, where I had carved my initials on the molding around the closet door. I looked for them but the molding had been replaced. The room had little baskets of sage on the bedside table and strange-smelling candles burned in the bathroom. This was my childhood bedroom and now there were old copies of *Architectural Digest* on a rosewood nightstand next to the frilly four-poster bed.

For better or worse my real life is here in Sitka now, with my roommate Todd and Jane Marie DeAngelo. Jane Marie moved from Juneau, nominally to be with me but the presence of humpback whales in Sitka Sound in the late fall and early winter helped. Jane Marie is a research biologist and the chief executive officer of Playing Around Enterprises. This was her day job so that she could fund her research. Playing Around Enterprises published a journal called, naturally, *The Playing Around Review,* which featured news, information, and advice on games. Jane Marie was a specialist in games: board games, card games, parlor games, even games to play in a car or boat during a long trip. The review created positive cash flow but the real money came from her catalogue of games and supplies. She took orders from all across the north: Alaska, the Yukon and even into eastern Canada. She specialized in finding the right games for individual social and cultural climates. She had games suited for Christian families living on the prairies of Saskatoon, and anarchist fishermen on the coastal islands of Alaska. She sold game supplies to the arctic villages and software on the latest computer games to kids all over the north. Although whenever she was given a chance, she would try to steer children out of the virtual world and back to the real one. Games, Jane Marie insists, are best played against another human, and suffer when played against machines. She currently has a friend helping her get started with shipping games to the Russian Far East. Games, Jane Marie says, are the way people sort their lives out and how they learn to appreciate the balance in all of their human relationships. As a species we have become so "over-evolved," entertainment is no longer the subtext of our daily lives but the reverse has become true. Our lives are the subtext of our entertainments. She maintains that this has been true for a very long time and that it is not just true for those of the idle rich but for all of those people who labor during the long days of summer so that they can survive the long northern winters.

I opened the door to my house and noticed there was a strange coat hanging on the rack in the entryway. The house, which could usually be counted on for some manic strangeness, was quiet but for adult voices speaking in a sober tone upstairs in the living room. I carried the dead chicken upstairs by the throat. I had forgotten why I was carrying it but supposed I needed it for some evidentiary reason.

When I cleared the stairs a well-dressed young man with extremely straight teeth and a nice haircut stood up and strode toward me with his hand outstretched.

"Well here he is, the sleuth himself. Hiya, Cecil, I'm Sonny Walters from Great Circle Lines. Gosh, I'm sure glad to meet ya. You know, I've heard a lot about you."

I stepped back and foolishly tried to hide the dead chicken behind my back. Jane Marie spotted my awkward moment and came to my rescue.

"I see you've been successful." She flashed a buttery

smile and reached around my back. "How our winged thoughts have turned to poultry," she added, then took the pathetic bird and disappeared downstairs toward the utility room.

"Mr. Walters wants to talk to you about a case, Cecil," Jane Marie's voice floated up the stairs.

"Gosh . . . a case!" Mr. Walters grinned foolishly and shrugged his shoulders as if he were a child star about to go into his tap dance routine. I sat on the chair that was nearest the woodstove. The stove was cold but the chair was the closest to me and would force Sonny Walters to sit opposite on the couch.

"Well, it's really not a case, I don't think. I suppose it's just a little problem we at the cruise line would like to have . . . oh . . . I don't know . . . fleshed out."

"Then you work for a cruise ship?" I said, and I realized that he had already told me that and so to cover I brushed imaginary crumbs off my lap. I was becoming more and more self-conscious of the dead chicken smell clinging to me. I knew the Great Circle Lines; their ships had been disgorging travelers onto the streets of town in grow- ing numbers the last few years. Tourism was booming in the island communities of southeastern Alaska. Most of the towns on the coast were changing over from the culture of resource extraction—logging, mining, fishing—to the culture of tourism. The seedy little boardwalk towns were becoming gaudy with the rust and gold of big money. Lei- sure was Alaska's new resource.

"You know, you've got a super place here," Mr. Walters said, looking around the upstairs of my house. There were dishtowels scattered on the arms of the couch and my room- mate's laundry was sitting in a heap on the table near the

kitchen alcove. I nodded and said nothing, not sure how
to acknowledge the "superness" of my living environment.

"Well, here it is, Mr. Younger . . ." Walters turned to me
and his voice dropped a couple of businesslike octaves.

"The main office of Great Circle Lines in Miami has
authorized me to hire a local investigator. But first I have
to ask: Have you been approached by any other cruise line
or shipping company to work for them in the past five
years?"

His shift in tone caught me off-guard. I shook my head
in the negative to indicate either that I hadn't been hired
by anyone else or that I didn't know what the heck he was
talking about.

"Good." He went right on. "I just want to make sure:
Have you been approached by Empire Shipping, out of
Singapore?" He stared at me. Waiting.

"No." I stumbled. "I mean, should I have?"

"Oh no. No." Mr. Walters waved away the thought.
"Empire is the company that owns our ship. I was just making certain we weren't, you know, reinventing the wheel
here." He stopped again, waiting, but this time there was
no thread for me to follow.

"Oh," I said conclusively.

"Well, Mr. Younger, the Great Circle Lines wants you
to help us in sorting out some complaints they've been
receiving over the last few seasons. We need it done, well,
you know, discreetly . . . I'm sure you are used to this kind
of thing."

"Sure." I said it too loudly and too confidently. This was
sounding like a real job with a genuine paying client. The
thought gave me something of a nervous sugar rush.

"Sure," I repeated. "Oh yeah. Discreet." I bit down on

my tongue just to stop yammering. "Tell me what you need, Mr. Walters."

"Oh, call me Sonny. Really, you know," he looked nervously around the room again, and I looked too, just trying to be helpful, "I mean my . . . father was Mr. Walters." He laughed nervously and I responded nervously. I knew why I was nervous, because I needed this work, but I had no idea what was making Mr. Walters twitch.

"Well, anyway, the main office has had some complaints about the medical services on one of our ships. It's the *Westward,* I suppose you have seen her. She really is a lovely ship, really. A converted steamship. I mean an old cargo ship that was refitted in the seventies. You know, this is a ship with a real soul. The soul of a world traveler. A fine old ship, not just a glitzy hotel. There is a beautiful main salon and a wonderful reading room and a small gaming room, a gym, and a classic old theater down belowdecks . . ." Mr. Sonny Walters was off and running, having found a comfortable topic.

"The *Westward* is just beautiful, really. Clean. And a great staff, of course. We have a terrific time on her. Of course, there is a lot of work and that really comes down to me and my staff."

I handed him his tea if for nothing else than to create a pause in the action.

"What is it you do, Mr. Walters?"

His young square face lit up. "Why, I'm the Cruise Director, Mr. Younger. My staff and I are in charge of the entertainment. I worry about your vacation so you don't have to."

I studied his face to see if there was any sarcasm creeping into the conversation but so far I could detect none. Sonny Walters appeared to be a cruising true believer.

"Sounds dreamy," I said and sipped my tea.

"Oh yes. Oh yes." Sonny went on haltingly. "We've had a terrific season so far but . . ."

"The complaints . . ." I offered.

"Yeah . . . Well, I frankly don't think there is anything to them. You know, we do all we can. But still the main office wants an independent investigation."

"Are people getting sick?"

"No, not really. I mean, there are problems. Heck, we have eight hundred passengers and three hundred crew members. There are bound to be some illnesses out at sea."

"Then?" I held my palms up in front of me. I was starting to lose my enthusiasm for this case already, and I hadn't heard the first fact.

"There is just a bit of controversy surrounding our ship's doctor."

I waited. Sonny looked down at the wooden floor. He did not go on. Outside I heard the low mutter of a fishing boat passing by close to the house. From the kitchen I could hear Jane Marie sharpening a knife on a whetstone. There was a rhythmic shiver to the sound that made me shrug my shoulders and take another sip of tea. I decided to wait Mr. Walters out.

"The company wants you to come on board and see for yourself," he said finally.

"Are you going to tell me any more?"

"Well, here's the deal on that." Sonny looked at me and smiled again with his "Old College Try" kind of confidence. "The company—Great Circle, that is—just wants you to come on board the ship and see for yourself, Mr. Younger. You can poke around all you want, enjoy yourself and experience all of the facilities—"

"Including the infirmary?"

"Of course. The infirmary and the ship's doctor, and if you cannot come up with any problems or anything, then . . . Well, then, I guess their concerns were unwarranted."

I took a deep breath. Of course, there were many things I needed to ask. I could have ticked off a long list of things I knew Sonny wasn't telling me.

"Sure, I can do that for you. No problem" was what I said instead.

Downstairs the door banged against the coatrack and I heard the even, heavy footfalls of my roommate upon the stairs.

Toddy came into the room with both arms filled with envelopes from the film-developing store. He'd been working all summer long at two jobs and it seemed that most of his discretionary income had gone into film processing. Todd was forty-six years old and he had just received his first camera. This may have explained his lack of discrimination as a photographer. It seemed that he was trying to document every visual element of his life.

He had lost his job at a local restaurant when, according to the manager, Todd had spent too much time engaging the customers in protracted philosophical discussions when he should have been doing salad prep. Now Todd worked as an aid for the local veterinarian, and for a landscaping company, where the most minute details of each yard, lot, and trimmed sidewalk had been documented photographically.

As a local kid from the neighborhood once noted, "Toddy ain't dumb, he's just smart in his very own way." I am his official guardian and I have long ago stopped trying to reconcile our differing intelligences.

Sonny Walters stood up as Todd came into the room and Todd stopped short. The envelopes of prints cascaded from his arms and scattered across the floor. Sonny looked alarmed at the scattered photos but Todd smiled and extended his hand as if nothing of concern had transpired.

"Why hello," Todd said, thrusting his massive hand even closer to Sonny.

"Hello," Sonny said tentatively. "Would you like some help with that?" he asked, simultaneously shaking Todd's hand and nodding to the envelopes on the floor.

"Oh no. That's okay." Todd smiled again, stared at Mr. Walters and said nothing. For several long moments Todd just stood and kept staring while he continued to rock back and forth on the balls of his feet. This, I think, was impressive to Sonny Walters.

Todd is just under six feet tall but his height is not that noticeable because he often stands with a pronounced hump in his back. Today he was wearing mustard-colored polyester trousers and a flannel shirt. The trousers were held up well beyond his waist by a pair of red suspenders that had the words *Alaska Logger* written on each one. Todd has what used to be called a crew cut before it was adopted by the young people in black who work in the bookstore coffee shop downtown. But the fashion feature that had defined Todd over the years was his thick black-framed glasses that had broken at the bridge some years ago. His father, who has long disappeared into the taverns of Ketchikan or Aberdeen, effected a repair with two stainless steel screws and a tiny plate that had a sharp edge on the outside corner. To mitigate the plate's sharp edge Todd had taped the joint with different layers of industrial tape over the years. The whole effect lent Todd the look of a damaged New Wave paperboy, kind of the friendly Road Warrior image favored by some urban youth. Only Todd didn't know that, of course.

Finally Todd bent down and picked up his photographs. He was humming "The Sheik of Araby," for some unknown reason.

"So then, do we have a deal?" Sonny slapped his hands together, turning away from Todd.

"How do you want to handle the travel? The expenses . . ." I paused and held my breath for a beat, ". . . and my fee." There, I had said it.

Sonny smiled like a man flush with cash, which I like to see.

"Well, the travel will, of course, be fully compensated. Food, stateroom, bar tab, would be covered by the ship, and I thought we'd just sign you on as an escort and pay you whatever your fee—in cash, of course—as long as we can come to some . . . reasonable understanding."

"Of course . . ." I smiled. "What kind of escort?"

"Ah . . ." Sonny said professorially as if he were about to begin his lecture on the finer points of living. "Many of our passengers are older women. Women, as you know, are longer-lived than men, and many women who like to travel are forced by circumstance to travel alone. The cruise line likes to provide escorts for them: men of good conversational ability, witty companions, and good dancers. It's a completely honorable thing," Sonny added seriously.

"Ah . . ." I said in return in what I hoped was a worldly way. The thought of an open bar tab and foxtrotting the

North Pacific with the sporty heiresses of America's industrial wealth was beginning to brighten my spirits.

"Mr. Walters . . ." Jane Marie's voice came into the room like a clarion call. "Do you know why males are generally shorter-lived than females?" Jane Marie had blood on her hands and there were feathers clinging to her denim apron. Her dark eyes flashed. Poor Sonny shook his head. By now Todd was sprawled out on the floor reviewing the photographs in one of the envelopes. Jane Marie stepped over him.

"The males of the species are generally shorter-lived because they expend so much of their reserve energy in trying to mate every possible female they come in contact with. Some of this energy goes towards display . . ." Jane Marie walked ever closer to poor Sonny with the bloody knife in her hand and Sonny tried to take a step backward but was stopped by the woodstove. I stayed put in my chair.

". . . Some of this display energy goes into activities you mentioned." She stopped, and, holding the knife in her hand, placed her fists on her hips. Her eyes were sparking now. "Dancing, card playing, joke telling . . . these are all forms of mating ritual and subjects of male display. Then, of course, this male energy is funneled off into aggression when the males are forced to compete for the attention of the females." Jane Marie was smiling sweetly now.

"But truthfully, Mr. Walters, do you know why men are generally shorter-lived?"

Sonny, being no fool, shook his head in the negative. Jane Marie let out a long breath and held the bloody knife to his face, still smiling as if she were presenting him with a diploma. "It's because the males often die as a result of their dangerous breeding behavior."

There was a pause and again Sonny said, "Ah." Then another long pause and then, "So then you're suggesting . . . ?" Sonny drawled.

"Your company would benefit greatly by having Cecil accompanied by his mate," Jane Marie replied sweetly. "And, of course, Cecil will benefit because if he goes on a cruise without me, I'd be forced to kill him." She held the knife tightly in her fist and batted her eyelashes.

So, telephone calls were made, along with some veiled threats and cajoling, and my little nuclear family was off to Vancouver, British Columbia, to board the SS *Westward*.

Actually, it had worked out as a bonanza for Sonny Walters. After Jane Marie put the knife down, he'd remembered that he was shy one lecturer for the cruise. Jane Marie had made a powerful impression with her knowledge of biology, and when he realized she also specialized in game strategy, he offered her a berth for one-half of what my salary was to be, which turned out to be more than the other lecturers were going to get but worth it if he could take it out of my pay.

Todd's berth took some cajoling and the rest of my fee. This would have been the second extended trip of his entire life, the first being a trip to Centralia, Washington, which involved an aborted bus trip and a string of bizarre rides on Todd's first-ever hitchhiking experience. But we couldn't leave him alone, mostly because he was rather indiscriminate on who he would invite home, and we couldn't trust that the house wouldn't be overrun with strangers upon our return. During one lunch hour this summer, I came home to find a church group from Indiana having lunch on our wobbly deck out over the channel. Then there was a Filipino gambling society that had to be asked to leave. No, Todd would be making the trip with us. So my fee was forfeited but there was still the bar tab, the midnight buffets, and the moonlight cuddling on the aft deck, tucked in a blanket with a hot toddy and a wedge of Brie on a cracker. Here was the summer of my discontent being made glorious by this Sonny Walters.

Of course, I knew he was lying to me. I figured the ship's doctor had probably maimed one of the passengers in some sort of blatant malpractice. The company wanted to fire him. But firing any doctor is problematic, especially one with a sweet gig. The company wanted to know how bad the news was. They needed some ammunition to either fire the doctor or cover the whole thing up. They just wanted a read on it before they had to act. This was fine with me. I'd just try and figure out what they wanted to hear, and give it to them. Anything to get me off the island. Anything to forget this summer.

We had two days to pack and make excuses for unexpectedly putting our real lives on hold for two weeks. Vernon Welsh, who ran the landscaping business, was so tickled with the thought of Todd on a cruise ship, he not only gave Todd the time off, he gave him some extra cash to spend on the boat. Then Vernon did something which seemed out of character until just after he had done it. He slipped me a check for three hundred dollars, pulled me aside and whispered: "For Christ's sakes get him something decent to wear. It wouldn't be right to have old Todd stick out on that ship like some goddamn retard." I took the money and Vernon slapped me on the shoulder as if he knew I could keep a secret.

Of course, I'm sure Vernon assumed that Todd *was*

a goddamn retard. In fact, once when Todd put diesel fuel into the riding mower, Vernon had used the words himself. But it was in character that Vernon would want Todd to be dignified if he were going on the ship. Dignity is what a tourist town needs most: Dignity is often the first to go.

We were to be tourists in our own country. Sitka, Alaska, had been the capital of Russian America, and we like to remember that when San Francisco was a tiny mud-rutted Spanish village, Sitka, Alaska, was the European capital of the Pacific, with nobility, chamber music, and the imperialist's naive sense that with enough guns and whiskey one could make anywhere home. There is a long tradition of tourism and adventure in Russian America. Some of the aristocrats I'm sure felt they needed to escape the Old World and thought of this Alaska as a chance to see their philosophies writ large. Everything a traveler sees or does generally confirms this belief that God is with them . . . again, as long as the guns and whiskey hold out.

From the era of the sail to the age of steam, European visitors would walk the boardwalks of Sitka and buy trinkets from the Tlingit Indian women who crouched against the log buildings and sold their baskets and decorated bottles. Small white children would cut their hair and sell their curls to rich widows from Philadelphia who thought it odd that such curly-haired angels could live in these far reaches of rock and ice. The kids would take their money, then add to it by crawling under the boardwalk out in front of the bar where coins fell through the cracks into the mud. Then, dirty and happy, they'd buy hard candies or peppermint sticks from the package goods store. With their money, the Indian women bought fishing gear or fabric or canning jars. But whatever it was, it always seemed a good trade and both sides seemed satisfied.

Today, Sitka is caught in the transition from the timber industry into something else. And the supply of people who want to see God in the landscape appears to be almost limitless. Apparently, we no longer need guns and whiskey to survive in the wilderness. Well, we like guns and whiskey, but apparently we need computers, cable TV, reliable power, modern schools, better guns, stronger whiskey, and more wilderness to make room for our new thirst for strangeness.

Jane Marie had students working on her humpback whale data and she had the ever reliable Mr. Meagles to take care of *The Playing Around Review*. She now had a mailing list of twelve hundred subscribers. She was publishing articles by writers from all over the north and even some flossy poets who liked her take on the world. The review came out monthly now, and her ad revenue was starting to pay almost all of the larger bills. The letters from readers were always lively and on target. Jane Marie says that if you asked readers directly to talk about a subject like sex or power between men all you would get is weird retreads of other people's opinions. But have them talk about games, in detail, and you get it all: faith, luck, randomness, and love. She continually ran articles on games that men should play with women and vice versa.

Mr. Meagles was at work on laying out the next newsletter and Jane Marie had hired a couple of kids to help with the mailings. Meagles was working on an article on Charades and the considerations when inviting friends to play it. This had been sparked by letters to the newsletter describing people's recent frustration at how hard it was to get a group together who even had heard of the same books and movies. This had caused some serious arguments and hurt feelings up in Barrow with a group of teachers who had huddled together to keep themselves entertained. This situation was just what Jane Marie loved to delve into. She had written the teachers back and asked for more details, ages, education, ethnic origins, and sex of the people in the prospective "Charades Pool" of Barrow.

On the way to the airport we stopped by her little office headquarters which was in a float house down near the float plane dock. Jane Marie had drafted out the Charades article, but Mr. Meagles was fiddling with the draft. Jane Marie stood behind him and looked into the computer screen. Mr. Meagles had been a venerable barfly in Juneau until Jane Marie placed him solidly in the party-gaming industry. He had been up most of the night working on this article. His hair was standing up on top of his head and he was chewing on the end of a pencil. In her earlier columns Jane Marie had already included the advice on limiting alcohol, including children in all the teams, and suggested having theme nights that the players could prepare for ahead of time. But the fights had apparently kept happening and the letters kept pouring in. "All of our friends are so dissimilar!" the letters kept calling out. "We don't know the same things" was what they said in one way or another.

Jane Marie put her hand on Mr. Meagles's shoulder and let out a long sigh. She said, "There is more to it. My guess is there will be a divorce by spring and the game will be moved. Just tell them to get along, for Christ's sakes. I'm going on a cruise."

Mr. Meagles waved to us as we left. He had a wild

sentimental smile on his face and it looked as if he were holding on to one end of a very long streamer thrown from the deck of a boat.

I didn't have any loose ends to tie up. We'd eaten the chicken. I told my friend the lawyer that a big goofy white dog was killing her poultry. Luckily, this lawyer was a dog person too, and was not of the Alaskan mind-set to either kill or poison the offending interloper. She'd called up the dog's owner and talked to him about rehabilitation prospects as well as sharing the cost of a new fence. She paid me two hundred dollars. I spent five dollars of that on a sports coat at the White Elephant shop, and the rest of the money on film for Todd's camera.

Todd took pictures through the window of the jet until I told him to stop. Todd is very compliant, but the problem with telling him to stop doing something is that he doesn't stop wanting. He sat in the window seat nervously eating honey-roasted peanuts, one nut at a time, rocking ever so slightly back and forth, then he would lift the camera to his eyes for just a second, then set it hurriedly down on his lap. All he wanted to do was take another picture but we had done a roll and a half just getting from Sitka to Ketchikan. Todd would be out of film before we boarded the ship.

I tried to tell Todd about Ansel Adams and about how he might travel for days and never take one exposure. Todd was not impressed. Todd had become fixated on photography after his last run-in with language. And I think this fits with a particular long-running theme in Todd's life. I think Todd wants to make contact. He'd spoken to his mother after her death and he assumed that all communication came from heaven in the form of words, but he had become frustrated with that. Now

he was onto images. Not that he thought he could send
his photographs to heaven or anything. "That's crazy,"
he said when I tried to weasel around the subject. "Cecil,
my mother is deceased. I mean how could she possibly
hold a photograph close enough to her eyes to see it?"
He looked at me with considerable pity.

No, Todd now was transfixed by the idea of capturing
images. It was more a question of time travel for him than
the transference of forms. He loved the idea of snipping
out something now and seeing it later. I discovered this
quite by accident when I was going through the mail and
found letters Todd was sending to himself. Address Sitka,
return address Sitka. In them Todd wrote letters to his
future self. Always very upbeat, with hopes for good things.
Always very polite. And he would include pictures. Pictures
of Wendell the dog. Pictures of our street or the house.
Some of ravens sitting on the roof line of the old hotel
down the block. Common images. And then I noticed that
in many of them he had somehow managed to put in the
time. The clock on the cathedral, or a reflection of someone eating lunch by the fish plant. In one, Todd had laid
an old pocket watch in the corner of the steps. This was
time Todd was documenting. It wasn't the images.

We arrived in Seattle and ran to catch our commuter
flight to Vancouver, British Columbia. We got stuck in Customs when Todd tried to have a long conversation with the
customs official. This was not a shakedown or anything; I
think the Canadian customs agent was just too polite not
to answer all of Todd's questions. We loaded our duffel
bags on a wobbly handcart, let the drug dogs sniff them,
and headed out to the bus stop. The Great Circle Lines
had provided a limousine service to the ship but the limo

had stopped running because we were late, so we took a taxi across town with a Pakistani driver who also was quite happy to talk to Todd for every minute of the drive.

Vancouver in the summer seemed so urbane to me. There was concrete everywhere and the warm scent of curried food in the air. There were oil paintings in a shop window. And on one corner there was a film crew with light scaffolds and blue boxes on wheels. I think I saw more people on the taxi ride across town than I had in the last six months in Sitka. Todd asked our driver about everything. Todd spoke slowly and probably too loudly, because he figured the driver didn't speak English all that well.

We arrived at the dock with only ten minutes to spare before the gangway was to go up. The cab driver let us off in the covered area inside the port building. Two buses pulled away and porters in red vests darted out to open the cab doors. One offered to carry the book I was holding. Todd grabbed his camera back and held it to his chest. Jane Marie walked around the front of the cab and began talking to the most senior of the porters, explaining to him which ship we were to be on and her position on the education staff. In the wall to my left was an oval window. I looked through it and toward the sky to check on the weather and my vision was filled with the *Westward*.

Of course I had seen cruise ships all my life, but knowing I was about to board this one gave it a romantic eminence I had never experienced. The summer of rain and dead chickens, of Grant and his girlfriend, of the endless debriefings by the police about his suicide, of my friends avoiding me at the coffee shop—all of these things were small now in comparison to the clean white hull of my life's new adventure.

The three of us walked up an escalator and through a long lobby covered in red carpet. At the far end of the lobby was a dais and a woman in a ruffled blouse and a steward's jacket. She was chatting with a young black man in a white shirt and tan trousers. They were laughing at some private joke as a family of four hurried with their own bags toward the entryway.

The father was clutching the tickets and the mother carried a large travel satchel stuffed with books and games. One young child dawdled behind, swinging her feet and spinning on the thin stems of her legs. She was humming a meandering tuneless rhyme and curling her long brown hair with her index fingers. The bigger girl walked with a pronounced stoop to her gait, and she shuffled her feet on the red carpet. The mother turned and snapped at the girls, and as the big sister turned I could make out her wide-set features, features I associated with Down's syndrome. This girl repeated her mother's words.

"Come on, Alicia, we'll miss the boat," she said in a flat monotone.

"All right, Carol," the mother said. "We'll take care of it now." And the mother put her hand on Carol's arm as the whole family eased to a stop at the ticket taker's dais.

The father fumbled in the pockets of his blue blazer, clearly agitated, and the woman scowled down at a manifest list. Carol started to stand up and down on her tiptoes. Looking anxiously over the ticket taker's shoulder, the mother held both of Carol's hands. Carol looked through the entryway toward the gangplank bridge to the *Westward's* salon deck. Her eyes were wide with some growing concern.

The father was having some trouble finding the last of his paperwork as several other people lined up behind us. Todd tried to take a picture of the ship from where we stood, even though all that could be seen was the edge of the aluminum gangway. Alicia stood by her mother and kicked at the back of her father's shoe.

"Stop it now . . . please," the man said as he put on his glasses and re-patted his pants pocket.

Carol said, "Too high!" and jumped up and down more vigorously. Carol could have been eighteen years old. She was a good two feet taller than Alicia. Alicia called out, "Mommmmm!" just as the father found the last of his paperwork and everyone smiled.

Everyone except Carol, who pulled back and bumped into Jane Marie. "Too high," Carol said, looking out to the gangplank that spanned twenty feet from the port building to the ship. The gangplank was approximately forty feet above the dock.

The father stepped aside and ushered little Alicia past him and she cantered past him toward the gangway. Passing me, Carol stepped on Todd's foot. Todd said "Ow," a little too loudly, I thought.

"God dammit now," the father muttered and the mother kept repeating, "Carol . . . it's going to be fine . . . excuse me I'm sorry . . . Carol, it's going to be fine."

But Carol bellowed "No!" Her voice echoed off the walls. Everyone in the terminal was watching. I stepped back to give them room and Carol twisted to get away from her mother's arm and the father lunged forward to grab her. "Now, we'll have none of that!" he said with building resolve in each syllable. As Carol twisted away, she lifted her shirt up, exposing the white flesh of her belly and her breasts. "No!" she declared and continued to pull back like a horse might, fighting with a fury that was not hysterical but beyond reasoning.

The woman from the cruise line waved to us and her voice tinkled over the commotion like a music box. "Why don't you folks come on aboard and we'll let them take their time?" We walked on through.

Both parents were holding Carol and the mother called for Alicia to come back but even I could see there was no chance of that. The mother turned back to Carol and held the frightened girl's face in both her hands and spoke slowly and urgently to her. The father breathed deeply and purposely did not look at any of the other passengers who filed past staring or trying not to stare.

Jane Marie took care of the paperwork. We were checked off the manifest in a moment and walking toward the gangplank.

But now there was something wrong. For some crazy reason I wanted to stay behind with Carol. Even though I wasn't afraid of crossing this bridge, I didn't want to go. I hated the gangplank; I hated the designers of the ship; I hated the cute girl in the steward's jacket. But mostly I supposed I hated Carol's father. I hated the resolve in his voice. His assurance which left no real question that we who had come so far would all be crossing that bridge no matter what we thought we wanted or didn't want. I hated the authority he had over Carol's life and for a moment I wanted to sit down like a burro just to show him that he didn't have that authority in mine. But of course I didn't, and when I saw Todd's grin as he stepped off into the carpeted main salon my vague anger dissolved instantly into sadness, because I knew with some intuitive sense that no one loved Carol more than her parents. Her father was harried and anxious about catching the boat, but still, no man loved this damaged girl with any more conviction than he did. Certainly I didn't.

So, when I saw them leading Carol across the gangplank with her eyes squeezed tight, I offered her mother my hand. But I was turned aside by four crew members who were smiling and joking as they helped the family down the final steps. As they pushed past me the mother smiled and raised her eyebrows to express both her embarrassment and her readiness for whatever was to come next. Carol opened her eyes and looked at the mirrored ball glimmering in a spotlight above the parquet dance floor situated in the middle of the main salon. Alicia was standing underneath it spinning on her heels, calling out, "Look, Carol, look . . . Stars, right here on our boat!" Carol put her hands to her face and laughed out loud.

The band on the back deck started playing a fanfare and a few people threw long streamers down to the dock. The tugs sounded their whistles and the *Westward* pulled slowly from the dock as I stopped crying and asked a black man in a white jacket if the bar was open yet.

3

Making Way

There was a large notice board on an easel under the archway from the salon deck to the fantail. There were notices for passengers and free copies of the shipboard newspaper, *Over the Horizon.* Big letters, printed right on the cork, promised, "TWO WEEKS ON THE SS *WEST-WARD:* THE BEST TWO WEEKS OF YOUR LIFE!" and in red letters: "DAY ONE: EMBARKATION, HAPPINESS ON THE HORIZON!"

Jane Marie was talking with a young woman wearing a sailor's cap as I pushed past a man in a short-sleeve sports shirt to make headway toward the Whipping Post Bar in the covered area of the fantail. My shipmate in the sports shirt dug a soft elbow into my ribs and said, in an irritated whisper, "Take it easy there, pal, we'll all get there at the same time." I looked over to him and saw that he had that crazed look of an overweight white man who had been pushed to his traveling limit and was in serious need of a drink. I let him lumber past. As I walked away I heard Jane Marie answering questions from the young woman in the sailor's hat.

"Yes, yes . . ." she was saying and then, "But you don't bring out the board games until everyone gets to know each other . . ." in a rather stern voice, and then I was out the door.

The band was packing up their instruments and moving back under cover. The docks of Vancouver were growing smaller. My friend with the fat elbows approached the bar and slapped his hand down against the polished ebony. "Well, by God, I hope to hell you have plenty of bourbon on this boat," he said loudly to the man behind the bar. The barman was as black as onyx and had a disturbingly cold but broad smile. "Plenty bourbon," he said, then lifted a glass of ice from under the bar and in one easy motion poured a double shot.

"Well," the big man lowered himself onto the stool, "that's the first goddamn thing that has gone right on this trip," and he made a vague gesture with his hand, circling it over the bar as if he were saying "Keep it coming" or "One for everyone." Just to be convivial I said, "The same," softly and, hopefully, unobtrusively.

The big man turned to me. His face was red and sweat had matted down the thinning hair he had told his barber to leave on top. "Women love this shit, ya know, buster?"

The drink came and I waited. The musicians were struggling to get the drum kit under cover before the rain squall hit. People were milling around on the deck looking at their passenger guides and trying to get their bearings. I could smell the big man's aftershave. I could smell the ocean and a faint hint of steamed vegetables. But mostly I could smell the bourbon.

The big man caught me staring at his drink and thinking I might be deaf, he worked again on his opener. "I mean they just *love* this shit!" He drained his drink and the cubes sounded to me like wind chimes.

"You mean they like drinking on deck?" I offered lamely.

He laughed loudly and slapped me on the back, making the circling gesture with his hand. Two more drinks appeared as if he were working on his sleight of hand act. "Shit, no, man." He held his drink to his lips and paused for effect. "I mean this cruising shit. They love it. Me? I'd rather just stay home, you know? I mean, give me my lawn chair, a game on the tube, and I'm happier than a pig in shit."

I held the cold glass and raised it solemnly: "To pigs in shit," I said respectfully.

I felt a strong hand on my elbow. "Hey there, Mr. Younger. It's great to see you here." I turned and saw the perky Sonny Walters smiling at me with his five-hundred-watt teeth. Behind him Todd was carefully reading his passenger information, but Jane Marie was staring directly at me. She was holding a diagram of a players tree for a gin tournament.

"Wow," I said to her. "It didn't take you long to settle in." I slowly put the drink down.

Sonny's hand pulled me easily from the bar and I waved gaily to the drink and its rightful owner, who had turned from me and was already showing the barman the pictures from his wallet.

"Listen," Sonny was whispering urgently in my ear, "we need to get a few things squared away before . . . before you get going on your investigation. One of them being our agreement about your bar tab and how that will be handled."

"I don't really care how you handle it, Sonny." I pulled

my elbow back and ducked through the sliding glass door that led us back inside to the main salon.

Sonny stopped walking. "Whatever . . ." He was reading a clipboard. Several older white women asked him questions and he answered them slowly and clearly and with his usual aplomb.

"Look . . ." he said as he turned to me and I stepped back. "I'm the Cruise Director here, dammit! Lots of people depend on me and I'm not going to waste my time holding your hand, okay? I was never in favor of bringing you on board. But . . . but . . . my authority was . . . overridden on this one and I suppose I'm just going to have to live with it. But right now I want you and your . . . *family* . . ." and he looked at Jane Marie, who was looking over the players tree, "to go down to your cabin. Unpack and wait there. Read the materials and familiarize yourself with the ship and the facilities onboard. You are eating at the second seating. I will talk to you before then. Now, if you'll excuse me—" And Sonny walked away quickly, straight into the concerned expressions of two couples from Davenport, Iowa, as announced by their ball caps and shirts.

Jane Marie pushed past me and mumbled, "Come on." She said it coolly. "Let's see if we can make it to our cabin without getting arrested."

"That Sonny Walters turns out to be a man of unexpected depth," I said, trying to preserve my dignity and hurrying to keep up with her. "Where the hell are we going anyway?"

Todd started to read aloud as we walked into a narrow passageway.

"'*The* Westward *was commissioned in 1957, and is a*

steam-generated electric-powered vessel. She is six hundred and seventeen feet long, eighty-four feet at her widest point, and carries a tonnage of twenty-three thousand five hundred. She is registered in Monrovia and has a carrying capacity of seven hundred and thirty-nine passengers and two hundred and twenty crew members, including the bridge, the boat crew, the engineers, the hotel staff, the kitchen staff, the entertainment staff, the educational staff, and the shore excursion staff, all of whom are here to make sure that this is the best two weeks of your life.'" Todd stopped reading and looked up at me wide-eyed. "Do you suppose that will be true, Cecil? I mean, will this be the best two weeks of my entire life?"

"Well, Todd," I said as I noticed we were now shoulder-to-shoulder with a crowd of elderly white people jammed into a narrow carpeted hallway all reading the exact same literature and looking around like baby chicks for the return of their mother, "this could well be the best two weeks of our lives . . . if we live through it."

Jane Marie pulled Todd by the elbow as the herd split up near the stairs. "I'm assuming we head down towards the steerage cabins," she told us, as I eased in behind a woman smelling of lavender who was reading her materials and stumbling on every third step.

Todd began to read aloud again as we walked as quickly as the press of passengers would allow. "'*The* Westward *is laid out in the style of the luxury liners of the grand era of sailing. Passengers should take a moment to familiarize themselves with the structure and design of the ship. Remember, as you face the front, or bow, of the ship, your left is the port hand and right is starboard. An easy way to remember is to think of the fact that "Left" and "Port" have the same number of letters.'"*

"What deck are we on?" I called out over the head of

the woman who was now grabbing onto the rail in the passageway.

Jane Marie looked down at the papers in her hand. "Acapulco Deck," she said.

Todd continued, "'*The decks of the* Westward *are conveniently laid out alphabetically, starting with the Acapulco Deck and moving upward toward the Horizon Deck. Also, if you notice the color scheme of the passageways, you will notice that each deck has its own color scheme, going from rich emerald green to a Mediterranean blue on the Dolphin Deck and capped off with glittering starlight silver on Horizon.'*"

I looked around the passageway. We were on Bermuda Deck. There were far fewer passengers. A couple with kids, who were skipping off down the strange pea-green carpet. The smell of perfume had given way to the much stronger smell of cleaning products, and then the faint hint of steamed vegetables. Cabbage, I thought.

On Acapulco Deck we stopped because there was nowhere else to go. The air seemed progressively warmer as we went down. There was more engine noise at this level but, truthfully, not near as much as I might have expected. The carpeting and the walls were a clammy gray-green with all the light coming from the buzzing fluorescent strips along the low ceiling. We turned left and walked some thirty yards toward the stern and Jane Marie found a door, on the inside of the ship, fitted a key, and stepped inside. Todd followed.

I swung around the corner with a certain assurance, then banged right into Todd, who was inches away from Jane Marie. Our three duffel bags were stacked on the square of carpet between the bunk bed and the one berth along the inside wall, thus taking up all of the available space. I think kidnapped heiresses who have been buried in the ground had more room than this cabin.

Jane Marie slipped along the wall toward the one dresser and lifted one bag onto the bunk, making some room to stand. Todd flopped on the lower bunk. I sat on my duffel in the middle of the stateroom. My elbow was on Jane Marie's knees and my legs lay just underneath Todd's resting body. The room was a strange sea-foam green that gave the close quarters the feel of a dimly remembered womb.

"Well. Cozy!" I said, not wanting to lose our vacation momentum.

Jane Marie was unpacking her books and placing them on the ledge above the top bunk. She had brought every possible animal and plant identification book for these waters with her. She also had some of her source books on party games. She unfolded a black strapless evening gown and a book for identifying moss fell out and hit me in the head. She stepped over me and hung the black dress in the closet after she mistook the first door and thus found our toilet-shower cubicle.

"Christ, Cecil," she grumbled. "This is not exactly what I expected."

"I wonder if this vessel is completely unsinkable," asked Todd as he took a picture of me reclining on our duffel bags.

"Absolutely," I replied in a chipper voice I was learning from Sonny Walters. "Come on, you adventurers. We're cruising now. None of the old rules of our shorebound lives apply."

"I wonder if they supply us with enough oxygen?" Jane Marie stood looking up at a small square vent that apparently pumped air from somewhere into our quarters.

"Sure . . . Sure . . ." I reassured her. "First, we need to become oriented." I slapped Todd on the leg. "Now which way is the bow?" Todd looked around our cell, then pointed vaguely to his left. "Good. Now, which bars are near the bow?"

Todd squinted at the information sheets on his chest. "The Compass Room and Fiddler's Green."

"Check. The stern?"

Todd flipped a switch on the wall next to him and he nudged the information sheets into the narrow pool of dim light. "The Great Circle Lounge, the Terra Nova Room and the Whipping Post outside on the fantail."

"Okay. We're on the bottom. Underwater, I'd say. Acapulco. What decks are the bars on?"

"Enterprise, Flag, and Horizon. Horizon is the top passenger deck. And I believe you are right, Cecil. I suspect that we are indeed underwater here in Acapulco. Intriguing, don't you think?"

"Absolutely, Todd," I answered, as Jane Marie picked up her moss book from my chest without smiling or saying a word.

"Where do I give my talks, Todd?" Jane Marie muttered.

"That's in the Great Circle Lounge on the Flag Deck. I think that is where we came from . . . where that interesting decorative ball was hung above the wood floor."

"Game room?" Jane Marie said absently as she scanned her own diagram of the ship.

"Uh, I think that is on the Enterprise Deck just below Flag Deck." Todd looked around our cramped space as if there was actually something with which to orient himself.

"I believe we are almost directly amidships and in the virtual center of the ship here. The dining room is also on the Enterprise Deck, four floors above us."

"How about the medical facility?"

"That's on our level. I think it is on the starboard side near the stern. We, of course, are on the port. I think."

"Good then," I said, pulling myself up. "I'm off to work. I'll see you up on deck."

Jane Marie took one step and crossed the room. She had her face in mine. Her eyes were squinting tightly down on mine.

"Mr. Walters told us to stay here," she hissed.

I looked around the space. "He was kidding," I offered.

"I don't think so." Her voice had a dangerous gravity to it.

"I'm not waiting here, Janie." And I turned my back on her.

She spoke and her voice softened, yet it was still rich with irritation. "If you start drinking I'm going to throw your sorry ass overboard, Cecil."

I did not turn or look at her. "Duly noted," I said, and walked from our quarters.

Behind me, I heard Jane Marie's voice. "You're going walking around dressed like that?"

I stopped short. I was wearing what I always wear, my canvas pants, a cotton work shirt and my new, used, sports jacket that, if it had actually fit, would have given me a kind of dapper English country gentleman sort of look.

"It would appear so," I said down to the leather boat slippers I was wearing.

"You look like a flasher. We're supposed to go to the captain's cocktail party later," she said before the door snipped off the last syllables of the sentence. I took a deep breath and set off down the pea-green carpet.

Some elderly couples were sorting through their luggage in the hallway ahead of me; I pushed past them. A woman was chattering something about closet space and I could hear ice cubes tinkle into an empty glass. The next stretch, toward the stern, was clear. It felt like the interminable hallway that appears always ahead of me in a recurring dream about running, running, and never arriving.

I was losing myself slightly in the mood of this dream when my shoulder bumped into an open door. I peeked in. Against the far wall of a cabin remarkably like ours was a blonde girl in a white shift. She was lying on the bed. What caught my attention was the paleness of her skin and the thinness of her arms. I watched her in spite of myself, just to see if she was breathing. She was. Her head was facing the direction of the stern; her right arm seemed as thin and pale as a maple branch just stripped of its bark. This arm was splayed out and curved backward over the edge of the bed so I could see the IV needle taped into a vein at her elbow.

I must have involuntarily sucked in my breath for I made some noise that drew her attention. She bent at the waist and raised herself up on her bunk as if she could float into the air. Pulling her hair away from her sunken blue eyes, she turned toward me.

"Excuse me," I said and I made some kind of awkward gesture with my hands to indicate that I was actually confused and not really a voyeur. "I was just looking for the ship's clinic," I added, hoping that would help.

This insubstantial girl smiled sleepily and pointed her wraithlike arm over her shoulder. From somewhere deep within a cloudy but pleasant dream, she smiled.

"Do you want some medication?" she asked in a

reedy voice. "I've got lots . . ." Her smile was broad and full of white teeth but was somehow distant and almost unfathomably sad. "Are you seasick?" She curled both of her arms like ropes around her shoulders and lay back down. "Mal de mer," she added in a long breath.

"No. I'm just not quite feeling up to snuff," I said. It appeared that the shipboard atmosphere was causing me to talk like Bertie Wooster.

The girl's eyes were closed. Her tiny frame moved gently with what I detected now was the gentle motion of the ship. She licked her lips as if her mouth was dry but she appeared to be asleep.

"I'll just pop off then," I said idiotically and waved at the sleeping girl. As I walked on down the hall I was grateful that I hadn't said "Cheerio!"

The passageway gently curved toward the center of the ship and there, near the end of the long hall, was a large double door. A poster board next to it said: "*Welcome aboard. Our shipboard clinic hours are listed every day in the ship's paper and are also posted here, above the door. In case of emergency please dial 911 (that's right, just like home) from any of the ship's telephones and our well-trained medical staff will assist you at any time of day or night. Tablets for motion sickness are available in a dispenser by the front door. Please wait to see the doctor if you are taking any other medication before you take any medication for motion sickness.*"

Written in a dark ink in block handwriting was:

"*There will be a get-together for the travel club, 'L'Inconnue de la Seine,' in the Compass Room, on Horizon Deck, this evening at 9:00 after second seating. We'll meet with the medical staff and get acquainted. See you there!!*"

A white man who appeared to be extremely fit and

perhaps in his early sixties strode up to the sign and stood close to me and read the board.

"Huh," he grunted. "Not until nine o'clock." Then he stuck a fabulously long black cigar in his mouth. He jutted the cigar out at the sign and waited. It became clear he was waiting for me to say something.

"I say, that's really quite some cigar," I offered, then I bit down on my tongue for fear that I was shifting down into some kind of Winston Churchill impression.

The old man snatched the cigar out of his mouth between his index and middle fingers. The log of tobacco stretched his fingers wide apart. He shoved his other hand out and took my hand in a crushing grip.

"Isaac Brenner. How are ya? You're damn right this is a cigar. You know what I mean? Now this . . ." He held the cigar before him as if he were weighing it with the full force of his arm . . . "Now this is a cigar. Cuban. Get them in Canada, you know. I'm going to smoke it before we get to American waters. This and all of his brothers and sisters." Isaac Brenner elbowed me so that we would both get the implication and he let the locomotive of his conversational style roll on.

"Stupid. This mess between the United States and Cuba. I mean, really, who does it help? Who does it hurt? I ask you. I was there, you know." He nodded to me. "Cuba back in the forties. Under Batista. Pigsty, I mean really. Tijuana? Nothing. Havana had the donkey shows, the drugs. Poor people everywhere. Now they ask why there is a revolution? Why the heck do they think there is a revolution? I mean, look around."

I looked around. There was nothing but the sign board and an Indonesian-looking man in a white jacket carrying an armload of towels.

My new companion pushed ahead. "So anyway, Canada has some sense. They stay open and they get these cigars. These stay lit. I mean it." Mr. Brenner saw me laughing and reached quickly into the breast pocket of his camel hair jacket and pulled out an aluminum tube the size of a model rocket.

"Here . . . Take . . . Smoke, you'll see. A perfect, long ash."

I took the cigar tube and sniffed it, which I instantly realized was a stupid thing to do, but Isaac Brenner accepted the gesture. "So. I'll see you upstairs at nine o'clock?"

He seemed to almost radiate good health as he stood before me bouncing on the balls of his feet. A massive thatch of white hair showed through the shirt he had casually left unbuttoned. I looked at him with something less than understanding. "Oh, God, no . . ." He smiled and slapped me soundly on the back. "My God, no. You look too good." And he laughed and moved past me. "Let me know what you think of the cigar. I'll be seeing you, young fella."

He lumbered off down the hallway waving the Cuban cigar over his shoulder like a torch lighting his way.

I walked to the last stairwell and went up four flights. At each landing the color scheme of the carpets and walls seemed to lighten. At the Dolphin Deck I was standing on a cerulean-blue pattern of waves. I turned and walked to the heavy door I assumed would lead me to the stern, pushed against it, and walked out into the wind.

I was standing on an outside deck of the bow. We were on the port side and I was looking out over the front of the *Westward's* bow lunging through the water.

The ship had built up speed and was coursing down a channel. There were low bluffs on the port side and pleasure boats like bathtub toys making "V" wakes behind them heading into the shelter of their port. Gulls wheeled overhead. The wind cut full against my body and there was the slight spattering of rain from a few thin clouds. The ship rose and fell into the waves. Each falling was accompanied by a rush of the white wave sliding from the hull.

There was a rope hung across the deck just before me, and on the other side were stairs down to the main deck where the docking winches sat. Four black men worked, coiling the thick hawser line used in docking.

I turned my back to the wind and pulled the collar of my jacket up. On the outer deck above me, Enterprise Deck, I saw the thin girl with the white arms standing out in the wind. Her arms were spread and I could see the IV needle still taped on the inside of her elbow. She spun in the wind and the white dress rolled and billowed around the bones of her legs, her angular torso. She held a champagne bottle in one hand and it seemed to weigh one side of her slender body down. She put her other hand to her face. Her hair was flying, in her eyes, in her mouth. She stripped the hair from her mouth with her fingers, then she patted her sunken cheeks. She wrestled the bottle over her elbow to lift it awkwardly to her mouth, drinking as if the bottle were a keg of corn liquor. The champagne spilled down the front of her white linen shift and I could see the outline of the ribs high up on her chest. A large white man with a beard came out behind her and cradled her in his arms and took her back inside.

I turned back and saw the crewmen below me looking up. They were laughing, all except one of them who looked to be saying something scolding as he went back to his work.

I hiked back to the stern and up one floor to the Enterprise Deck.

Couples were standing in small groups holding drinks
in plastic cups. Most of the men were dressed in slacks and
blazers. The women wore colorful slightly ethnic-looking
dresses—rust, gold and burgundy. There was laughing and
the rolling surf break of conversation up and down the
stairwells and out into the halls. This was the holding area
for the first seating of dinner. There was a table set up
to distribute complimentary drinks but only if you were
assigned to the first seating.

I continued on up the stairs until I found myself on
another back deck. Here was the Whipping Post Bar.
Feeling proud of myself for my first successful circumnavi-
gation of the ship, I settled back on a corner stool and
ordered a champagne cocktail. This was after all a depar-
ture, and who was I to cut across the grain of all of this
festivity?

Here were the true drinkers of the voyage. Men in
leather vests drinking beer all day long and women who
drank vodka slowly and continually. Perfume, cigarette
smoke, the clatter of glasses on polished wood, and the
tinkle of ice. This was the atmosphere of endless vacation
that had lured all of us on board.

A woman with silver-white hair and a low-cut blue blouse
that was the upper half of what I could only describe as
some kind of formal golf wear snubbed out her cigarette
and asked the man next to her if he were traveling alone.
The man brushed back what hair he had left and sat up
as straight as he could. "Not for long, I hope." And we all
cackled and raised our glasses to toast our wit.

I drank the champagne and the bubbling feeling of

optimism rose up into the forepart of my brain. Someone asked me what I did for a living, and for some inexplicable reason I told him I was an investment analyst. The silver-haired woman slid over and curled her shoulder into my chest and cooed theatrically, "Oooo, now this is the man for me. I need all the stock tips I can get." Again we all laughed.

"Save your money," I said with as much disdain for those distant markets of the world as I could muster, "and never listen to anybody with less money than you have."

The woman leaned back and batted her black whisk-broom lashes. "Now you're talking . . ." and she tipped her glass as her eyes took a walk over my body.

"This is my eleventh cruise," she blurted out to all of us. "I love cruising, you know. I hardly even go home any-more. I can afford it. Why not see the world and be waited on a little? We earned it, didn't we?" she asked and draped her powdery white arm across my shoulder.

Of course she knew I was lying about being an invest-ment banker. One look at my ratty clothes probably told her that. But this was flirting, and flirting, after all, expects a certain amount of tolerance for deception. In fact, at these early stages of flirting, lying is preferred. These lies, like the fake yawn, or the over-close examination of some-one's jewelry, are just the groundwork for boozy seduction that may or may not subsequently happen.

Somehow I missed the first dinner seating. That was okay because I was supposed to. But then I missed the sec-ond one, which my new friends and I at the Whipping Post took rather philosophically. We ordered some strange-looking deep-fried finger food while my friends told of their earlier ports of call. I heard about strange taxi rides in Hamburg and dishonest restaurateurs in Papeete. We laughed and smoked and drank like old college chums.

The evening came down like a curtain and the boat rolled through the sweetening sea. We were leaving sight of land. Somewhere distantly off our stern were the lights of an unknown Canadian city. I imagined all those ardent working-class poets and the friendly policemen sitting down to their dinners of boiled beef or whatever the indigenous food of Canada was, then I ate another morsel of the unknown fried food.

There were lights just off the stern illuminating the pure white foam of the wake. Gulls dove in and out of the glare and their shadows streaked across the lower deck. I watched the gulls as I listened to my companion, whose name was Elaine from St. Petersburg, Florida, enumerate her extraordinarily bad luck with husbands. But when I looked back to finish my cocktail and dip one more niblet into the spicy tomato sauce, I realized I was alone at the bar and Elaine had apparently finished talking and was gone.

I tried to walk into the Great Circle Lounge but the door was barred and a very pleasant Filipino man in a white jacket told me the captain's cocktail party was happening and that I had to enter the lounge from the bow side. The pleasant man made a strange gesture with his hand over his shoulders. He made the gesture several times and when I tried to decode it he explained, "Jacket, sir. Jacket."

"No, that's all right. I have one," I told him as I fingered the dirty collar of my second-hand coat and started to weave toward the outside deck.

My fellow passengers were lined up in the passageway

outside of the Great Circle Lounge. They were all in their finery, tuxedos and black dresses. They were all waiting to enter and be presented to the captain. The end of the line curved down the stairs and out of sight. I leaned against the bulkhead to steady myself although the motion of the ship was slight. Just as I was about to launch back in the direction of the Whipping Post I saw Todd and Jane Marie.

Todd was in a black suit with a white shirt and tie. He stood straight. Somewhere he had taken on a new pair of fashionable wire-rimmed glasses. He was looking down and smiling attentively as a young woman spoke to him in an animated fashion. Todd looked wonderful. He seemed more dignified than I had ever imagined him. He still had his camera around his neck and the pockets of his suit coat bulged with extra rolls of film, but still, I was amazed because he looked so dignified and at ease. For some reason, now I was irritated with him.

Jane Marie had her arm casually draped through Todd's arm and I watched her for a moment and was overwhelmed by my drunkard's sense of wonder which is always slightly tinged with self-pity. Her black dress hung just off the crest of her shoulders and clung down her torso, stopping midway down her thighs. The fabric sparkled slightly and had a soft texture that invited touch. She wore just a little lipstick and maybe something on her eyes but perhaps her eyes had always been that intense.

It has been my experience that to love a beautiful woman is to live in fear. I walked down the stairs toward them.

She saw me and did not smile.

"You missed Sonny," she said flatly.

"Damn the bad luck," I said.

"He wants to see you." She would not look at me.

"He's probably not far off."

Jane Marie took my hand. Although she wasn't looking at me, her voice eased into a soft intimacy. "Cecil, I know we've been kind of . . . out of touch these last few weeks. But this trip . . . maybe we can do something about that."

A black steward walked down the stairs balancing a tray of champagne glasses. Jane Marie was struggling to continue her sentence. I took two flutes of champagne and offered her one. She took the glass but still would not look at me.

"One toast," I said and held the glass up to her. "To whatever it is we have to do . . ."

Jane Marie shook her head sadly and gave the glass to the young woman who was talking to Todd.

"You've got to snap out of this, Cecil. This summer . . . this thing with Grant . . . Don't try to tough it out. Don't go Bogart on me." And she rubbed the back of her hand against my cheek.

"Don't worry, doll. I've never toughed out anything in my life." I tried to smile, but she turned away suddenly.

A woman in a blue silk dress charged up to her and started asking questions about the bridge tournament. I walked along as the line inched toward the captain of the ship. Another steward took our glasses before we walked through the cut glass and brass doors of the Great Circle Lounge. The door opened and I saw the liquid blue-green light of the interior of the lounge. I saw a gray-haired man in a short white military-style jacket. He was being photographed with a Japanese couple. The band was playing "Three O'Clock in the Morning." Jane Marie went in before me and I took one step behind her when someone grabbed my arm and jerked me out of line.

Sonny Walters was standing with his handsome face

reddening rapidly. He was wearing a perfectly tailored pale blue tuxedo jacket with padded shoulders. He jutted his face in front of mine.

"This is a formal reception, Mr. Younger. It is absolutely not acceptable for you to be here dressed like this."

"Lend me your coat then, Sonny," I slurred and leaned into him to avoid a steward rushing by with an armload of empty glasses. Sonny moved me into a small dark area behind the bandstand.

"This is just not working. We've been to sea a few hours and already you are screwing up—excuse my French—the program."

Sonny ducked his head away and steadied his perfect hair with a shaking hand. "I'm going to put you ashore at the next port, Mr. Younger. I need your friend Ms. De Angelo, but you and whatever he is . . . Todd . . . will be put off on the dock and you can very well fly back to Sitka." Sonny was trying not to sound peevish. The thick baritone voice was slipping up an octave.

He turned and disappeared behind a black curtain. I peeked around it. In the room behind the curtain a mirrored ball was spinning. Darts of light cut across the parquet floor, shattering on the glasses stacked near the bar. Todd was taking a picture of the spinning ball. The pretty dark-haired girl who'd been talking to him earlier came over and asked him to dance. He looked at her as if she were offering to set him on fire. The band was playing "Tuxedo Junction" and the girl took Todd's hand to lead him out on the dance floor.

In the corner near the bar an elegant black man in a white tuxedo and red cummerbund was leaning close in to Jane Marie, admiring the string of pearls around her

throat. She turned her head and her long throat made
a lovely arch as she smiled up at the spinning ball. She
smiled as if she were warming herself on the man's breath.

It was nine-fifteen as I walked away from the Great Circle Lounge. I climbed the stairs. The Gallery Deck was a
lighter blue and the Horizon Deck was a spangle of sand-
shaded fabric. Chrome encased the light fixtures and large
windows looked out over the dark water where the lights of
the ship reflected off the waves. I turned toward the bow
and stopped at the signboard on the easel at the entrance
to the Compass Room. It read:

WELCOME, MEMBERS OF
L'INCONNUE DE LA SEINE TRAVEL CLUB!
RECEPTION 9:00 PM TILL WHENEVER!!!
MEMBERS ONLY, PLEASE.

Under the printing was a drawing of a young woman's
face. Her eyes were closed and she had a slight smile. Her
hair was pulled back from her forehead and the muscles
of her face were relaxed. The drawing was eerie: a few
lines of ink on white paper, but her face had an almost
hypnotic quality of repose. I don't know how long I stared
at it because I became lost in some vague dream: thinking
about Todd downstairs in his black suit. And Jane Marie's
entreaty to me to get back in touch. Then about Sonny's
threat to bump Todd and me off the ship in Ketchikan.
I stared at the drawing of the girl and felt that nothing I
could do would change anything.

I looked up and through the door I saw the white girl
with the skinny arms. She still had a champagne bottle and
she was dancing with her eyes closed. She opened her eyes

and looked at me standing there outside the door as if I had fallen out of the sky.

"Hello," she said in her hazy voice and she walked out into the hall. "You look sad. Did you find the doctor?" Her eyes darted under her drooping lids. Her gaze wandered over my face. Then I realized that part of what gave her face such a pale expression was she had no eyebrows at all.

"I wasn't really looking," I told her and pointed into the Compass Room. "Are you having a party?"

"No." She shook her head slowly and then came forward, putting both of her arms around my neck. She held me as if we were dancing, pressing her head against my chest and swaying from side to side. She smelled of lemon soap and when I put my hand on her back I could feel the sharp ridges of her shoulder blades.

"There is nothing to be afraid of." She said it softly. "Do you know that?" She lifted her head back and looked at me. For an instant her expression cleared and her eyes were steady on mine. She looked quizzical and at the same time deeply concerned. "There is nothing to be afraid of."

She leaned forward and kissed me. Her frail body trembled; her lips were so thin and dry that it hardly seemed like a kiss at all. She licked my tongue, then my lips. Her mouth, but for the slight hint of champagne, tasted like ash.

Someone tapped me on the shoulder. It was a large black man wearing a white jumpsuit. He smiled broadly.

"Mr. Walters asked me to find you, sir. He wondered if you would like to watch the film being shown on the television."

Mr. Brenner came from the Compass Room with the huge cigar still in his mouth. He gestured back into the room and the large white man I had seen on deck with the spinning girl came and wrapped his arms around her and they disappeared back into the Compass Room and closed the door. The pale arms of the girl hung loosely at her sides and her eyes were closed. I felt a massive hand on my upper arm.

"Please, sir." The crewman said. He had a thick French Caribbean accent. He turned me around and we started toward an elevator that was held open by another crew person. We stepped in and the crewman pushed the A button all the way at the bottom.

"What does that mean?" I asked, nodding toward the door. *"L'Inconnue de la Seine?"* The door shut quietly in front of my nose. The hydraulics of the elevator squealed slightly.

The big Caribbean man said, "It means 'The Unknown of the Seine.'"

"Who is the girl in the drawing?" I asked, still nodding toward the party that wasn't there now but rising above us.

"That is her, sir."

"Who?"

"The Unknown, sir." And he smiled broadly, showing two rows of perfect white teeth but for the one gold cap adjacent to the left canine.

I stayed in our room watching Kevin Costner's *Field of Dreams*, while Jane Marie danced at the captain's reception. The warm room and the rolling of the ship made me sleepy. I hardly woke when my roommates came in. They were laughing and telling stories. Todd threw off his suit and clambered up to the bunk above me. I watched Jane Marie take off her pearls and unzip her dress in the bathroom. She said nothing to me as she lifted up the blankets of her own bunk.

She lay there silently and after a few moments she said, "Goodnight, Cecil," and then rolled over.

There was no port or natural light in our stateroom so I had no idea how late or early it was when my eyes came open again. I could not sleep soundly for fear of the strange dream I was having. It was something about the girl. The pale girl who had kissed me. The Unknown.

Sometime either late or early, Jane Marie woke up and went into the bathroom and threw up. I asked her if she was all right and she said something about seasickness, and the closeness of the room. I felt the room sway and closed my eyes against my own nausea.

When I next woke up, there was a slurred voice clipping through the public address system and there seemed to be a lot of commotion in the hall. People walking hurriedly and whispered voices outside our door. I pulled my pants and a T-shirt on and left the room. The fluorescent lights in the hallway buzzed like insects. I could hear the thrum of the engine somewhere deep in the body of the ship and there seemed to be more rolling to the hull. I definitely felt queasy. I padded down the hall.

I tapped softly on the door. When there was no answer I tried the handle; it turned easily. Inside I could hear chamber music playing. Vivaldi. *The Four Seasons.*

I opened the door and she was lying back with her head propped on four pillows. This time her IV was hooked up. There was a stand next to her bunk and the empty shriveled plastic IV bag hanging like rotten fruit.

Her wig was off and the light glared off of her scalp. She had an empty bedpan on her lap. Her bald head was bent back; her eyes were open and unblinking. She was quite dead.

4

Off the Coast

Cut the Miss Marple shit, Cecil." Jane Marie shuffled through the wildlife books piled in front of her on the table.

It was morning. I had followed Jane Marie and Todd up to Flag Deck where the breakfast buffet was being served. We sat at a round table near a window on the starboard side watching the near shore of British Columbia slip past. Jane Marie stopped looking at her books and spread cream cheese on half of a toasted bagel. Todd sipped from a tankard-sized glass of orange juice, then suddenly lifted his camera to take a photograph of God knows what.

"This is not Miss Marple shit. I'm telling you this girl was dancing up on the Horizon Deck last evening and by morning she was dead."

Jane Marie placed some salmon lox on her bagel. "Well then, did you tell anyone else about this . . . ghost woman?"

I speared a forkful of sausage patties. "Yes, Miss Employee of the Month, I did. I went to the doctor's office. No one was there. I found a phone and reported it to the

ship's operator and they thanked me very much. Then I
went back to the girl's cabin. It was locked."

"What room was she in?" Jane Marie asked. Her brow
was furrowed and she looked as if she were working out a
problem in her head.

"Acapulco 800, between our room and the clinic
entrance. It's still locked."

"Have you spoken to Sonny Walters?" Suddenly she
reached out and gripped my wrist. "800? Are you sure it
was Acapulco 800?" Her grip tightened.

I tried to pull away and as I leaned back in my chair I
felt a hand on my shoulder. I looked straight up and saw
the inverted image of Sonny Walters smiling down on me.

"Well, good morning, everyone. Sleep well?" His voice
was bright in his stage whisper. As I looked around I
noticed that at least two-thirds of the people eating in the
buffet room had their eyes on Sonny. Men in golf clothes
and older women with Cartier scarves all watched him
walk and hung on his every word.

"Well, that's just great!" he said, keeping up the patter
even though we hadn't answered him. Then in a lower
voice he whispered to me: "Mr. Younger, I think we should
talk in my office."

"Moonlight Bay," Jane Marie said loudly as it burst from
her memory. Sonny Walters winced and I could feel his
fingers tighten on my shoulder.

"Moonlight Bay . . . I heard someone say that over the
public address system . . . 'Moonlight Bay, Acapulco 800.'
I'm sure of it," Jane Marie insisted.

Todd took his camera down and nodded at me in
agreement.

"You know, come to think of it, Cecil," Todd said slowly,

"that is correct. I heard it very distinctly. 'Moonlight Bay, Acapulco 800,' just as Jane Marie has remembered. I thought it was quite unusual and that is perhaps why it registered so clearly in my memory."

"Okay then . . ." Sonny's voice was building in frustration and his hands were now pulling me by my armpits. I was being pulled to my feet and Todd snapped a couple of pictures of this. Sonny smiled winningly but said through his teeth, "Not here. Darn it. In the office." It was eerie how he could communicate anger to me and hearty equanimity to the rest of the room. Several women in the far corner watched him and I could tell their hearts were melting as if they wanted to adopt him. Sonny had a strange effect on the majority of the cruisers. This was, I would later learn, part of the stock in trade of a perfect Cruise Director: complete and utmost control over everyone's sense of happiness. A Cruise Director must radiate it: Fun, Adventure, Possibility. Fun was more like it. Fun as a religion.

As soon as he shut the door to his remarkably small office, he turned and his face both hardened and aged. "What in the Sam Hill do you think you're doing?" he said as if he were holding a gun to my chest.

"I was eating my sausages and toast. Until you created a scene out there." I pointed to the closed door, heightening my dramatic presence. I hoped.

"Oh . . . yeah," Sonny said petulantly. He flipped over his trash can in one well-practiced move and sat on it. But in the next moment he paused. Then he looked worried. "I didn't really make a scene out there, did I?" Now I had him worried. Even his perfect teeth seemed to pale, as if that were possible.

"Naw." I waved a reassuring hand at him and sat down

and put my feet up on his desk, thereby taking up most of the available space in the room. "Sonny, you hired me to look into—"

"*I* didn't hire you," he interrupted.

"Okay." I held my hand up in my best "no argument" gesture. "Your *boss* hired me to look into the situation with the medical facilities on this boat. Well, the first day out I get drunk and there is a dead girl in Acapulco 800 and you are starting to lose your trademark good sense of humor. Now you can bounce me off the boat, but that won't be until at least tomorrow when we get into Ketchikan. So why don't you tell me just a little bit more about your problems?"

Sonny sat silently. Scowling, his boyish good looks turned down like a cracked egg: sort of a Pat Boone about to puke.

"I suppose I could talk to the captain . . ." I said finally.

"No!" Sonny said, both exhausted and pleading. "Don't talk to the doggone captain!" He bent and flicked the tassel on his loafer. Then he straightened and brushed some imaginary crumbs off of his lemon-yellow crewneck sweater. "It wouldn't do any good anyway . . ." He sighed, most of his anger gone now. "There are three companies that operate this ship, you see, Mr. Younger. I work for the cruise line company. We basically charter the vessel from a larger company. I work for the Great Circle Lines. We're in charge of the ship's itinerary and the entertainment. The captain and his crew work for the Empire Shipping Company. The captain operates the boat, and is in charge of all deck staff, crew and the ship's officers. I am the head of the cruise line on board. I direct the entertainment, shore excursions, and the social staff. Then there is the hotel manager who is in charge of the accommodations and dining on board. You don't have to worry about them because they really contract with us. So, in effect they report to me. But the captain—no, the captain works for Empire and he is very clear about his authority. You can't go talking to him. The captain doesn't even know about you, Mr. Younger."

By now all petulance was gone and Sonny picked at the cuticle of his left thumb. He was clearly rattled and would not meet my eyes as he went on talking.

"My boss in Miami, the cruise line boss, directed me to report on the . . . Moonlight Bay situation . . . but he made it clear that Empire Shipping is *not* to catch wind of our investigation." Sonny waved his hand around as if engulfed by a swarm of gnats. "Everyone is so, you know, afraid of . . . oh, I don't know, bad publicity and lawsuits, that sort of thing. My boss wants me . . . and you . . . to handle this situation before it gets out of hand and the shipping company finds out and pulls out of our charter agreement."

I nodded. "Okay, so the captain and the shipping company mustn't know. Now, tell me about the Moonlight Bay situation."

Sonny stopped picking at his thumb. He looked me square in the eyes in what could have been an exercise from one of his acting classes.

"'Moonlight Bay' is the term we use when we have had a death on board. We have a protocol, Mr. Younger. When there is a death, the stewards know to secure the room immediately. If there are relatives, we assign a member of the entertainment staff to comfort them. We take care of the body and the paperwork, and we try to do it without alarming any of the other passengers. Death on board a ship can ruin a person's vacation experience," he concluded grimly.

"I can imagine," I said, sounding more sarcastic than I had intended.

"Listen," Sonny said, and he lowered his eyes, "I know you think I'm ridiculous. I know that because I feel ridiculous when I do this job. Especially when I first started out. I mean . . ." He looked sadly at the clutter of schedules and contracts on his desk. His clothes hung on the edge of filing cabinets. "I mean, I had some luck in musical theater. I had been up for some good roles. I had a really decent cabaret act. I've always been old-fashioned . . ." His voice faded away. "I take this job seriously, Mr. Younger. Our passengers are not the super-rich. We are not a top-of-the-line tour. These people have saved a long time for a once-in-a-lifetime experience. This is just an iron tub floating around on the North Pacific, for gosh sakes. It's up to me to make it . . . exciting, romantic . . . Whatever crazy expectations our passengers bring with them it's up to me to make them happy. It's my job. I do take my job seriously." His voice had a quaver to it.

"So . . . a Moonlight Bay really fucks up your job," I said sympathetically.

"To say the least." He managed a weak smile. "And there are more and more of them. We had six on our last tour." He looked up at me, his eyebrows arched and his eyes sad. "That's six in fifteen days. Boy, oh boy, that's tough, let me tell you."

"What's going on? Why the increase?"

"There is a trend everywhere. Of course, some of it is our demographics. We have over seven hundred passengers on ship right now. The median age is sixty-four years.

We are bound to have incidental deaths. Elderly people who are not as well as they hoped to be for the trip, heart attacks, strokes, we've even had our share of 'cafe coronaries.' You know, choking on that last big bite of roast . . . But that doesn't explain all of it."

The ship started to roll from side to side; Sonny looked at his watch. "We're headed for open water. We'll have some motion for the next four hours or so." He turned back to me. "AIDS has something to do with it. We started noticing a few years ago that we were getting younger men traveling alone and in pairs. This makes sense; cruising is a very comfortable way to travel. Particularly if you are taking medication and have to regulate your activity. We have more and more passengers who are ill. Men and women coming on board knowing they are approaching the final stages of their disease. We predicted this and tried to accommodate it. More cultural events, educational programs, more activities for the mind and the spirit, if you will. The medical facilities were upgraded. But recently . . ." Sonny stood and pushed past me to his desk. He lifted a sheaf of papers and flipped through them. ". . . we started noticing a pattern of nonpayment."

"What?" I asked, not sure I was hearing him right.

"Nonpayment. People were going first cabin, Horizon Deck, and opening huge bar tabs, and then before disembarking they were choosing to end their lives. This is bad enough . . ." He paused. "But they're putting it all on their credit cards," he said with the kind of scolding tone of a schoolmaster.

"So they're dying and stiffing you on their bills . . ."

"Worse," Sonny said dramatically. "They're stiffing the credit card company. Many of these passengers are single males. They've used up all of their money or dispersed it before they come aboard the ship. There is no estate to go after."

"The card companies still pay you. Why is this a problem? . . . Well, other than it might dampen the festival atmosphere, with your passengers dropping like flies."

"It's much more serious than you may even imagine." Sonny's voice was headed up another octave. "The credit card companies are threatening to stop honoring our accounts."

"So?"

"What do you mean—*so*? Mr. Younger, nobody writes checks for reservations. No one travels on *money*. If we couldn't take credit cards, we're basically out of business."

The ship lurched once to port and a sheaf of papers fell off the corner of Sonny's desk and scattered on the floor.

"The credit card companies are asking that we take steps to address the situation."

"Can you stop people from killing themselves?" I held my hands out, palms up.

"There's more to the picture. There are now tour groups. Groups dedicated to providing services specifically for this clientele."

"L'Inconnue de la Seine."

"Exactly. These travel companies are growing more and more popular. They help their clients prepare, and they find the right ships and tours to travel on. For some reason our ship, and particularly the Alaska voyages, has become more and more popular with these groups."

"What does your ship's doctor say?"

"Now we are getting to the point. The ship's doctor is an officer of the boat. He works for the vessel company. He

works for the *captain*. The doctor really is not very helpful
to us."

"He won't answer questions?"

"Not about this subject." Sonny shook his head sadly.

"So . . ." I spoke slowly and clearly, knowing this might
be the only contact I would make with Sonny. "You want
me to check out the ship's doctor. You want me to find out
if he is doing anything to encourage these . . . Moonlight
Bays."

"I think he gets a cut from these tour groups. I just
know he is profiting from this." Sonny was showing more
peevishness now that the subject of death and credit card
fraud was out in the open.

"And if you can take whatever dirt I come up with to the
ship's company, you might get him fired. Then you hopefully find a doctor who will make the ship a little less . . .
hospitable for the death tour industry."

"You have to understand, Mr. Younger. Everyone is welcome on our ship. We can't afford to get the reputation of
being unfriendly towards passengers with special needs."

When I had first met Sonny Walters I'd assumed he was
what he appeared to be: a good-looking and shallow twit,
in the mold of a singing towel boy who had been given too
much authority. Now I was beginning to get the sense that
there was something more going on with him, but I wasn't
sure I wanted to find out what. "Why didn't you just tell me
this when we first spoke?"

"For one thing, I was hoping we wouldn't really need
you. I don't know, I was hoping it would just go away. I
wanted to get you on board and break you in slowly. On
these two-week trips, you'll see, there is a longer break-in
period. A longer settling-in period. This death, this girl in

Acapulco 800, came too fast. They don't usually start dying until much later in the trip. Usually until after Ketchikan or Sitka."

He smiled professionally.

I stood up and wiped my hands together, acting as if I were ready to go. Sonny sat quickly back on his overturned wastebasket and waved me to sit back down again.

"The culture on board ship is very interesting, Mr. Younger . . . Cecil, there are some things you should be aware of. The ship's crew—that is the sailors and the officers, the people who actually make this thing *move*—these people are part of a union. No one else on board is union. Both companies, mine and the hotel contractor, have worked hard to keep it that way. The hotel and restaurant staff is made up largely of Filipino and Indonesian workers. On this cruise we also have a large number of Caribbean islanders. The Filipinos are great workers and they're perfectly suited for the job but the thinking in the industry in the last few years is not to let the Filipino workers form a majority or you can see we'd be right back in the union problem . . ." Sonny stretched his hands out before him, as if imploring me.

"The ship's crew is similarly a mix. The captain is a Serb, the first officer is Panamanian, the chief engineer is Polish, and there are a growing number of other eastern European sailors on board. The lower down you go into the ship, of course, the more islanders you'll find."

"What about the doctor?" I asked.

"The doctor is an American," Sonny replied without showing the least of a smile. "He stays to himself mostly. He eats the first few meals with the captain and passengers, but after that he has his own schedule."

"Does he have a good record in treating most of the patients? I mean, is he good at what he does?"

"The passengers love him!" Sonny enthused. "That's another reason we have to be extremely delicate in this matter. He's great with them. He's treated all kinds of conditions and made people comfortable. Some of our wealthy passengers have even tried to set him up in private practice in their own hometowns. I mean, he has a following!" Sonny was wide-eyed.

The ship lurched again to port and Sonny stood up, looking again at his watch. "Listen. I'm sorry about our rocky beginning. Just try to settle in. Find out what you can about the doctor." He pointed to the door and smiled. "I've really got to be going. I've got a ten o'clock presentation and then some entertainment on the schedule. There are a million people looking for me right about now. It should tell you something that they'd never think of looking in my office, huh?"

I decided not to answer that question. Instead I asked, "What's the doctor's name, and where do I find him?"

"His name is Allen Edwards. Doctor Edwards. He keeps clinic hours. Get sick if you have to. You'll find him soon enough." Sonny opened the door and disappeared. The door closed.

I looked around his office and my eyes fell on a back-lit publicity photo of Sonny: Faded blue wash with a halo of light surrounding his boyish hair. The door opened again and Sonny himself stuck the hair back into the office.

"Oh . . . I forgot to tell you. Gee, I'm sorry but your bar privileges have been cut off, Cecil. At least until Ketchikan. We'll just see where we are then. Okay?"

"You mean in Ketchikan?"

"Exactly."

"That's easy, Sonny. We'll be in Ketchikan."

He smiled winningly and pointed his index fingers at me, six-gun style. "Ouch . . . Good stuff." He squeezed his imaginary trigger fingers, then disappeared again.

Out on the fantail, passengers were stepping through their paces at day one's aerobic class entitled "Making Friends." The song "Getting to Know You" was blasting out of a pair of speakers near the stern. Two dozen or so participants, mostly fiftyish white women, were stretching their arms above their heads and swaying. "Getting to Know You" shifted into a thumping disco beat and a slender, older woman with a remarkable helmet of yellow hair began to lead the group. The sign said she was our exercise "clinician," Tricia. Tricia had the smallest, tightest butt I've ever seen. She snapped out cues to the assembled.

"Good now, two three, back now, four five, go nice and easy back to one . . ."

The sunlight was pale and milky. It was perhaps sixty degrees and it could rain at any time but that wasn't a concern to the exercisers. We were outbound, past some rocky headlands. The ship had a gentle but pronounced roll. Gulls wheeled in the eddies of air behind the stern. Occasionally one would dive down into the foam, come up with something and then, working awkwardly to pull away into the air, glide back to the others.

Todd was exercising. He had his new tan slacks rolled up and his shoes off. For whatever reason, Todd is spectacularly uncoordinated. Although he tried to keep time with the disco version of "Getting to Know You," he was consistently at least three commands behind the others. He waved and floundered around like a broken windmill but with each effort Tricia would smile at him and give her own legs an extra kick in his direction. "Good! . . . Good!" she told him. "That's it. Perfect. Now up a little higher." The song ended and everyone clapped and shook their arms to their side. The woman working out next to Todd was dressed in shiny tights and pink leggings with a T-shirt that read "I'm spending my grandchildren's inheritance." She patted Todd on the back and said, "You're doing just great." And Todd beamed at her as he awkwardly imitated the last of the stretching exercises. "I love doing this," the woman gushed. "I just feel I can eat all that much more." She laughed unashamedly and so did Todd.

The music changed to something by the Miami Sound Machine and I couldn't bring myself to watch. Jane Marie was sitting in a straight-backed chair with her feet propped up on the port side rail. She wore a spaghetti-strap shirt with her sweater bundled in her lap. Her dark glasses were perched on top of her head and she scanned the ocean with her old green rubber-armored Zeiss field glasses. She looked like a movie star. Carole Lombard, maybe. I pulled up a chair next to her.

"I lost my bar privileges," I said.

"Do tell . . ." She kept scanning the ocean. The shadow of a gull brushed the white skin of her shoulders.

"That's not to say you couldn't buy me a drink now and then," I said out to the Pacific.

She put her field glasses down on top of her sweater and looked at me as if I had just peed on her foot.

"Not me, pal. I'm looking to keep my privileges. I'm going to meet some people on this trip." She picked up the binoculars. "If you ask me, I'm pretty well positioned here to make some contacts. This is a good spot for a single woman."

"Yeah, too bad you don't know any single women." I tried to sound amusingly sarcastic and confident at the same time.

I looked out to sea. The waves rolled in undulating columns with only a slight chop on top. The horizon was a wavering line dividing the gray sky from the gray sea. The sun was blocked by a cottony gauze. My eyes ached to find detail. It was a mild, mild day.

"There!" Jane Marie stood up and pointed.

Five hundred yards from the ship, the slick black form ploughed the surface of the sea. A quick puff of breath came from a blowhole just behind a round pumpkin of a head, then the dagger shape of a long dorsal fin.

"Killer whales! Port side. Nine o'clock, five hundred yards!"

About a dozen of the exercisers ran to the rail. The Miami Sound Machine kept churning. Tricia kept right on with her routine. Several of the passengers kept doing their leg lifts standing at the rail. Back under the covered bar there was a flurry of activity and I heard someone call, "Whales? I'll drink to that, by God!" and gales of laughter.

There were seven animals. One large male with the tall dagger-shaped dorsal fin. Two juveniles. Four females or perhaps young males. They traveled swiftly, on a course parallel with the ship. As each came to the surface, the white of the head marking and saddle patches rippled through the green water. Their backs curved in a smooth muscular motion. Dorsal fins sliced like blades into the surface. The whales stayed near the ship for perhaps forty seconds. Then they dropped behind, cut across the wake, and were gone.

A young woman stood with an older man near us at the rail. The woman had dark hair and eyes. She tried to keep her eyes on the whales long after they had vanished. "I've never seen anything like them . . ." she said softly, almost to herself.

A gray-haired woman in a turquoise workout suit lit a cigarette and looked at me quizzically. "Whales?" she said. "That's it?"

I shrugged my shoulders apologetically and the turquoise woman drew on her smoke and walked back inside. I could hear her athletic shoes squeak on the decking.

Still scanning the sea, Jane Marie had walked to the other side of the ship. Off to my left was a woman with long frizzy dark hair. She was sketching in a book. Her hand worked furiously. I walked over and looked across her shoulder. She had scrawled several lines but, amazingly, the lines captured the motion of the swells and the big animals cutting through without showing the whales themselves. It was as if she had drawn the sound of their breath. She looked up and caught me staring at her drawing.

"Have you ever seen anything like it?" she asked breathlessly.

She was not instantly beautiful. Her teeth were crooked and she was overweight, at least overweight for a fashion model. But her eyes were large and they had this crazy glitter to them. Instantly, I was almost afraid to look straight into them, worried that something would be looted clear out of my chest. Her face showed no hint of suspicion or distrust. The sun broke out from the clouds and I almost attributed the reemergence of light to some power in this chubby girl's spectacular eyes.

"I mean *whales!*" She grabbed my hand. "*Whales*, on our very first day out. Can you believe it!"

"No, I can hardly believe it," I said with as much conviction as I could muster.

"I'm Rosalind Kench." She twisted her hand around into mine, pumping a more formal handshake. "I used to live in New York. The City, right in the middle of the City, it's incredible, isn't it? I mean the City. Well, really it's incredible because I've just moved to Portland, Oregon. Lake Oswego really. It's fabulous there. I never thought the world was so green, really I mean, it's a *different* kind of green. Vermont, New Hampshire, of course, are both pretty green, but there is something about the light on the Pacific. The evening light especially, of course I love the light on the Cape, particularly in the morning, but this . . ." And Rosalind dropped my hand and spun around. Her arms took in all of "this," which I guessed was the western edge of the Northern Hemisphere. "But *this* is, well, you know, different . . ."

Her voice trailed off and as she came around to face me again her expression fell. She stared down at my feet and I realized suddenly that her eyes had an odd kind of presence. As if they were flashlights that could only cast shadows. She bit her lower lip.

"I'm babbling, aren't I?" Her voice was soft and she would not look at me. "Oh God, I've been babbling. Please say something quick so I won't say another word." Her hands started to shake.

"You have very strange and beautiful eyes," I said without knowing why.

Rosalind Kench squeezed her eyes shut as if we were playing hide-and-go-seek and she was "it."

"Ooooh, that's . . . sweet, but now I know you're making fun of me." She kept her eyes closed and we stood together on the deck silently. I started to shift on the balls of my feet thinking that maybe I was supposed to go hide now.

"My name is Cecil Younger," I said and I took her hand as she had mine and pumped her forearm up and down in a greeting. Rosalind opened one eye a crack.

"Hello, Cecil. That's a very interesting name. What kind of work do you do?" The other eye opened slightly and I could feel something in my chest fall into shadow.

"I . . . well, I . . . actually I'm retired."

"Really! You seem young to be retired. You must have done very well for yourself, if you don't mind me commenting, I don't mean to pry. I mean . . . I'm sorry." And she squeezed her eyes shut tight again.

"No. No, don't worry. I don't mind. I'm retired . . . I'm retired because of certain health problems."

Rosalind opened her eyes and clutched my forearm with both her hands. I felt her breath on my neck. I didn't dare look into her eyes.

"Isn't that just the dickens?" she said.

"The dickens?" I echoed.

"Well, you know, the body. I mean, we're all just machines wearing out. I mean, if you think about it too much it just gets incredibly depressing." She pulled on my arm to get my attention and unwittingly I looked down into her dark eyes.

"I know this is going to surprise you," she said slowly and solemnly as if we were about to share a forbidden intimacy, "but I'm *not* going to ask you about your health. I just *hate* that. I mean, I've been going through it myself and I hate to have to answer questions. Not that I mind sharing but it's just when you tell people about your illness then they feel like they have to tell their own story and before you know it you're talking about bladders or uterine cysts, for Pete's sake."

"I hate that." I tried not to think about a uterine cyst, which was turning out to be impossibly hard for some reason.

"I'm just going to say one thing," Rosalind continued in the same solemn tone, still gripping my forearm. "You look really good, Cecil. So just keep doing what you've been doing. It's working." And she winked, leaning back and giving me the covert thumbs-up of a co-conspirator.

I nodded toward her sketch pad. "What kind of work do you do?" The gulls whirled close to our left and she spun to see them. "You must be an artist," I continued, awkwardly trying to look back into her eyes even though she had turned away.

"Oh Gawwd." She brushed her dark hair out of her face. "I'm an illustrator. I mean, I do books. Well, now I've got just one book." She turned back to me, smiling. "I mean, it's really great. This is my very own contract. This book I'm doing now. It's my own." Her face fell again. "But I'm way behind on it. I mean, that's what this whole trip is about. You see . . ." She looked out over the stern wake. "I've spent the whole darned advance on this trip. I thought, you know, it would be good for inspiration. But I don't know. I've got all my stuff with me. I just don't think I can do it." The gulls banked to the west and receded into that gray horizon.

"What's the book?" I asked her.

"Oh, I don't know. It started out a good idea. I mean,

they liked it. The editor liked it. She said the marketing people were *wild* about it."

"Just what is it they are wild about?"

"Angels," Rosalind said in a whisper. *"The Encyclopedia of Angels.* Portraits and descriptions."

She said nothing for a while. I shifted on my feet again, scanning my knowledge for all the interesting conversational hooks I could use for "Angels."

"Oh," I said rather smartly.

"You're right," Rosalind said. "It's a dumb idea. But I started it. I've been reading all the stuff. I mean, people are crazy about Angels. I've read all the stuff and I've gotten started. And *now* I've spent every cent of the whole gosh-darned advance and I don't think I can do it." Her voice disappeared into the wash of wind.

A large seabird came into view from our starboard: huge wingspan skimming the tops of the swells, curving and looping on the slightest change in the wind.

"Isn't that an albatross?" I asked Rosalind.

"I think so." Her eyes followed the invisible lines the bird's wingtips cut into the wind. Her head turned with each curve the bird made across our wake. Rosalind followed the albatross so intently it was as if her own personality had dropped away momentarily.

"I understand they can go days without a beat of their wings," she finally said.

"Angels?" I asked her.

"No, silly." And she looked at me shyly. "Albatrosses. I don't even want to *think* about Angels today." The tips of her fingers brushed my wrist. "Do you know where the clinic is? I swear I was there once but I'm not sure how I found it."

"I do." I said this with the air of an old salt. "I'll walk you down there."

We walked past a group of people standing in the full wind on the back deck. A dark-haired woman with a silver scarf lashing the air around her head held a champagne flute in her thin hands. I heard her saying to the four men clustered around her, "Don't even talk to me about hunting. There *is* no literature of hunting. All of that fake sensitive crap about killing animals. It disgusts me. Same with the whining businessmen on the farms. This is no literature of farming or hunting. It's just boys being boys." The men in the group stood silently as I walked past them. Rosalind came closely behind me. As we turned into a stairway, I turned and looked back at the group. The woman was flattening her hair and clutching the ends of her silver scarf as she finished the last of her drink. "Well then . . . what's next, gentlemen?" The four men laughed. I closed the door behind Rosalind.

I swear I had to clear my ears, too, by the time we made it down to Acapulco Deck. The motion of the ship was an odd sway in gravity, making walking unsteady and tempting seasickness. I walked past my stateroom and down toward the clinic. I stopped at Acapulco 800, apparently too abruptly, for Rosalind bumped into me. She braced her hands against the foam-green walls.

"I didn't know they even had rooms down here." She had her eyes closed and I could tell she was trying to peel back the tentacles of motion sickness.

"I'm just going to try my room," I told her and then tried to turn the knob of Acapulco 800. It was still locked.

"Damn! I forgot my key," I said hurriedly and walked

toward the clinic. The ship lurched to the port and our bodies pulled against the walls. We were both using the inside handrail when we turned the corner to the clinic.

Men's voices were arguing. "Don't tell me about the numbers. I don't want to hear any of that."

The door was open through to the examining room. There on the table was the pale girl from the evening before. She was dazzling in her colorlessness, as if she were already a spirit of pure light. Standing above her was the large white man with the graying beard I had seen with her last night. He had on a military-style mess jacket with braided epaulets. A stethoscope was draped around his neck.

He spoke and his voice was deep and soothing. "I understand, Isaac. Please don't misunderstand me . . ."

Then the doctor saw me and he was clearly startled. He quickly turned and in one motion zipped up the green rubber bag in which the pale girl rested. Her hands lay crossed over her sunken chest. Somehow the light in the room seemed to dim. The doctor turned and swiftly kicked the door shut in my face and I found my nose within an inch of the metal door.

"Just one moment, please," I heard the doctor's voice say distantly behind the closed door. There was a long silence. Then the doctor walked out the door, pulling the bottom of his jacket down and rolling his shoulders to straighten the fit. "I'm very sorry," the doctor said and he placed his hand reassuringly on my shoulder. "I'm dealing with an extremely serious situation. Everything is fine, but it just needs my attention. I'll be able to get back to regular clinic hours soon. I'm sorry, but why not check back with us later? Why not come back in say . . . forty-five minutes?"

"Was that girl dead?" Rosalind piped up over my shoulder.

The doctor winced ever so slightly. "It's a very serious case. But actually it's working out quite well. Everything is fine and I'll be able to help you soon. Please just check back with us later." And he stood silently in front of us. The conversation was clearly over.

"Right then," I said cheerily and taking Rosalind's hand, turned and walked away.

"Wow. She really looked dead to me," Rosalind said in a stage whisper as we shuttled down the narrow hall. "I couldn't see very clearly but it looked like—"

"I think you're right," I interrupted. I started fishing in my jacket pocket for my wallet. "Why did you want to see the doctor, anyway? Are you okay?" I asked Rosalind.

Her eyes arched in sympathy and she touched my arm. "Oh, I'm fine really. I just . . . well, I just worry that I'm sick all the time actually. I mean, I just think about it a lot, you know. I mean, I've got my share of . . . but . . ." She held her palms up in front of her face as if fending the words off. "I don't want to talk about it. Yuck. Yuck. Yuck." Then she hugged me quickly. "But thanks for asking, Cecil. That's sweet."

Together, we walked up to Acapulco 800. My State of Alaska Organ Donors card is the perfect laminated weight and flexibility for sliding against the latches of most old hotel rooms. I disentangled from Rosalind and fished my card out while at the same time trying to shade my hands from her. The bolt clicked and the door swung open with a slight pressure from my shoulder. There was no top bolt and no door chain. But what there was were four legs on the bunk near the back wall with a bright light shining down on them. A shiny black torso and muscular legs thrusting. Two thin shapely white legs topped with red patent leather pumps spread wide and forming a truncated "V" above the black man's shoulders. His company-issue coveralls were down around his ankles. Her flowered panties were on the floor between us. He was too concerned with his own motion to hear the clunk of the door. Not so with the woman beneath him. The talons of her bright red fingernails flew against the skin of his back. Her eyes, wild and hazy with sex, cleared instantly with panic. His voice groaned, with intense expectation. She was pushing and sucking a scream between her teeth and into her lungs.

In two beats he opened his eyes and then followed her panicked gaze over his shoulder to me. Then he did an odd thing; instead of pulling up his pants, he dove into the bed and buried his face in the pillows at the foot of the bed.

The woman's face came into focus. She tugged a blue raincoat down across her rumpled dress and thrust her hand between her legs to cover herself, but as she tried she was thwarted because the young man's exposed bottom was lying across her lap.

"Excuse me!" she said with breathless dignity. "But is this your room?"

"No. It's not," I said and bumped squarely into Rosalind, who was pushing hard against my back and craning against me to see. Not wanting to miss out on the details this time.

I closed the door. Rosalind was breathing hard and balancing on the balls of her feet.

"Wow," she said, "I guess you know where the excitement is on this ship."

5

Day at Sea

The boat rocked with an uneven rhythm. Behind the closed door of Acapulco 800, I heard the shuffling of embarrassed people hurriedly dressing. Rosalind stared wide-eyed at me as we both watched the knob on the door turn slightly, then stop. The door did not open. I could hear them both breathing on the other side, or perhaps it was my own breathing, but they never came out. I tried to make conversation with the people on the other side of the door. I apologized again and told them that I just needed a few things out of the room. No one answered. No one spoke.

My plan was to wait for them. Maybe confront them in the hall or follow them to a place where we could talk. Rosalind said she had to get up on deck for some air because the motion down in the warm hallway was getting to her. She promised to see me later. Then she turned and walked down the passageway with both her hands touching the sides for support. I stood by the door, prepared to wait however long it took to talk with the romantic couple, but the family from the gangplank with Carol and her young sister Alicia came rumbling down the hallway as if they were bison.

Before I could disappear, the little girl was holding my hand.

"Hello," she said and down by my hip her freckled face smiled up at me. "We're going to our room. Wanna come see it?"

The father was blustering by me. "For heaven's sake, Alicia. This man doesn't want to see our room."

Alicia's mother was in some definite distress. She leaned against the wall as her husband held her by the elbow.

The father turned to me. "Seasick. I'm afraid," he explained curtly. "She says she wants to lay down in her room. I told her I thought it would be better up on deck looking out."

"No." It was all the woman could manage.

"Hello!" Carol said very loudly in my ear. She stood hunch-shouldered and flat-footed very close to me. Her wide-set eyes stared at me without seeming to focus.

I nodded, smiling. "Hello."

"I don't feel so good," Carol said loudly.

"I'm going to my room," the mother said and walked away. "Come on, girls."

Then, without warning, Carol leaned forward and threw up on me. She leaned back and covered her mouth. Alicia stood back and shrieked. "*Eyuuuue!*"

In many circumstances I don't mind being thrown up on. Although I am not all that proud of it, there was a time in my life when every weekend was marked by some form of either vomit, urine, or blood. I was a social drinker, and I was just part of a strange society. But this was somewhat different. First, I was working. I was trying to watch the door, and I wanted back into room 800. Second, Carol's sickness had created an atmosphere that was intolerable for her mother. For as she came forward digging desperately in her black leather purse for a tissue to hand Carol, she was overcome and then put the contents of her own stomach into the purse. And lastly, if I was trying to remain somewhat inconspicuous this was not going to help, for out of seemingly thin air there were cabin stewards with damp towels all over me, as if I were a terrier being attacked by rats. The stewards must have a finely tuned sensitivity to the sound of retching for they were on us in an instant.

The poor father was holding his wife upright. Carol was standing up straight but she started to cry. I think she was more surprised and afraid than anything. Her father looked at me beseechingly. A young steward was on the floor at my feet wiping and cleaning the short-napped carpet.

I spoke to the father in my chipper country gentleman voice. "I'm just going to pop upstairs and get some air. I can take the girls with me. They will be fine. We'll come back later. All right then?"

"Good. Good," the father said. "Alicia. You know where the room is. Watch out for Carol and remember—both your feet stay on the deck. No climbing. Understand?"

Alicia must have had an iron stomach, for she showed no signs of seasickness. She nodded and smiled sweetly. "Come on, Carol," she said and we three walked to the passageway up to an outer deck.

"Thank you," I heard their father say as the mother had another go at emptying her stomach into her purse.

◙ ◙ ◙

In a few minutes we stood on deck. Alicia had gone
through formal introductions as we had walked up. This
included the exchange of full names, eye contact, and
hand shaking. Then, after asking after my home, she
allowed how she and her family lived in Baltimore, Mary-
land. This, she said, was where she was going to begin the
fifth grade next fall.

A slight rain spattered down. Carol closed her eyes and
took deep breaths. She was not feeling well and her features clamped down in unhappiness. She rocked back and
forth and moaned, "Icky, Icky, Icky."

"She'll be okay, Mr. Younger," Alicia assured me as she
hooked her arm through mine in a shipboard gesture
that I instantly recognized only after she had done it.
"She was born that way. She doesn't know any other way,
so it doesn't really bother her." Then she repeated the
litany of explanations I imagined she'd had to learn for
strangers.

"Carol's eighteen years old but she doesn't learn things
the way other people do," Alicia said, and then she added,
"I know my states and capitals and, of course, I can name
all the presidents." She looked down the front of her
sweatshirt with a delicate air of well-enforced modesty.

Down off the lower deck toward the stern, I saw two
stewards pushing a hospital-style gurney with a covered
bundle through a hatchway. It was just a brief glimpse.
It looked like they came out momentarily to position
the gurney around a tight inside corner. Then they were
gone.

"Well, then you must have enjoyed traveling through
Seattle, the capital of Washington," I said to Alicia, staring
at the closed door.

"Please," Alicia said rather patiently. "Seattle is *not* the capital of Washington. That would be Olympia."

We stood at the rail and looked out at the waves. The massive engine of the ship was a slight hum under our feet and the air was a gray wash of the sounds of foaming water under our bow. Nothing broke the calm surface of the undulating swells. Alicia stood at the rail next to me. Once she lifted her sneakered foot to the second rung of the railing and shifted her weight as if to stand on it but she didn't.

A young woman in a white crewneck sweater with the company logo stitched on it rushed over to us. "Well, hi there!" she almost bellowed as she leaned down to talk to Alicia. "I'm Becky. I'm the kids' social counselor and a little birdie just told me that you might not be feeling so good. Is that right?" Everything about Becky's voice and appearance suggested she had been raised among hard-of-hearing simpletons.

"Feeling well," Alicia said. "I think you meant 'feeling so well.'"

"Of course, honey. Ohhh, you are just the smartest little thing!" In the next second both Carol and Alicia were gone with the vivacious Becky amid discussion about a kids' makeup party. I didn't catch the details because, as they walked through the passageway, Mr. Brenner and his cigar came on deck.

"Hey. What did you think of that cigar?" he bellowed. The cigar was down on top of my dresser near my wallet and keys.

"Great," I said, and cast my eyes down as I always do when I'm lying . . . a facial tic which has made it impossible for me to play poker in either Sitka or Juneau.

Mr. Brenner's camel hair blazer flapped back in the wind. The hair that was delicately combed across his scalp lifted to the Pacific breeze and he ran his fingers across his head, pushing everything back as if to say, "To hell with it."

He sucked on the cigar that was roughly as big as a young boy's forearm. He stared out across the water. There was nothing to see, yet he kept staring with that contemplative railside gaze.

"I saw you last night outside the party," he said at last to the ocean, hoping, I suppose, I was listening. "You're not with the tour. I thought you were when I saw you outside the clinic, but you're not with the group, are you?"

I stepped up to the rail with him as if we were two old drunks staring down at our reflections in the water below. "The group?" I asked the ocean.

Mr. Brenner tipped the burning end of his cigar in a self-conscious gesture. "L'Inconnue de la Seine," he said in a stilted French accent. "The group." Then he said nothing.

The sun shattered down on the webs of water streaming away from our bow. A lone gull flew down to the wake and tumbled into an eddy of wind, then lumbered away behind the stern.

Mr. Brenner cleared his throat, then started speaking clearly and slowly. "There was a girl's body fished out of the Seine. I don't think it was any later than the eighteen eighties. Paris, France, you know?" He looked at me quickly and I nodded so he would go on. "This girl had a remarkable face. She was dead. People assumed she had killed herself. Her expression was serene and very beautiful. The authorities brought in an artist to take a plaster cast of her face. They used this image to try and identify her. The girl's face was so perfect, her death mask became an object of art, almost an object of worship."

"Was she ever identified?"

"Well . . ." Brenner drew out the word, considering something, but then he charged on. "No. Never was." He shook his head slowly back and forth as smoke billowed from his mouth. "She is *L'Inconnue* . . . The Unknown. Her image became the object of cultlike significance all over Europe. This was in the nineteen twenties, between the wars. Almost every student in Germany and France had a copy of her death mask in their room."

On a deck below us, someone opened a door and music from the ship's jazz band leaked out into the Pacific. I heard laughter and glasses clattering. Then it was quiet again.

"You see, L'Inconnue was like sex, drugs, and rock and roll. Before there was rock and roll. This dead girl seemed to say that it was better to die peacefully and take your beauty with you. Some used her as a cult of youth. Others claimed that she was the beauty that remained in the moments after death. But finally she is *inconnue*. Unknown . . . unknown and beautiful, of course."

"So this group you are traveling with does what? Sex, drugs, and rock and roll?" Brenner was now only a profile against the gray horizon. He had a broad smile. His dark eyes were hidden under crescents of flesh. He took a long breath.

"L'Inconnue de la Seine is a travel group based in the Netherlands. It promotes tours for people with terminal illnesses."

"What? Like a Hemlock Society?" I asked.

"Naw." He shrugged dismissively. Another door opened

and the music once again took the air. "Naw. The group provides support. It makes arrangements for any special needs. Helps with shore excursions and makes arrangements with the ship's medical staff to help with any treatments you may be undergoing. It's a pain in the ass to travel if you are feeling bum and have to lug around a trunkload of medications. Lots of people just give up. They stay at home or in some stinking nursing home. The *Inconnue* gets people out to enjoy the beauty of the world." He gestured toward the water. "I love it." He sucked on his cigar. "You can tell we're headed north, can't you? We're headed toward Alaska. God, I can hardly wait."

"So you have a terminal illness?" I asked.

"Ah Christ . . ." He fanned the smoke in front of his face dismissively. "Prostate cancer. Who the hell knows? Doctors are such pip-squeaks, don't you think? I mean, the only thing they tell you for certain is how much it is going to cost. *Wait and see . . . Wait and see.* That's all they ever tell you. I'm sick of waiting."

Mr. Brenner turned to me, eyebrows raised. "What do these doctors know? They're all so damn young. I'm convinced that my cysts are older than my damn doctors. You know what I'm saying?"

I shook my head to indicate that I did, but now I was trying to shake Mr. Brenner's prostate out of my mind.

"Why does the group choose this ship?" I asked him.

Brenner kept watching the sea. "Partly the destination. There's something in the north that thins out the blood. The stone and ice. It's dramatic and inspiring." He drew on his cigar, then went on. "But also they've got good medical staff on this ship."

"The doctor helps the people end their lives?" I asked without a change of tone.

Brenner turned and looked at me critically. "The doctor is supposed to help our people carry out their own wishes. He is here to serve the patients and help them in relieving whatever suffering that is in his power. He serves the patients and not . . . anyone else."

The prow of the ship lunged into a swell and the deck rolled down and to the left. The sea gave a great hissing sigh.

"At least that's the theory," Brenner spit out.

Music came out across the water again, followed this time by the fanfare of a saxophone and trumpet. Brenner grabbed my elbow as if he was going to impart something terrifically urgent to me.

"Have you ever heard Sonny the Cruise Director sing? I heard him down in the Caribbean. Oh my God, I tell you, he's good. I think that's his music. We better get down there," he gushed and pulled me back inside.

The Great Circle Lounge was crowded with perhaps three hundred people. There was a raised bandstand and almost a full circle of low-backed couch seats. Most of the seats were taken. Theater lights hung on poles above the bar. A sound booth was located in the back, near the men's room. Waiters brought drinks and took orders. Brenner abandoned me with a wave over his right shoulder as he gaily stepped over people's laps to grab a seat near a group of people who waved and wiggled closer together to make room for him.

Alicia, Carol, and the vivacious Becky were sitting at a round table near the bar. Alicia was sipping a clear carbonated drink through a straw. Becky was clicking her thumbnail against her glass and scanning the crowds for someone else. Carol sat with her shoulders hunched around her glass. Her mouth was open. She watched the band and the light sparkling off the bell of the horns. Occasionally, she would groan loudly and snort with an overloud laugh. Alicia slipped her hand over Carol's, as I'm sure she had learned from their mother. Carol squeezed her sister's hand and made an effort to stay quiet.

The band was Margie & the Navigators. Margie was of indeterminate age but definitely prewar. She wore black slacks and a maroon sequined jacket. She played the piano and her silver-blonde hair bobbed just out of her eyes. She had a lit cigarette in an ashtray and a glass of water next to her piano. The other Navigators were a smattering of different eras. The drummer looked as if he could have played for Bob Wills and the Texas Playboys. He was an old white man with great big square glasses. The bassist could have sat in with Erect Nipples—the band, not the condition. As natural as Margie looked in her gig clothes, the bassist seemed uncomfortable, as if his tuxedo was giving him a rash. The saxophonist's skin was drawn tight over his skull and he kept time with his chin while he played with an irritating tone that felt slightly out of tune. He seemed the most confident onstage, as if he were in a deeply stoned dream, but his playing seemed stiff, and in several places resembled honking rather than song.

Margie & the Navigators played "I Had a Dream, Dear," which had been one of my father's favorite songs. I had never known that it was a real song actually performed by other people. I had always assumed my father had just made it up. I saw a hand waving in my direction. Jane Marie sat near an aisle on the far side near the bar. Todd sat next to her, and on the other side of her sat a slender, and very well dressed, black man.

When I worked my way over there, neither Jane Marie nor her companion offered to get up. Todd took his eyes briefly off the Navigators and squeezed closer to the center. I was able to sit with half a cheek on the couch, one man away from Jane Marie.

The woman I had assumed was in love with me whispered across the chest of the black man. "Cecil, this is Nigel. He's an investment banker from London."

"Hello," Nigel said in an irritating Denzel-Washington-doing-Shakespeare kind of way.

"Nice to meet you," I replied and cast my eyes down at his soft leather loafers and his tailored cuffs.

I was in the mood to hate every second of Sonny Walters's act. I figured he would play up the irony. Try and stay hip both ways; Bill Murray doing his lounge singer routine with a few tearjerkers from *Les Miserables* or *Cats* thrown in.

Sonny walked out wearing a lemon-yellow sports coat and a pale blue silk tie. His teeth were straight. For some reason I still held that against him, maybe because he had the kind of handsomeness my mother always wanted me to have when she picked out my clothes.

Sonny in fact was an extraordinary singer. He sang a series of ballads in an unsentimental baritone. He looked at each member of the crowd and he didn't fake a thing. His voice didn't waver with phony longing. He didn't have to oversell a single lyric. There wasn't an ounce of self-awareness or cheap sentiment. He was giving his audience exactly what they wanted without apologies. He sang old songs about complicated love and longing. I didn't know I had missed these songs until I heard them.

As he sang, Sonny leaned against a high stool and he did not loosen his tie. In the quiet passages of the tunes the women in the audience did not move, they did not breathe, only drawing deep breaths when Sonny did, as if he were pulling the phrasing of the song through his lungs and theirs. When he ended, the applause was urgent. They needed him to sing one more. Always. One more.

A waiter came close to my left side. He offered me a champagne glass and I took it. The ball in the middle of the room was turning: Threads of light spidered around the room, flecking every surface. Sonny was singing "Make Believe," his voice reassuring as a flannel quilt. I jumped slightly as I heard the voice of the waiter, crouched close to my elbow.

"Sir. Excuse me, sir."

When I turned, his face was close to mine. A thread of the light cut across his ebony skin. He had a clipped British accent. His expression was grave.

"I'm sorry, sir. But I have a message for you." He took the bottle of champagne out of the slush of cubes. "I know nothing of this. I have just been told." The young waiter was breathing deeply and for a moment I thought he might hyperventilate.

"I've been told to tell you . . . to forget what you saw." The waiter held my eyes with his. He had strange gray eyes, the whites masked with a thin film. He did not say anything more. I was confused. I was about to speak when the waiter looked down into the mouth of the silver ice bucket. So strong was his hold on my eyes that I looked down, too.

"Just forget what you saw, sir," the waiter repeated in a whisper.

The ice cubes had a dull glitter in the bottom of the ice bucket. Buried down in the cubes was a human hand. The pale white palm faced up as if it were scooping ice out for a drink but at the wrist was the shaved nub of bone surrounded by tattered skin and red meat. Severed tubes of the blood vessels hung limp in the water. Stray light scattered around in the ice and my head felt strange as if I had just now noticed the movement of the ship for the first time. The hand was like a glowing ingot banked down in the coals. I couldn't take my eyes off of it. When I started to reach for it the waiter stood up and walked quickly away. Sonny finished his set and took his bows. He held his microphone in his right hand and blew kisses with the left. The crowd clapped and clapped and clapped.

6

Ketchikan

In the early morning the *Westward* docked in Ketchikan. The ship was tied to the dock in the middle of downtown. The downtown area of Ketchikan is cradled against the side of a mountain. A stream flows down the center, breaking the view into a "Y." There are some new dockside tourist buildings that could exist on any dock in any tourist port of call, but one block back from the water are the soggy wooden hotels where loggers and fishermen still pay by the week, and several of my friends have been known to pay by the hour.

The passengers of the *Westward* were scuttling forth into Ketchikan like an invading army. Plastic raincoats were buttoned up tight; those without a hood were pulling their collars up over their heads. They held cameras in their free hand as they took off to find that perfect memento, under twenty dollars, that would bear witness to their adventure. The rain came down as hard as unwanted manna. Great skeins of water pearled off the clogged roof gutters.

I was watching the scene from the concrete bunker of

the court building. Tourists spread, grouped, and moved like drops of water forming into streams. Some were off to the old-fashioned salmon bake, others would paddle kayaks. Many would walk the streets and gawk at the old houses that had been bordellos back in simpler times. Today, chunky white women wearing feather boas and red garters passed out handbills for the old-time whorehouse gift shops. These women were happy to have their pictures taken kissing your husband's bald head, or to mug provocatively for your camera. In the stream the salmon were pushing up the river to spawn and die. At low tide the river hissed over the rocks and the sound of water rolled downhill and collided with the rattle of buses and the crying gulls.

I actually love Ketchikan. It may be one of the friendliest and least pretentious towns in Alaska. It's also a great town for crime. Its citizens have a certain passionate, brawling kind of drunkenness that sometimes spills out into the streets. Sitka, on the other hand, seems much more uptight. There, our drunken brutality stays decorously at home. Despite my affection for the working-class vibe of Ketchikan, however, Jane Marie wasn't getting off the boat. She was not only attending to her lecture notes but was helping set up a tournament of Alaskan Charades in which teams would act out various animals, geologic and natural features of the Alaskan coastline.

Todd was staying on the ship, too. I think he knew he might run into his father in one of the waterfront bars, and as little emotional insight as Todd had at times, I was certain that prospect went into his decision to stay on board and watch the video presentation of Ketchikan on the ship's closed-circuit TV.

◙ ◙ ◙

I was mulling all this over as I stared over the downtown area from the court building. I was being verbally abused by the local coroner and I wasn't listening. Instead, I watched a young woman in a tank top weave unsteadily in the rain from one bar to another. It was nine in the morning.

"Get a grip, Younger," the coroner said as I stood on my tiptoes to watch the young woman turn and shake the wet spikes of her hair under the eaves of a bar. Her shirt was soaked clear through and she laughed, throwing her head back as she turned and entered through the swinging doors.

The coroner was a woman in her early fifties. She had black hair and was attractive in a disarming way that is peculiar to many women in Ketchikan. For some reason women in Ketchikan always make it seem that anything is possible, given the right combination of events. They are game in the ways that more delicate or urbane women usually aren't. Perhaps that was why I watched the wet woman disappear into the bar. I wanted to imagine what would come next. I tried to get her out of my mind as I made an effort to listen to the coroner.

"No, I didn't actually see the body of the girl brought off the ship," she continued. "Christ, I'm not a ghoul. I have the doctor's report. I have the family's request. I have the ship's officer's report. I just sign off on the death certificate and then release the body. The death happened out at sea. I have no real jurisdiction to order an inquest, even if I thought there was cause for one."

"What she die of?" I was still standing on my tiptoes at the window.

The coroner sighed. She looked down at the papers. "Cecil, I'm not supposed to talk to you about this but . . . Christ . . ." She rifled through the papers grumbling to herself.

The coroner was an old client. I had worked on her divorce case years before when she had been an attorney in Juneau. She had been a contract lawyer and had been married to the Governor's special assistant. There had been a young daughter who had been the apple of both parents' eye. The case was noteworthy for its slow-building ugliness. When wealthy young professionals divorced, no matter how much they protested their amiability, it was usually good for lots of billable hours. Anyway, I had been loyal, and had listened with sensitivity. I had also produced the pictures that allowed her to keep the kid, so I deserved at least a little confidential information.

"It says she died of respiratory failure as a result of her ongoing medical condition and treatment," the coroner said.

"Ongoing medical treatment?" I turned away from the window.

"She had AIDS, Cecil." The coroner's eyes were beseeching me to let this thing go. "She was very sick and stopped breathing."

"Did she have both her hands?" I asked.

"Oh, for Christ's sakes. It says nothing about her hands."

"Just look, will ya?" I said, then added, "Or just let me look, if it's too ghoulish for you." I sat down across the desk from her.

She scowled, again reviewing the papers. "Left hand or right hand?"

"Are those my only two choices?"

She looked at me with a kind of peevish glee. "I'm asking because there is a note here that says there was a 'medical artifact' on her right wrist. That usually implies that some surgical or emergency treatment was used when trying to treat her. Emergency tracheotomies or something like that. I have to admit I rarely see anything like that noted about the wrist. But if she had collapsed veins from her other treatment they could have tried to stick her anywhere when they attempted to resuscitate her."

"They never tried to resuscitate her."

"Well, the doctor on board said he did. He claims he treated her at eight-thirty A.M. ship's time yesterday morning. That is the time of death."

I had seen the pale girl much earlier than that in her stateroom. She had been dead then. Eight-thirty was about the time that Rosalind and I had caught a glimpse of her being zipped into the bag. I didn't mention this to the coroner. I wasn't sure an official investigation would help me, or my clients, at this point.

"What was her name?" I asked instead.

"Her name was Traci Lord. With an 'I.' She was from Virginia."

I sat up straight. "Come on—Traci Lord? Like in *The Philadelphia Story* Traci Lord? Cary Grant, Jimmy Stewart . . . remember?"

The coroner smiled and looked at me, her brown eyes cloudy with memory. "Yeah, I loved that movie." She made her voice quaver in a passable impression of Kate Hepburn's Yankee drawl. "'Remember, Mike, with the rich and mighty, always a little patience.'" Then she snapped out of it and stared down at her papers.

"Anyway, that's what it says. Traci Lord," she said.

"So where is she now?" I asked.

"She is at the funeral home. Her family has been notified."

The funeral home was also headquarters for a cab company. The back lot of the warehouse looked like an automotive graveyard. There were rotting minivans and station wagons sinking up to their axles in the mud. There was an incredibly ugly dog chained to an engine block by the corner of the metal shed. My friend Felix, the mechanic, and occasional hearse driver, was cuffing this creature and talking baby talk to it. I interrupted him.

"What the hell kind of dog is that?" I asked as I stepped on top of the rusted hood of a Buick Regal that was floating in the mud.

"Cecil, you wouldn't believe it, man," Felix said, oblivious of the rain. His large moony face showed piano-style gaps in his teeth. "This old dog has made me a shitload of money this summer. I tell people off the ship he's a wolf. They go apeshit, man. They pet him and have their picture taken and I get 'em to charter tours in my cab. I'll have a string of two-hour tours just because this old butthead is sitting in my front seat."

"Is . . . it . . . a wolf, this butthead dog of yours?" I asked, not wanting to seem even more stupid and effete than I already had.

"Fuck no, man. I tell you, I bred this malamute bitch . . . Well, you know, *I* didn't breed her." He smirked. Felix ran with a crowd that got a lot of mileage out of dog-fucking jokes. Of course, I did too, so I listened intently as Felix went on, "But I *had* her bred with a . . . now get this: This is the genius part of the deal . . . I had her bred with a big fucking RAT!"

"Felix . . ." I said slowly, standing in the rain. "You didn't have a dog bred to a rat. It's not possible."

"Nugh huh!" he said loudly. He had his head cocked to one side and he looked blankly at me as if he could not figure out how the universe had spawned someone as dumb as I was.

"Anyway, Felix . . ." Then I paused and added parenthetically, "You might be right," because I was going to ask him a kind of touchy favor. "You've got a new corpse that came in the front door, off the *Westward.*"

"Yeah . . . ?" he said, drawing it out and looking suspiciously at me.

"I need to take a look at her, Felix."

"Yeah, sure. No problem." He stopped playing with his dog and started walking into the back shed. I jumped across what looked like a shoe-sucking mud hole and followed.

Once inside we crossed behind a wall of chainsaw posters and several file folders that were mysteriously turned on their sides. Felix stopped short and grabbed my arm.

"Hey, wait a minute!" he said as if I were putting one over on him. "Are you going to have . . . sex with her?"

I knew he was serious by the way he had used the words "have sex with."

"With whom?"

"With her . . . You know, the package off the *Westward.*"

"I wasn't planning on it, Felix," I said slowly, letting each word sink in. "Why, does that change something?"

"Naw," he said as he kept walking, waving his hand distractedly above his head as if he were fending off thoughts. "Oh, naw. I had a guy come in here once and offer me two grand for that. I just thought . . . you know . . ."

"Anyway, I don't have two grand, Felix," I said.

"Well, you know, I just thought I'd ask," Felix said in a very businesslike manner. He rubbed his hands against his elbows. "Burrrr. Man, I feel cold all of a sudden. Wonder what that's about?" Then he turned the light on.

Coffins on their metal stands were scattered around the concrete garage like Foosball tables. A polished mahogany one near the garage door and a white child-sized one near the sink by the radiator.

Felix looked around, agitated. He peered into a shiny gray coffin that had pink filigree around the hinges. Then he scratched his head. "Hey!" he yelled into the dark hallway that leads to the front and more formal part of the funeral home. This was an area into which Felix was never allowed to set foot unless he was in his driver's uniform.

"Hey!" he yelled again. "Where's that package from the *Westward*? The green bag on the gurney?"

The voice of a woman came floating out of the dark. "Jesse drove it out the road. They wanted it taken care of pronto. Had to get it on the next plane. Extra money in it. Jesse took it out the road, soon as it came in."

"Hey, man." Felix shrugged at me. "She went out to the crematorium. They burned her. Sorry." He shrugged again. Then he added, "You want another look at my dog?" He offered it with a kindly tone in his voice and I know he just wanted to make up for my disappointment. Felix is a good guy.

But I declined. Just to cheer him up, however, I half-heartedly inquired about having sex with his dog, saying that I'd always wanted an heir. But Felix was not amused. I could tell he took my question as a sign that I doubted his story about the rat.

◙ ◙ ◙

Sonny Walters was in a fuchsia jogging suit. He was pedaling a stationary bike by himself in the shipboard exercise room. During the port call in Ketchikan, he could stare out through a square port and look down toward the mouth of the channel where float planes crisscrossed their wakes in the pelting raindrops.

"I'm telling you, Cecil," Sonny puffed, "there is no one on the ship's manifest named Traci Hepburn."

"Traci Lord," I corrected.

"Yeah, right. Traci Lord. No. There was no one on the manifest by that name."

"Come on, Sonny, who was in Acapulco 800?"

Sonny stopped pedaling, turned, and swung around sidesaddle on the stationary bike. He kind of looked like Ricky Nelson in *Rio Bravo*. He wiped his forehead with the bottom of his sweatshirt.

"That's what I'm trying to tell you, Cecil. There was *no one* assigned Acapulco 800. That stateroom is hired out as an extra to that travel group—the *Inconnue* or whatever."

"Sonny, you have one less passenger today. Get it? There's been a death in the family. Someone won't be at her place at second seating or whenever she was eating, and you're telling me there is no real record of her?"

"What I'm telling you is that I don't have any record of her. Did she sign up for a shore excursion? I don't think so. Did she ask me for escort services? No. How about did she sign up for exercise class or weight lifting? No, I don't think so. Maybe that's because she was too busy dying of AIDS."

Sonny's complexion was reddening as a result, I assumed, of peevishness.

"Sonny, she had to have a passport. She must show up on the manifest."

"You have to talk to the ship's officers. They maintain the manifest. The first mate would have written a report on the death. He reviews the doctor's report, writes one of his own, and shows them both to the captain. They will advise me of any changes to the manifest later. If at all. *They* run the boat, *I* run the vacations. Get it?"

"Sonny, I tried to talk to the first mate. He acted like I didn't exist. He assumed I was a passenger. He brushed me off like lint. Get me an introduction, will ya?"

Sonny was now doing curls with the thirty-five-pound free weights. "Cecil, I told you we never told the boat company about hiring you. We couldn't. I mean it looks like we're spying on our own business partners . . ."

"Which you are . . ." I sat down on the seat of the bench press machine and unwrapped a stick of gum.

"Well yeah, but you knew that going in. The worst of it is I think they are up to something!" Sonny toweled his forehead.

"They?" I asked him.

"Empire Shipping." He started puffing. "The first mate and the captain. They seem like they are agitated. The captain had a car waiting for him when we arrived here. That's unusual. I don't know, Cecil, they may be doing their own investigation, as far as I know. But that's it—I don't know. I suppose that's why we hired you."

The pedals of the stationary bike squeaked and I didn't say a word as I felt the full force of Sonny's superiority.

"Anyway, I can't get you an introduction," he puffed on. "What you need is a copy of the report."

"The first mate's report?"

"Right. Officially they're called fatality reports but they are referred to as Moonlight Bays."

"Come on."

"Really." Sonny shook his head in all solemnity. "Cecil, we can't go around *talking* about people dying. Talk about putting a damper on the trip. Also, you just don't know how fast rumors can travel and get distorted on board ship. So we use the code and we file reports. You need the Moonlight Bay on this girl who died in Acapulco 800."

"So you can say over the public address system or phone system . . . ?" I was trying to grasp this.

"Exactly." Sonny was breathing hard but still pulling the weights to his chest. I was chewing gum in time with him. "I've already told you this: We say 'Report to Moonlight Bay, Acapulco 800' and everybody knows what to do and our passengers stay relaxed."

It was beginning to dawn on me that few things in life were as important to Sonny as the relaxation of his passengers. I chewed my gum and watched him pump iron and as he pedaled I was wondering if there was any place to get something to eat on board the ship.

"So this extra room that the tour group has, they use it for sex or what?"

"I don't know." Sonny grunted. "I never pried into what they did there."

"Well, some old doll was pumping one of your sailors there the other morning."

Sonny dropped the weights. "What!" He stared at me just as Felix had. "What did you say, Cecil?"

"There was a passenger. A woman, she was down in room 800, you know, Sonny, she was making the beast with two backs with one of the guys from the boat crew." I tried to illustrate with some hand gestures.

"Are you absolutely sure it was a crew member?" Sonny was more agitated than I had ever seen him.

I took a step back. "I don't know, Sonny. He looked like a crew person. He had his white coveralls around his knees. I didn't get that much of a look. They were not expecting company. What's the problem?"

Sonny shook his head from side to side while he wiped himself down again. "There are three hundred crew members on this boat. Besides my staff and the people working the tables and in the bar, have you seen any crew members."

I thought for a minute, remembering the scenes I had observed on the ship. There were drinkers and blue-haired ladies, professors and sick people, but no one that looked like they were working for a living. "No," I said. "I guess I never thought about it, but, no, I've never seen any crew members."

"Crew are expressly forbidden to have any social contact with the passengers. None. They are not supposed to be on deck the entire trip. They can go out on the working decks after dark. They can go ashore. But other than that, they are supposed to stay at their station or in Freetown."

"Freetown?" I offered Sonny a stick of gum but he declined.

Sonny stood up and walked to a diagram of the ship on the wall. In every public room on the *Westward* there was a diagram of the decks with red dots with the words YOU ARE HERE. Sonny pointed. "Around the sides of the hull are the ABC decks, you know—Acapulco, Bermuda and all the rest—this is where the passengers are. The crew lives here in the center of the ship. They have their kitchens, their showers, and a rec room all on the inside. This is Freetown. Passengers are not allowed there, and the crew are not allowed on the ABC decks. If they break this rule, the whole trip is deadweighted."

"Meaning?"

"Meaning the crew person is sent home immediately and he forfeits his pay for the cruise. Nothing for the whole trip. And nothing with this company ever again."

"Seems kind of harsh. I mean, it all looked consensual. Possibly even romantic."

Sonny held up his hand as if he were a judge who had heard it all. "Believe me," he said, "I don't doubt that for a minute. I know what my passengers are like. Some of them want it all. But there has to be a strict separation. There are social considerations. These crewmen come from very different backgrounds from our passengers. I mean, most of them could buy a house back home with just the jewelry some of the passengers wear. We can't have them sitting at the bar together. We've never had a serious theft on board and that is because we don't put temptation in their way."

"That's white of you, Sonny."

"Don't judge people you know nothing about, Younger. There's more than just that, there are the health concerns. We have crew members from Thailand, from . . . Haiti, for gosh sakes. Do you know what happened on one of our competitors' ships?"

I shook my head no, but for some reason I had a feeling I was still going to find out.

"A passenger made a claim that he had contracted a sexually transmitted disease from a crewman." Sonny rolled his eyes. "I mean, it was *herpes,* for gosh sakes, but he filed suit and their next season's receipts went down the well. It's like finding a rat in the soup, you know what I mean?"

The ship's horn blared out from the stack and bounced back from the mountains. The mooring lines were slipped from their massive cleats and winched on board. The ship pulled away from Ketchikan in the pouring rain. The fan-tail bar was in full swing. The regulars who seemed to have staked their turf when we set sail were laughing and toasting their luck as the tug released the ship. The blonde woman in the silk pants stood out a foot from the eaves of the covered bar and let the rain blubber down her face. Then she tossed her hair back and laughed.

In the Great Circle Lounge, Toddy was setting the timer on his camera and running around to have his picture taken with Margie & the Navigators. He snapped two pictures, trying to get the timer to work. A librarian from Rock Island, Illinois, on her way to the bar, showed Todd the right timer switch. He thanked her, then threw the switch and ran around by the bandstand where the Navigators were hanging around after their in-port rehearsal. The shutter clicked before Todd made it to the saxophone player, who still appeared to be deeply stoned.

The Great Circle Lounge spanned the width of the ship. On each side were floor-to-ceiling windows covered with thick shades for the performances. The shades were open now as the *Westward* headed north up Clarence Strait, along the western edge of Revillagigedo Island. Several people sat in the low-backed couches and chairs swiveled toward the window. Three women with binoculars slung over their necks sat at attention. One of them still had her sou'wester rain hat on. They all scanned the shoreline with their field glasses.

On the opposite side, Alicia and Carol's mother was sprawled in front of the huge plate-glass window. There was a plate of shrimp and an empty margarita glass on the table next to her. She was slouched down in the chair with a spy novel sprawled on her chest. By the bar Carol and Alicia were laughing and joking with one of the barmen. He was making chains of origami cranes that the girls wore in their hair. Carol spun and laughed between the chairs. Carol's mother looked up sleepily and saw her daughters laughing and then closed her eyes again. "This is good," she muttered.

In the farthest corner Rosalind sat with her legs tucked under her with her sketch pad laid out on her lap. She sat in a pool of milky sunlight and each time she looked up her eyes were dull and unfocused. When she saw me she brightened and smiled.

"Hey!" she said and sat up straight, covering her sketch pad with her elbows. "You find anything out?"

"No." I sat down across from her. One of the birdwatchers snapped her binoculars to her eyes and pointed; the others followed suit. "How are you doing?" I asked Rosalind, and brushed her hair from her face, then felt her forehead with the tips of my fingers.

She blushed, and touched my hand. "I'm okay. I felt a little queasy down there. I went for a walk in Ketchikan. I'm great now." She smiled at me.

I turned away.

"Is anybody talking about that girl we saw in the doctor's office?" I asked her quickly.

"No. It's weird. I haven't told anybody what I saw but I

just asked around about the woman in Acapulco 800 and no one knows a thing. They say the room is empty."

"Her travel club books it."

"Kingfisher!" all three of the ladies said at once.

Rosalind smiled at them and looked back at me. "Yeah, well, the crew has been tearing that room apart. There has been a lot of activity all day. I tried to get in to see the doctor myself. You know, just to check in . . ." Her eyes wandered toward the windows.

"Raven . . . raven . . ." one of the birders murmured without much enthusiasm.

"The doctor didn't have much time. He was very busy," Rosalind said absently. "There are lots of sick people on this boat. Have you noticed that?"

"Yeah. I have," I said intelligently.

Rosalind shivered. She touched her throat as if checking her glands. "Gives me the creeps. I don't know. I've been feeling kind of crummy all day."

"You look too good to be sick," I deadpanned.

She looked down, embarrassed, her face reddening again. "Cecil," she said seriously in a way that made me cringe. "Cecil, you are attached, aren't you?"

"Attached?" I said and for some terrible reason all I could think of was the severed hand in the ice bucket.

"Yeah, I guess I am attached," I said absently.

"I think that's terrific." Rosalind brightened. "I met your friend. Jane Marie. I was thinking of going on one of those Charade teams. But you know, I just don't know. She seems really nice. Smart and thin, and pretty and everything."

"All that's true," I said and then, "But she does not have strange and interesting eyes and I don't think she knows squat about Angels." I touched her hand and she laughed.

I looked over and Todd was taking another photo of Margie and chatting with her as she shifted from one foot to another obviously wanting to leave.

"Oystercatcher!" one of the birders shouted and then pumped the air with her fist. "Yes! Yes! Yes!" The other two slumped slightly in disappointment.

I turned back to Rosalind. "How are the Angels coming?"

"Oh," she wrinkled up her nose and looked distastefully down at her sketch pad. "I'm being bad, I'm afraid."

I moved closer to her and she wriggled in discomfort but she lifted her elbows off the pad. As I leaned into her I felt the shadow of her body's heat. I could smell her hair and the trace of lemon soap on her skin.

On the paper she had drawn an angel with its wings pinned against the pages of a book. A giant woman in glasses reached toward the angel with a probe as if it were a biological specimen. The drawing had some intricate details: structures of wing feathers, the folds of the robe, the hinge of the eyeglasses. Other details were left out, or cartoonish. The angel appeared to be asleep, its head bowed to one side, its expression vague. Behind it dozens and dozens of other angel specimens were tacked into display cases.

"Eagle! Eagle! Eagle!" All three birders were on their feet. They danced on their thin legs, swiveling their butts around, while they trained their binoculars on the point. Beyond the window an eagle settled on top of a broken spruce tree. The bird tucked her wings and thrust her chest out as she scanned the water with the air of a haughty predator.

I felt Rosalind put her hand into mine. "Have you ever seen anything like it?" She sighed.

I watched the eagle's perch disappear past the stern. "Never one exactly like that," I answered and looked down at my shoes.

She squeezed my hand and bent her head closer to mine. "I have something to ask you, Cecil."

My chest tightened. I kept ahold of her hand.

"Later in the week there is going to be a dance featuring seventies music. I . . . I was wondering . . ."

I closed my eyes because I didn't even want to think of the possible ending for her sentence.

"I was wondering if you could still, I don't know, if you could still flirt with me a little bit."

She buried her head in her hands. "Just a little bit. Even though I know you are attached. It would help, you know, make it so I wouldn't look like I'm so, I don't know, pathetic."

"You are not pathetic." I took her hands away from her face. "And I would be happy to flirt with you if it would help."

"You could even act heartbroken, Cecil." Her voice brightened. "It's kind of like chumming for sharks. I just need some blood in the water."

"So if I hang around acting interested and heartbroken, you think this will help with your chances of meeting available men?" I asked just to clarify.

"Oh you bet it would," she said excitedly. "I've been on other cruises. I've seen it work. But . . ." And she paused. "There's another thing. Can I pencil you in for that dance towards the end of the trip? The seventies night. I really want to go and I need some backup if things don't pan out with someone."

"I'd be honored." I said it without much conviction.

In my universe there are drinkers and dancers. And the two should never intermingle. I have always been with the drinkers, self-conscious introverts who crack wise about the music and sneer at the dancers while at the same time they are consumed with envy. Dancers love their bodies and open themselves to the music. Gravity is my enemy. It conspires with my body to make me look stupid on the dance floor. Why did she have to ask me to dance?

"I'd be happy to go to the dance," I said and never took my eyes off the carpet.

"Hey, you guys. What's up?" Jane Marie said over my shoulder.

I was holding on to the tips of Rosalind's fingers. She smiled up.

"Hi, Janie. Cecil has agreed to let me break his heart," Rosalind chirped.

"Some trick." Jane Marie slumped down next to us. "Did he agree to go to the dance with you?" she asked and Rosalind nodded happily.

"I told you he would. Don't get your hopes up, although he is perfect for the job." Jane Marie put her hand on my knee. "With Cecil as your date you should be motivated to find a real date." Then she looked toward me, smiling.

"Cecil, I'm glad you made it back on board." Jane Marie's eyes were arched and I think she was showing real concern. "I was worried you'd get hooked up with some of your buddies in Ketchikan."

Rosalind said, "You know people in Ketchikan! How exciting! What do they do there?"

For some reason she seemed so sweet I didn't really want to tell her about Felix.

"They're in transportation," I said, then dropped her hand and stood up to face Jane Marie.

"I'm going to the bridge," Jane Marie said. "I've been given bridge privileges. I'm going to talk with the captain about where the best spots to see marine mammals may be. I can take you along, Cecil, if you don't do anything dumb." Jane Marie finished her sentence staring at the beaming Rosalind.

"Go. Go," Rosalind said, beaming. "It will be really neat. Maybe you'll see some whales!" She was so excited she could hardly contain herself. "I have to go down to the clinic anyway. I'll see you later. Bye bye."

And she was gone.

"Come on," Jane Marie said to me. "I'll help you." The ship was rolling underneath us, her engines sounding like the air sucking out of a mine shaft. One of the birder ladies shrieked out, "Another one. Eagle! Eagle!" They started doing their myopic bird dance, shuffling their feet and keeping their binoculars still. Carol and Alicia danced in the center of the lounge with the paper cranes in their hair and their mother smiled contentedly out the window to the rain.

The bridge ran the width of the upper deck with the helmsman's station in the center. It was a smaller steering wheel than I had expected, more like the wheel you'd find on a sport utility vehicle than a twenty-three-thousand-ton vessel. The *Westward* was winding through the passageway of the islands, making way to the outside waters so as to come into Sitka from the west. All along the inland waters there is a US pilot who is in charge of the navigation of the ship. He does this by law and with the full cooperation of the captain. As

we came on the bridge the pilot was giving headings to the
Helmsman in a clear strong voice. The Helmsman was a
short dark-skinned man in a white ship's uniform. He stood
erect at the wheel and studied the compass and the rudder
indicator laid out in front of him. All the other eyes on the
bridge scanned the horizon. The pilot was a tall athletic
man dressed in a sports coat and a red tie. He could have
been a basketball scout or a senior detective. There was
nothing much nautical in his appearance.

The captain was a short, stocky man in his sixties, perhaps. He wore a military-style sweater with gold braided
epaulets and white pants and green rubber clogs. He had
enormously bushy eyebrows, which gave him an owl-like
countenance. When we entered the bridge all the men
who'd been scanning the seas turned and stared at Jane
Marie. They all smiled, and the captain stood up, taking
her hand in both of his.

"Yes. Yes," he said in a thick eastern European accent.
"This then is the new professor, our native guide. She is
the famous Whale Woman who knows each of her precious
animals by name. I am captain of the *Westward*. Captain
Minosh. This is my first mate, Mr. Calbran . . ." He gestured grandly to the tall, very fit Panamanian standing by
the Helmsman's elbow. The first officer nodded solemnly
to Jane Marie and lowered his eyes. The pilot pushed forward and shook her other hand with a cowboy's vigor and
said, "I'm Pete Smith. I've heard all about you." And he
pumped her hand like a well handle, while Jane Marie
blushed crimson. I apparently wasn't there.

Finally, the captain turned, and without fully acknowledging me, gestured for me to step forward. "Come, come," he
muttered and I stood several steps behind Jane Marie as she

looked over the chart the Mate had spread on a table near the back curtain of the communications room. Jane Marie pointed to areas on the map and spoke of sea lion rookeries and the seasonal distribution of humpback whales. The pilot scanned the course ahead and called a new heading, saying, "That will be left to two, eight, zero then, Captain," and the captain would murmur his agreement and the Helmsman said, "Aye sir. Left. Two. Eight. Zero." The ship then swung farther from the rocks breaking a quarter of a mile on the right.

"How then is the fishing in Sitka this year?" the captain blared out in my direction.

I shrugged because I really didn't know. I had seen a lot of blood on the docks near the fish cleaning tables so I figured I could make a guess. "Great!" I answered.

The captain, still looking ahead, nodded. "I'm going to catch a halibut, you know." And he gestured with his arms as if he were pulling in a fish. "Halibut is the most perfect, you know. I will bring it here and there will be so much I will share it with all of you." He swung his arms dramatically from his chest and everyone on the bridge burst into laughter. This was apparently a very old joke among the ship's officers. But no one said a thing. The ship rolled on and Jane Marie now scanned the course and I picked the cuticle on my thumb.

I broke the silence awkwardly. "Did we lose a passenger back in Ketchikan?"

Now for the first time the captain turned and looked at me. His great brush of eyebrows rose above sparkling eyes. "Lose a passenger? Sir, this is not a Boy Scout troop. We do not lose passengers." The first officer smiled just slightly as if a joke were percolating deep down in his memory.

"Well, I was just asking because, you know, I met this woman last night, she was, well, you know, very attractive and now I don't think she is on the ship. She was in Acapulco 800. I was just wondering if she had gotten off the ship."

The captain again stared out over the bow of his ship. On each side of the inlet, ragged gray rocks lay everywhere below the surface. His ship weighed twenty-three thousand tons and there was no slamming on the brakes.

He turned to me and smiled again. "You are Mr. Younger from Sitka, yes?" The captain studied me for a moment and then flickered a look to his first mate. "Mr. Younger, on these trips you should remember, if you find yourself with a beautiful woman in your arms you must keep close watch of her, for the next morning she is likely to be in the arms of another." He held my eyes with his until I looked away, and I realized he knew my name without having been introduced.

"Well!" Captain Minosh clapped his hands together and walked past me to the cart table with Jane Marie. "Tell me then about these great rubbery friends of yours." And he put his arm around her shoulder.

7

Freetown

There are only a few expressions used by television private eyes that I have ever heard in real life. Although I've heard of going on a "surveillance," I've never been paid for a "stakeout." Guns are usually guns and never "gats" or "pieces." Sometimes they are weapons and only occasionally are they very useful at all. But one term I have a fondness for is "being made."

"Being made" is to be recognized for what you really are. I once knew a private investigator in Fairbanks who was tall and very thin, wore a short leather jacket and had his hair in a ponytail. He even had a scar across his lower chin. This private eye would walk into a bar behind anyone he was supposed to be following and would stand in the entryway long enough to make sure that everyone in the place saw his silhouette in the brightening light behind him. All heads would turn, all eyes would appraise the ponytail, the scar, the bulge in the black leather jacket. Heads would bow and go back to their drinks. Then he'd turn to me at his elbow and mutter, "Shit, we've been made."

Well, of course we'd been made. More people go to a college basketball game than live in the entire city of Fairbanks, Alaska, and the bar scene was a tiny village of close friends. Of course they recognized him, and of course they knew that he was working on a case and he knew they knew. Notoriety was the only perk he had. He liked being made. It was the whole point of the exercise.

I, on the other hand, do not like being made. I suppose I have never really recognized myself for what I am, and particularly don't like to have others see it. Of course, surreptitious work in the small villages of Alaska is rather pointless. Most village people know what I'm doing in town before I step off the floats of the airplane. But on a tour ship I thought there was a possibility, however slight, that I might be able to slide around unmade. Stupid, I know.

Being made usually comes with a glance. A look that tells you that someone is not buying whatever pose you are trying on. It is a look like no others. It jolts you like a hold on a wet power line. It says "I know the truth about you even more than you know about yourself."

This was the look Captain Minosh had given me. If Sonny Walters and his cruise company had hoped to keep my presence on the *Westward* a secret they were going to be bitterly disappointed.

I walked out of the bridge and down past the Compass Room on the Horizon Deck. Jane Marie said she had to meet with some team captains. She turned to go, then turned back suddenly.

"That Rosalind, she's nice, huh?"

"Yeah," I said as noncommittally as I could.

"You have a crush on her?" Jane Marie asked, biting her lip.

"Naw," I countered. "Just blood in the water."

She looked quizzically at me. Then her mood changed. "How about that captain saying I was a native guide. What's that all about, you think?"

"Maybe he's never laid eyes on a real Alaskan woman," I joked.

Jane Marie laughed and waved me off, then disappeared around the corner of the passageway. I had no idea where she was going and that left me with a slight panicky feeling.

In the lounge, Toddy was trying to set up another group shot. This time the crowd was much larger. Rosalind was there, and Mr. Brenner. They were standing with others of Todd's new friends, all crammed next to a bust of Captain Cook. Some in the crowd had drinks in their hands and held them high above the shoulders of the people next to them. They awkwardly tried to bend and push themselves closer together. Todd balanced his camera on the ledge near a drinking fountain and clicked off a couple of frames as he tried to set the timer. Men shouted and women laughed. Todd kept fussing with the camera and as I stepped forward to help him, I ran into the chest of a very tall and solid black man.

"Excuse me, sir," he said slowly and quietly and it was only then that I noticed he was holding a folding knife with a thumb latch next to a talon-curved blade.

"Please, sir, step this way with me." The tip of the knife blade had cut through the front of my sweater and I could feel it needling my skin. I stepped backward and then turned the corner. Along the wall of the companionway was a blue metal door with a white sign which read, AUTHO-RIZED SHIP'S PERSONNEL ONLY. My traveling companion reached over my shoulder, opened the door, and pushed me inside.

The door shut and we were standing on a metal stair landing. The noise of the ship's engines was louder here. So was the faint smell I had picked up on the first day. This smell was of boiled vegetables and sweat, cigarette smoke with a hint of disinfectant, and fresh paint. Doors clattered shut all around me. The shadows slanted away from dozens of bulbs inside glass domes. We had stepped into the industrial center of the ship. This was Freetown.

I looked up into his face. He was shiny black and the whites of his eyes were bloodshot as if he had not slept in days. His expression was extreme and severe but there was a boyishness in his expression that meant that this act was more motivated by fear than from some kind of dull meanness.

"Sir, you shouldn't have gone to the captain now," he said slowly. "You don't know what you have done."

"This is true," I agreed and I raised my left hand up to my belt, lowering my right slowly.

The black man's whole body trembled. The knife wobbled in the air just under my sternum and felt as if it were working deeper into my skin. The man let out a long breath.

"I need this job," he said at last as if he were going to cry. "I need that money, too."

"I'm sure you do," I said and pushed up with my right hand as I jabbed with my left.

I had meant to grab his forearm but ended up grabbing the blade of the knife instead. The sharp blade slipped through my hands and cut down to the knuckles of my right palm. At first, I could not feel the cut and was confused by the splash of red that flowered on the black man's tunic. My heart sank when I thought that I might have stabbed him by mistake. Then I looked at the bright flash of bone and we both listened to my blood drip on the metal stairwell.

We were smiling at each other, thinking, I hoped, that this would end things and we could go on with some sort of reasoned explanation for the craziness that had just transpired. Then he lunged his knife at me and ripped across my chest and I tumbled down the tight circular stairwell. I yelled and rolled down the metal grating. I remember other voices and ringing footfalls on metal. I folded my hand under the sweatshirt and ran down one of the gray-painted metal halls. There were bare pipes and gauges. Red fire extinguisher boxes, coiled hoses, and axes with sharp metal points. Brown men in coveralls with bandannas around their heads. Pointing and yelling. A poolroom, lots of cigarette smoke, and a dark lounge where men were playing cards. One bulb hung from the ceiling and some of the men had hand towels draped around their necks. Hot and loud voices yelling at me, and the engines were getting louder and the heat more intense.

I opened the vault like door to a paint locker and tried to stuff myself inside. Hands worked the door and I blundered on, running to another tight spiral staircase, dark at the bottom, and I fell again, wrenching my back and my shoulders as I fell and tried to curl around my cut hand.

I came to rest in a pile of sooty rags. I could see the flutter of flame reflecting on the surface of one of the large gauges. The footsteps came fast and the voices were like the flutter of cheering from a passing train. I rolled to my side, twisting to see the staircase. The man with the blood-spattered tunic came first, the knife still in his hand. He reached down and yanked at my hair, turning my throat up to the light. Behind him, the other men fell silent. I could hear his breathing above the gravelly throb of the ship's engines. The knife, with my own blood on the blade, came down to my eye level and his torso blotted out the light.

From over my right shoulder a pipe wrench came down hard on the blade. The knife clattered across the diamond-plated metal floor. Men started pushing back up the stairs. I heard someone move behind me and then the wrench was raised again.

"Cyril, you must be out of your mind, man." The voice that came from behind us was deep, with a rich Caribbean accent. "Have you lost all of your senses? First, you breeding the sheep up there, now what? You going to kill a sheep down here? What is this craziness, man? Do you really expect us to watch you do this thing?"

Cyril sat down on the stairs. He looked sheepishly down at the blood on his shirt. He held his palms up wide to the man behind me as if beseeching the court.

"But, Mr. Worthington, now. He's no regular sheep, sir. He some kind of police. I hear them talking. He works for the companies, sir. He's asking about the doctor." As he said this last, Cyril made a gesture as if he were giving a shot with a hypodermic. "Asking about the doctor. You know, sir."

I rolled over and saw Mr. Worthington standing over me protectively with the head of the pipe wrench weighing in his left hand. He was an older man with a broad face and high cheekbones. He was very, very black and his eyes glittered a startling blue. He was covered from head to foot in soot. The white of his jumpsuit was smeared evenly in blackness. He had a yellow band around his forehead that was soaked clear through with sweat.

"And what about the lady you were breeding up there in the hotel the other night?" Mr. Worthington asked Cyril. "You telling me she wasn't a sheep then?"

"Aw, Mr. Worthington," Cyril protested. "You know, sir. She gave me money. She wanted it. You know how they are."

"I know exactly how they are, Cyril," Mr. Worthington said crisply and with a tone of some self-satisfaction. "I know exactly how they are. And what were you going to do then when she gets embarrassed about being found out and says that you raped her, then?"

"I know. I know," Cyril moaned and hung his head.

"No, you don't know, Cyril. You are surely dumb, man. You appear to have lost all of whatever sense God gave you."

"What about *him* then, sir? He's the only witness. He's been to the captain. I can't just let him run around now, especially with this business about the hand and all, now can I?"

I was actually rather pleased the subject was coming back around to me.

"I will be taking care of all that," Mr. Worthington said and that appeared to be final, for everyone began walking back up the stairs, wiping their hands either on rags or against the sides of their pants as if they were well rid of our confrontation.

Mr. Worthington rolled me over. He gently uncurled my palm where the sticky crust of blood was turning into a rind around the cut. The new blood continued to spread like an oil slick down my bone-white skin.

He shook his head. "Oh man, this is no good. You better come with me then, sir. I'll take you to my quarters. There is no one who will mess with you there." Mr. Worthington helped me to my feet. After the adrenaline stopped pumping I could feel the cuts on my scalp and the stiffness in my legs and shoulders. I was unsteady as I followed him down the narrow, howling passageway.

We moved past walls of gauges and through tangled jungles of pipes. The engine sound was louder of course but also more distinct. I could sense the pulse of the ship now, the gradual chug-chugging of the shaft turning the huge propeller.

Finally, we came to a sealed metal door and we walked into a quiet hall. The walls here were metal and painted white. There were four doors on either side and Mr. Worthington stepped into the second one. I had no idea where I was on the ship but I had a sense that I was well below the waterline.

He took some books off of a straight-backed chair and motioned me to sit. The room was tight, with the bed and the chair and a dresser near the tiny closet. In the closet was a small refrigerator and on top of that stood a statue of the Virgin. Taped to the walls were photographs of children. Some wore school uniforms in formal portraits, but there was another showing the same children gamboling along a dusty red dirt road, squinting into the bright sun with a row of pastel wooden buildings behind them. As I sat on the chair I suddenly felt dizzy. I closed my eyes but the images of the children still clung there. Mr. Worthington held my hand lightly. I could feel his breath on my palm, as he lifted my injured hand for inspection.

"Ayeeee! This is a bad cut, you know. I don't know what

THE ANGELS WILL NOT CARE

I can do for you. But I do it anyway. Wash it off then." He poured some bottled water and he scraped the rind of blood. The muzzy pain was strange enough, but what was worse was to see and feel how my hand now was two folds of separate skin that moved and wriggled at odds with each other. I gritted my teeth and looked again at his photos.

There was a tiny child laid out on a bright blanket. The child's hair was pulled back and tied with a yellow ribbon. She was a big girl to be stretched out like an infant. Her expression was vacant.

"That is my angel child," Mr. Worthington told me as he followed my eyes to the photograph. "That is Martha. The doctors told us she was to be born dead. But just at the last minute she came back to life. She is a miracle girl, you see, sir."

Mr. Worthington could not stop the bleeding. The towel he had placed on my lap was now scarlet. He stopped trying to scrub away the blood and he reached into a trunk under his bed and took out what looked like a fruit jar of black goo. He took off the lid and knocked on the bottom of the jar, and then from seemingly nowhere he took a small propane torch, lit it with a sparker, and held the blue flame near the glass.

"Not too hot, you see, sir. Just enough to spread." Then he took a large spoon and dolloped out some of this warm goo onto my palm. At first, the sensation was pleasant enough. Then the pain began to build, as if small fish were chewing off my hand. I tried to jerk my hand away but he held it in a viselike grip.

As I began to lose consciousness I could feel him fanning the torch over the numbed stump of where my hand had been.

◎ ◎ ◎

I didn't know what time it was when I woke up. I didn't
know what day it was or, in fact, what position of the sun
the ship was enjoying. I did know that it was hot. I knew,
too, that the room was moving and that my hand was being
nibbled by a swarm of enraged fire ants.

There was a kindly looking white man sitting next to
me on the bed. He was studying my hand. For some reason I was under the impression that this was a good man,
maybe Santa Claus or God, although I'm not sure why.
His beard was well trimmed and he was not particularly
overweight. It might have had something to do with the
fact that the last hornet that stuck me apparently was
some kind of benevolent bee, his serum allowing my
hand to go numb.

"What the devil did you put on his hand, Worthington?"
the God-Santa demanded.

"Iodine and tar, sir," said Mr. Worthington as he studied
the white man's work with the interest of a devotee.

"Well, to tell the truth, I think it did the trick. You stopped
the bleeding all right, and I don't think there is much worry
of infection. But you surely made a mess of things. I doubt
that even this acid solution will get it all off."

I tried to sit up but neither the men on the bed nor the
muscles in my body would let me. I recognized the God-
Santa now as the man I had seen outside of the clinic.
He turned and looked around to see my open but barely
focusing eyes. Now, I could make out that he in fact didn't
have much of a beard but one of those fashionable several-
week growths that men who were beginning to lose hair on
their head seemed to be contemplating more and more.

"Hold on now. If you stay still, I can get the last of it out. I've put in some temporary stitches and as soon as I get this hand cleaned up I'll take them out and get something of a more permanent nature in there." He turned back to his work. I said nothing but I think I heard him mutter, "Worthington, there is plenty of suffering in this world without you bringing me more. Don't you think?" I didn't hear if Mr. Worthington replied or not.

"I'm Dr. Edwards, by the way," the bearded man said. "And you are Cecil Younger, the much talked-of private detective."

Christ, I thought. Even unconscious down in the hold somewhere I had been made. This was not a good thing for my reputation.

"What was the Great Circle Company thinking? To hire a private detective, for crying out loud. What were they hoping to find?"

The doctor wiped his hands with a clean towel and nodded to Mr. Worthington to hand him the tray laid out on the dresser at the feet of the Virgin.

"They say you are killing some of the passengers. This, I suppose, is bad for business," I replied as I lay staring up at the beautiful blank stare of the little girl taped to the wall. "What did you say her name was?" My voice broke up like a distant transmission.

"Martha." Mr. Worthington smiled. The skin on his face was jet black but shivered with light.

"Martha," I said. "The angel girl. Yes, that's it."

"Are you a little light-headed, Mr. Younger? I gave you a shot of Demerol and a local, too. I thought you probably had enough pain on this day."

"Yes. Thank you," I told the doctor. I was thinking of

Rosalind and Martha the angel girl. Getting them mixed up in the slurry of my memory, I suppose. "So. Do you?" I blurted out.

"Do I what?" Dr. Edwards said softly, intent on his work.

"Do you kill your patients?"

"Am I killing you, Mr. Younger?" he said, never taking his eyes off his work.

"It doesn't feel like it." I dreamily took in a breath and felt a narcotic kiss in my brain.

"This is true. I am not killing you and you are not ready to die. These are two independent and true facts. I don't want you to hurt, and, from the appearances of things, I show more concern about your bodily suffering than you do. How did you get in such a mess?" Dr. Edwards's gray eyes looked sympathetic but tired. Behind him I could see Mr. Worthington looking grimly at me.

"It was a misunderstanding. A stupid accident. No real harm done," I said lazily and Mr. Worthington looked down at his own hands.

The doctor cleared his throat and his voice took on more of an official tone. "I understand that you owe something special to Mr. Worthington. But you see, Mr. Worthington is a member of the ship's crew. He reports to the chief engineer and to the captain. Nothing you can say about him would risk his status on this ship. You see, Mr. Younger, unlike you, we are not under the thumb of the Almighty Sonny Walters." And the doctor smiled. Then just as suddenly he stopped smiling.

"Mr. Younger, someone mutilated a body while it was still under my care. I suppose you know about this?"

Here, I wobbled my head noncommittally. The doctor talked on.

"This could have been very, very bad, but I was able to at least partially rectify it. This is not a game, you see. Mr. Sonny Walters thinks it is. I imagine you do too. I have people in my care. These people have the most serious health concerns. I consider their proper care to be the most critical thing a doctor can do. I can allow nothing to interfere with my duties: no intrigue, no games, nothing. Do you understand that?" He was staring down at me with a gravity I can only recognize in looking back on it.

"Just an accident," I repeated. The doctor took his needle and tweezers, asked Mr. Worthington to hold my fingers apart and then began to sew.

"What is it you do, Mr. Worthington, besides practice medicine?" I asked the black boatman, not wanting to engage the doctor while he sewed my hand.

"I am an oiler and the crew chief of the boiler men. I make this thing run."

"That is literally true," the doctor commented and he tucked and pulled on the threads.

"I've worked on ships for thirty-five years," Mr. Worthington continued. "I worked on ships we fed coal into the furnace. I worked on ships with cotton sails and Manila rigging. I tell you, man. I know ships."

"What of your family?" I stared up at the white ceiling.

"I see my family once, twice a year. I give them all my money. They build houses. They buy land. I'm a rich man, you see. You just don't see it here."

"And Martha the angel girl. Doesn't she miss you?" I asked.

"Sure she does. I know she does. We save all of the spare money and someday we go to the clinic in Minnesota and we see all the doctors there. It is only such a small part of

Martha's brain that is hurt. I know that by now they can fix her. It is money, that is all." Mr. Worthington dismissed the seriousness of his grief with a toss of his head, as if he were spitting away a drop of sweat that had worked its way to his lips.

The doctor finished up. He cleaned his hands and packed away his instruments into what looked like a gym bag. "You should let this breathe. Call me and I will look at that hand tomorrow. I do not want you anywhere near my clinic or near my patients. They have an absolute right to their privacy. I will not have you snooping around. Is that understood?"

He did not wait for an answer but turned to Mr. Worthington. "I'm glad you came for me. Thank you for that. I don't know what I'm going to do about all of this . . . this spying. But as far as I'm concerned, the matter of how Mr. Younger received his wounds is closed as long as . . ." Here he paused and looked gravely at Mr. Worthington and at me. ". . . as long as nothing else happens to reopen the issue."

I was not sure quite what was meant by that, but apparently I was being told to go and sin no more. I was about to thank him but the doctor was gone. Mr. Worthington stared down at me and smiled a great comical grin. "Cyril is a pure fool, man. But I don't think he will try to hurt you anymore. I will put out the word if you will agree that this ends this thing." Mr. Worthington made a gesture as if he were washing his hands and wringing them dry.

I struggled to my feet and tried to make myself steady. "There is nothing more between Cyril and myself as far as I am concerned," I assured Mr. Worthington and held my hand out awkwardly to take his but withdrew it as soon as I looked at the bulging Frankenstein stitches across my palm. He patted me on the arm and led me out the door.

We could have been walking through the boiler room of any old school building in turn-of-the-century New York. The pipes clattered and the metal floor underneath us rattled. There was the ever-clinging smell of cigarette smoke, sweat, and cafeteria food. Mr. Worthington led me around a labyrinth of catwalks and corridors until we came to an elevator. When the car came he reached in the doors and punched the button. I stepped inside and he smiled at me, holding his great broad hand up in a wave. The doors closed as I tried to think of something to say.

The doors opened and I stepped out into the hallway next to the Compass Room. A harpist dressed in a silver lamé evening gown played a slow Irish air on a full-sized orchestral harp. Four people were playing cards, one frowning deeply and tossing her hand into the center of the table. The others were chuckling softly. Mr. Brenner dozed with an empty brandy snifter balanced loosely in his hands. Beyond the glare of the ship's lights, I could see the lights of a town strung out like several small necklaces in the purple summer evening.

8

Sitka

The captain let the chain run about six in the morning. The anchor nestled into the mud of Sitka Sound as I woke up in my bunk. Todd was snoring like a sucking intake valve, and Jane Marie was nowhere to be seen. Her wildlife books and her slide carousel were gone.

The ship's newspaper *Over the Horizon* had been slipped under our door. There were short entries about various happenings on the ship with all of the daily scheduled events as well as the background report on our current port of call. I held the sheet in my good hand and sat on the edge of my bunk with my knees propped against the dresser, as I read about my own little town:

The setting of Sitka is spectacular. Overlooking beautiful forested islands scattered around Sitka Sound, Sitka has a charming harbor and downtown area. On a clear day, the mountains of Baranof Island, behind the town, and the volcanic cone of Mount Edgecumbe on Kruzof Island are in full view. There is a certain sophistication about Sitka, with two colleges, excellent museums, bookstores, galleries, and the National Historic Park, containing one of the largest exhibitions of Tlingit and Haida totem poles in existence.

All of this was accurate, of course. The paper went on to outline the history: how Sitka had been settled by the Russians and had in fact been the first capital of the territory. Alaska Day is celebrated here on October 18 of every year to commemorate the transfer of the territory from Russia to the United States. All of which is looked on rather caustically by the Tlingit citizens. At the time of the original transfer, the Russians had been beaten back to living in one small stockaded area where their forts and leaky cabins, which the Americans so grandly called "castles," were located. The Tlingits were incredulous as to what all the celebration was about when the official transfer took place. After all, what harm could be done by allowing white people to trade a small square of land inside a barracks back and forth? No one with any sense could believe that the white men really thought they owned it all. This was absurd.

And of course it continues to stay absurd. I imagine the "certain sophistication" of Sitka applies to the wet T-shirt contest and the belly sliding across the barroom floors on Alaska Day, when all the white people in town get drunker than skunks and celebrate the lasting perfection of it all. They didn't have to fight for it. They didn't even have to buy it from the Indians, they just claimed it, in a written language no one could read. This could not be happening and yet some hundred and thirty years later it still is.

I stumbled down to the gangway where the first of the crews were putting the tenders into the water. These boats would ferry anyone who wanted to go ashore into town. I was home and I needed to get off the ship.

I shuffled into a long line of people in plastic raincoats with cameras around their necks and tote bags folded over their arms. I wore a clean sweatshirt and some pants which were not stained with blood. As I approached the open door I saw Cyril standing in the entrance of a hall. He was tall and silent. When he saw me shuffling slowly in line he locked his eyes on mine and when I kept my eyes on his, he made a low bow as if to acknowledge my presence. Very softly he said, "Good morning, sir. Have a fine day ashore." And that was all.

The tenders were somewhat larger than a lifeboat. They had white hulls and orange roofs with plastic windows. The "sheep" dutifully filed in and sat in wooden benches somewhat more cramped than sitting at an elementary-school desk. There was a light breeze from the southwest; the little boats rolled like tubs. There were handsome young men and women in ship windbreakers talking into radios and looking at things written on clipboards. There were passengers asking for the totem walking tour and others about the wildlife cruise. The whale watcher was confused about which boat to wait for and she bolted from her seat just as our little boat was about to cast off from the ship. The boat's officer was Indonesian, I think, and he nodded and smiled as the woman spoke loudly to him about the whales and about the correct boat to be on. The officer nodded and smiled, then nodded once more, and gave the throttle enough push to ease the little boat back to the hull where the whale-watching woman frantically disembarked. Several of these small boats would be going back and forth to the ship all day long. Each trip took about twelve minutes, but no matter how often we were told that, there was always some mild atmosphere of hysteria about being left behind.

I had never come ashore from the sound in this way, and I had never woken up at home after falling asleep at sea. I was unhinged and started slapping my pockets looking for my tickets. My wallet. The key to my room and the little plastic credit card that would allow me back on board. I had the tickets, which it turned out I didn't need, but I didn't have the card, which I did. I had my wallet, but I didn't have a coat and although the weather showed some promise, that promise could always be broken in favor of more rain. I felt scattered, as if I had my stuff thrown all over the floor of a football stadium. This looked like my hometown, but how did I get here? What time did they say the boat was leaving?

The peak of the mountain that stared down upon Sitka was visible through a hole in clouds shaped like dirty tufts of cotton. Sun cut through and landed straight on the center of town, which is where the little main street divides to go around the Russian Cathedral. I had lived here in Sitka some seventeen years and it had just occurred to me I'd never had a really good look around the cathedral. My legs were unused to solid ground. I found the steadiness of it and the openness of the spaces unnerving. On shipboard I had gotten used to the narrowness and the straightforward navigating of walking down halls. Now I had choices. But I didn't know what to base these choices on. So I just followed the people in front of me. They were shipmates, after all, and they seemed to have been paying attention when I was not, and besides they were walking with such decisiveness.

So, I blundered through the day. I saw the Russian Dancers and the Tlingit Dancers. I stayed in the crowd and ate some salmon and a sourdough roll. I walked through the museum and took photos of my shipmates standing in front of the bronze statue of Lord Baranof. I didn't see anyone I knew. I did see Rob Allen, a young guy I'd played soccer with some years ago. Rob was walking briskly around in his heavy leather coat, talking into a hand-held radio and trying to get a word in with one of the skippers of his wild-life-watching boats. I waved to Rob and he smiled and waved without recognition, as he would at any tourist, then moved on. I broke away from the crowd for a moment and walked down to my house. I had planned to check my messages, maybe get the mail, but I had forgotten my keys. There was something sad about my little house, built on pilings over the industrial beachfront of the old Indian village. The fuchsia blossoms had fallen from their pots and curled like piles of dead insects on my porch. Wet papers lay soggy like rotten leaves. I know the smell of a closed-up house. I knew what mail I had waiting for me. Fuck it. I was on vacation. I was cruising. I walked back down the street and decided to find the perfect T-shirt for Jane Marie. Maybe that would put us back in touch.

I had to assume Jane Marie was back on the ship going through her slides for her lecture on "Alaskan Mammals: From Top to Bottom." I decided she would check the mail later. But I didn't suppose it mattered.

The one person who recognized me in Sitka was Marilyn at the bookstore. As soon as I walked in, she reached under the counter.

"Cecil. I'm glad you're here. You know we still have that book you ordered on Etruscan art." She hefted the tome up on the counter with the thud of a side of beef.

"Come on. You know I never ordered a book on Etruscan art. For Christ's sakes, I don't even know where Etrusca is." She'd been trying to sell me the book all summer. I tried to skirt past her to the coffee shop.

"Cecil, come on, this is an expensive book. You don't know what these guys are like. We'll get killed on the shipping alone if we try to send it back."

"Hold it for me. I'll take a look at it when I get back from vacation."

Marilyn stood in front of me. She had red hair and flaming yellow fingernails. Her necklace looked as if it had been made out of miniature car parts.

"What do you mean . . . *back*?" she demanded.

"I mean *back*. I'm taking a cruise, if you must know. I'm here as a visitor, so be nice, or I'll turn you in to the Chamber of Commerce."

"No way!" Marilyn screeched with delight and she turned to yell into the back room. "Hey, Don! Cecil is in off of one of the ships!"

So, there was nothing to be done after that. The usual layabouts and underemployed denizens of the Back Door coffee shop came pouring out of their booths and gathered around me as if I were giving out gold coins. Several noticed the glove on my right hand but they easily accepted my "bad paper cut" explanation, having seen me through so much damage in the past.

Now I was a tourist and I had been "made." But I took some comfort in the fact that this time I had been made as something I was halfway trying to be.

Todd walked through the door with a new ball cap and I swear a creased T-shirt on over his usual sweater. He snapped shots and tried to get a group photo together but that soon disbanded after everyone became bored with the waiting.

I told everyone that I was just invited along aboard ship as Jane Marie's guest and that she was working hard as a naturalist. I told them wild stories of champagne brunches and hot crab cakes at dawn: Wanton revelry at sea with rich widows and days of overindulgence. Of course, these were all lies and everyone knew they were lies as soon as the words tripped my lips, but such is the pleasure of irony: It's the only way we can ever really have it, however briefly, both ways.

Finally, the small crowd cleared and I went back to the coffee shop. I drink coffee here because the people I owe money to rarely set foot in here. I mostly borrow money from people with some to spare and the people who frequent the Back Door rarely have any extra. So I'm usually safe.

Todd sat with me briefly but said that he couldn't stay. He said that he was going to go run to the vet's and see how his dog Wendell was doing. He said he needed to "get a shot" and I assumed that meant he was going to get a picture. Todd was slumped in one of the straight-backed chairs, with his camera around his neck and his T-shirt bunched up around his stomach. The duct tape on the bridge of his glasses was frayed and it looked as if he had run to the tender before shaving this morning. Apparently he was saving his new glasses only for shipboard gatherings. He let out a long sigh.

"I think travel is an immensely broadening experience. Don't you, Cecil?"

I said that I had to agree and watched as Todd walked out the door at the same time as Dr. Edwards came in it.

Edwards saw me and nodded, then stood in the line beside the baked goods to place an order. Behind him came an extremely slender man who was probably young except that his age was hard to pinpoint because of the ravenous thinness of his frame. He walked with a cane and slowly took the table next to mine. He eased himself down into a chair with a great effort and then, breathing deeply, gazed around the room as if only now was he at liberty to take in the view. The doctor joined him and while setting his coffee cup down asked the thin man, "Would you like something to drink, Paul? Something hot?" Paul closed his eyes in careful thought.

"Chamomile tea, I think. Thank you," he said softly.

I could hardly take my eyes off Paul for he seemed a ghost already. Impossibly thin, with wispy hair. His face and his eyes were overshadowed by the skull pressing tightly on his skin. Paul turned to me.

"I understand they have a wonderful bookstore here. Is that true?"

Yes, I said, it was, and I pointed rather stupidly to the door where the bookstore began.

"Do they carry much poetry?" Paul asked as the doctor set down the tea and sat in the bench seat against the wall.

"Yes. I think they do have a very good selection," I said.

"I've been thinking of a poem. It's very weird. I can't get it out of my head. It starts, 'Lay your sleeping head, my love, faithless in my waiting arms . . .' Then I can't remember the rest." Paul closed his eyes again. "I want to say 'In it wait till judgement break excellent and fair.' But that's not it. Dickinson, that's what that is. Oh God, that movie with Meryl Streep." Paul opened his eyes. He laughed and stirred his tea. "My mind can take some trips," he added, laughing.

"The poem you want is by W. H. Auden," the doctor said. "It will be in his collected works."

"Auden. Yes. That is it." Paul looked at me comically. "It's a good thing there's a doctor in the house. The motherfuckers know everything." There was an edge to his voice, an anger that was so opposite from his countenance that I pushed back in my chair a little. Dr. Edwards smiled and sipped his coffee.

"I had a friend who loved that poem," Paul told me. "He read it all the time. I was thinking if I could find it, I'd read it to my dad tonight."

"You're traveling with your dad?" I asked.

"Oh yeah," Paul said and he puffed out his chest with a little self-mockery. "He's getting on, you know. So we're doing our father-son adventure. I never made it as a Boy Scout, you see." Paul looked at the doctor again. "No merit badge, but maybe some chamber music on the quarter-deck will do." He used his cane to stand up, slowly. He fumbled in the pocket of his tentlike coat and threw a five-dollar bill down on the table. "I'll see you on board, then." And Paul walked into the bookstore.

I said nothing for several moments. Dr. Edwards looked down into his coffee cup. Finally, he took a breath and said, "Paul thinks I hover."

I said nothing.

"So, how's the hand?" The doctor shrugged off his mood and lifted my hand. I had covered it with a loose-fitting glove liner I used inside my winter boating mitts. He took the mitt off and looked carefully at the bandage.

"Keep this clean. Soap and water should do. I got most of that tar off but God knows I don't think I got it all. Keep the wound clean and keep it open to the air as much as possible. Are you going to be continuing on this trip?"

He asked the question with such intensity that I gave a start and jerked my hand away from him.

"I expect so. My friends are on the trip. And I've never been told otherwise by the all-powerful Mr. Walters. I think I'll just hang around and wait to see how many people you kill and mutilate."

I don't know why I said it. The sentiment just sort of snuck up on me. The doctor shook his head sadly. At first, he looked irritated; then he looked profoundly tired. Not as tired as Paul, I must say, but tired nonetheless.

"It's all very easy for you, isn't it? No one comes to you in pain, do they? Have you ever fixed anything, Mr. Younger? Did you ever ease anyone's pain, even for a moment?"

A tiny girl with short black pigtails came over to our table and held up her library book. *"Snow White,"* she said proudly.

"I see that, Sarah. It's beautiful," I said to her. Sarah's mom owned the coffee shop. Sarah had been very understanding about the whole mess with Grant McGowan's suicide, but then she was three years old.

"I'm sorry, I don't know why I said it," I told Dr. Edwards.

He reached over and touched my forearm. "We all want to forget that we are mortal. I don't blame you really. I didn't ask for this . . . this situation, either. They come to me, more and more of them. They want to avoid the kind of industrial fading away that is waiting for them in the hospitals. More and more of them and I don't know what to do . . ."

His hand was shaking on my arm and his head was bowed down so that I could not see his eyes.

"Have you ever seen a botched suicide?" he said, still looking at the floor.

I had, in fact, but I didn't want to interrupt.

He labored on. "Brain damage. Disfigurement. Pain and permanent dysfunction. People will do these things to themselves."

"Why are they botched?" I asked. "The suicides?"

He stared up at me now with a coldness I wasn't expecting. "Ignorance, mostly. They don't understand the biology of it. The mechanics." He sat back, looking more composed. Looking almost professorial. "Ignorance and ambivalence, I suppose."

"Ambivalence," I echoed and Sarah, who had veered away to another table, sat on the floor by my feet and opened her book, calling out made-up words in a singsong voice, pretending to read.

The doctor brushed aside his last sentence, as if it were an annoyance. "And about that mutilation. The hand. You know, I had nothing to do with that. Someone else is responsible. And I think you know who."

I spread my hands wide and spoke slowly. "Why did you do nothing to bring the problem to anyone's attention? In the coroner's report, you listed the hand as a medical artifact. Now why is that?"

The saxophone player from Margie & the Navigators walked into the coffee shop. He looked at the doctor and me, then quickly turned away as if he were hurt by the sight of others off the ship. He ordered a cup of espresso in one of those tiny little cups and sat at the table opposite from us and unfolded a *New York Times*.

The doctor leaned his head close to mine. "I have very specific instructions, advanced protocols on file for each one of my patients. I am committed to carrying out those instructions." He took a deep breath and looked over at the saxophone player, who was now flicking his fingers on the edges of the pages of the newspaper. "In this instance . . ." the doctor went on ". . . the patient had made it explicit. She wanted to be cremated before the sun set. It was her very specific wish. She told me that was one of the reasons she chose Alaska. The long summer days. I could not hold up everything for some kind of rinky-dink investigation of what should be a shipboard matter anyway. It would have been a disaster. It would have disrupted the schedule, for God's sake. The captain would have never stood for that."

"The captain knows nothing of your . . . practices?"

"The captain runs the ship. He handles problems. We have had no problems so far. If there are problems, Empire Shipping handles them." The doctor played with the handle of Paul's cooling cup of tea.

"What was the girl's name?" I asked him suddenly.

The doctor slumped as if unexpectedly winded. "Oh," he groaned and ran his hands through his hair. "Her name was Beverly. She had no family. At least no family she wanted to claim."

He looked at me and I saw again how tired he was. I was vaguely aware of the saxophone player's newspaper trembling ever so slightly.

"Why was her name changed on the death certificate?" I pressed on.

"I had nothing to do with that." The doctor stood up and left abruptly. The saxophone player's eyes followed him out, then went slowly back to the paper.

I didn't have the money for the book on Etruscan art and neither did I have any for coffee. I left the coffee shop and walked back toward the ship.

The afternoon had worn on and the mountains behind town were starting to lighten with the slanting of the long sunset. The snowfields were small this time of year, but the forests were a vivid textured green up the slopes. Blue sky rimmed the gray rock, and the clouds held a glow that seemed about to survive the setting sun. As I crossed the street I looked over to the Russian Cathedral. Paul was walking painfully up the stairs. He had a thick book in his hand and he lugged it as if it were a steamer trunk. I turned through the alley where a garbage can had spilled. The ravens were hopping in and out of shadow, bickering over the scraps left in the plastic dishes from someone's box lunch. One very large bird sat on the lip of the can and lectured the others in full voice, but none of them seemed to pay any mind.

I had made Dr. Edwards nervous, and defensive, and this could only be a good thing, if I was really going to make some headway for the all-powerful Sonny Walters. I was assuming that Cyril had stolen the hand and had used it as a graphic illustration of what awaited me if I snitched on him about his little love tryst in Acapulco 800. This was old business as far as I was concerned. I had no real beef with Cyril. He was scared and I couldn't blame him.

I made it to the public dock for the second-to-the-last tender of the day. I stood with tired fishermen and whale watchers. There had been humpbacks out in Eastern Channel not far from where the *Westward* was anchored, and the passengers were ecstatic. Once we made it on board I had a snack from the sandwich buffet and went to our room. Jane Marie had been there. Her books had been rearranged and her rain gear was gone from the closet. I walked to the boat deck and made sure that Todd had signed in and then went to the observation deck above the Horizon Deck. As I walked the stairs I heard the anchor chain drumming against the steel hull and the engines shuddered under foot.

On deck, Jane Marie was standing with her old Zeiss binoculars around her neck. People were bundled up against the cold; some held their faces to that thin northern sunlight. Several held drinks in their hands. The ship eased away from its anchorage and we moved gradually out of the western passage toward Saint Lazaria Island and the outside coast. The sun was going lower in the west and the mountains behind us flared red and then purple. Paul was on a deck lower than us, sitting with a blanket over his lap, reading to an older gentleman at his side. As Paul read, the old man awkwardly reached over and lightly touched the young man's knee. Paul stopped reading for a moment, then touched his father's hand. He let his hand linger there for a moment.

Rosalind came on deck and stood next to Jane Marie and asked questions as they both scanned the water for mammals. Mr. Brenner smoked the great log of one of his cigars.

The first blow came to our port side and the crowd gave a noisy cheer as if the first pitch had been thrown in the World Series. The whales dove and lunged, breaking the surface with their great rubbery flippers. People from Detroit toasted them with their martinis and a couple from Denmark yelled "Bravo!"

I walked over to Jane Marie and put my arm through hers. She squeezed close against me. "I heard you cut your hand. Are you okay?" she asked me as she continued to scan the water.

"I'm beginning to think there are no real secrets on this boat. I have no idea why they need a private snoop."

Jane Marie laughed and pulled me closer. Rosalind shrieked and pointed. As everyone turned, a whale breached completely out of the water, spinning as it did so that its huge flippers twisted around its pleated belly. It seemed in slow motion, this forty-ton animal, as it crashed down with a thud, sending breakers rolling in every direction.

People on deck cheered. Some of them hugged and laughed; others just leaned against the rail with that far-off expression that seemed to look both inward and outward at the same time.

As we passed the basalt upwelling of Saint Lazaria Island, the volcanic ash of the cone of Mount Edgecumbe glowed a deep red. Auklets and tufted puffins labored by on their inefficient little wings and a peregrine falcon cut tight, fast circles down from the black-faced cliffs. We came within a hundred yards of the island, and inside of the basalt caves, cormorants held up their wings to dry, as if posing for a photograph.

Jane Marie answered questions as fast as she could. People shouted them out. Wanting to know. Needing to know, and she told them. Sometimes in plain language, and sometimes by admitting she didn't know the answer, but always giving them more to fill out their images. More information to flesh out their memories and the stories they would tell of their one great trip to the northern Pacific.

I looked back for one last look at my tiny little town. It was a strange feeling, for I knew that I was neither away nor at home. Looking at my home as the passengers must be seeing it: A fairyland, a place where fish always bite, and whales always gambol, and where strangers always welcome you in. Of course, this was not completely true, but on this mild evening no one wanted complete truth. Least of all me.

9

The Hubbard Glacier

That night the *Westward* worked its way north, staying well offshore until daylight when the captain planned to be entering the tidewaters of the Hubbard Glacier. The swell was moderate from the southwest. The weather was turning northeast, a high-pressure front pushing down from the northern interior. In the lounges of the ship the parties were in full cry, with a keening abandonment as if time were running out all over the world.

In the Terra Nova Lounge there was a dating game for the singles on board, where the young Master of Ceremonies from Sonny's social staff was asking embarrassing questions. The Whipping Post had a Caribbean beach party with a steel-drum band and a limbo contest with everyone dressed in parkas and straw hats. The Fiddler's Green lounge featured an operatic tenor singing bawdy sea songs, while there was an all-request sing-along in the Compass Room. In the Great Circle Lounge, a jitterbug contest and costume revue took place under the mirrored ball.

When I peeked in, Mr. Brenner had paid Margie & the Navigators to play "Hava Nagila" for the second time. I was guessing this by the bills that were stuffed down into the bell of the saxophone and into the top of Margie's hot pink sequined bust. Mr. Brenner had his shirt unbuttoned and was dancing alone in the middle of the floor; in a circle around him the other passengers in their spangled headbands and short fringed dance costumes were clapping and stomping their feet. Mr. Brenner was dancing with his arms spread wide. He danced and spun, then knelt down on one knee to reach a bottle of brandy on the floor with his mouth. To the cheers of the crowd he clamped the bottle in his teeth and hefted it above his head; brandy streamed down the side of his face and throat. I closed the door and went back out on deck.

Stars pressed down out of the sky. The sea gave way to the weather, changing from ink-black felt to a rolling glitter of waves. The dark purple outline of the Fairweather mountains rose to the east and the sky here in the gulf seemed a calamity of bright objects.

I could hear the steel drums on the fantail and prismatic laughter of passengers off the stern. In a moment the doors to the lounge opened and the blaring fanfare pushed Mr. Brenner out onto the starboard deck with me. He was dabbing his forehead and swabbing brandy off his neck. Someone had draped his camel sport jacket over his shoulders.

"What are you doing out here, young man?" he said in a much quieter voice than I was expecting. "All of the pretty girls are in there. They are waiting for you, my boy. It's your life—don't waste it out here." He looked at me sternly and I shrugged my shoulders.

"Ah. Moody, moody, moody . . . I should have known that about you. That first night. You're thinking about her then, the girl who kissed you that first night?"

"She's dead," I told him.

"Dead. Of course she's dead. What? You think she's avoiding you?" Brenner fished into his pocket and found a cigar tube. "They told us." He spoke as he lit the great cigar. "They told us you were a Shamus. That true? You asking questions about people dying on this ship. That true?" A squall of smoke wrapped around us from his cigar.

"Are you going to die on this trip, Mr. Brenner?" I asked him.

He stared at me defiantly. "You know how old I am?"

I shook my head assuring him I didn't.

"Eighty years old. That's right!" He stood flat-footed and posed for me.

This was remarkable, if true. My guess would have been in the mid-sixties.

"That's right, young man. I've seen the best of this century . . . and the worst, too, let me tell you: the war, the camps, America, Israel . . . everything."

"You don't look like you're dying of prostate cancer." I tried to head him off.

"Ugh! It's an old man's disease."

"So you want to kill yourself because of it?"

Mr. Brenner sidled up to me at the rail and we both looked over toward the outline of the Fairweathers.

"When I was a little boy, my parents were gone. Very bad. You know . . . Nazis." He spit out into the sea. "I had been sent away early. I lived with my aunt in Hungary for a time and then in Jersey City. I never really knew what they had been through, my family, only the stories and a little book of pictures. I didn't think much of it. I studied hard in school. I worked hard at everything I did. I made several wives miserable, I grew up to be very rich, you see, because I never wasted any time being happy. Oh, I was a bastard, young man. I don't mind telling you this is true. Then a doctor tells me I have cancer. This cancer may kill me and it may not. Suddenly I feel giddy. I drink. I travel. I love the women. Oh, my poor wives! I was such a prick. I only wish they had known me when I was dying!" He sucked on his cigar and the smoke bloomed like incense from a censer.

"So, you think your guilt about . . ." I began. But he slapped my arm.

"Hush. Don't talk about Freud. He's a witch doctor. There never was any science to that man. No! All I'm saying is I spent most of my life feeling crappy that I was alive and I'm not going to spend one second like that again."

"Then why travel with the club?" I asked, thinking of L'Inconnue de la Seine and their very high death rate.

"That girl, when she kissed you the other night, I know you can't forget her. Isn't that right?"

"That's true," I told him.

"You can't get that girl out of your mind because she knew exactly who she was and what she was doing. She was savoring the last passionate moments of her life and every ounce of that passion was in her kiss."

"Or so we'd like to think," I said softly.

"Ah, my boy, but you are a cynic, aren't you?"

"Not really. I'm just wondering why a man with such vitality would want to die just now."

Mr. Brenner's eyes flickered and he turned back out to sea. He put a foot up on one of the bars of the rail. "I am vital because I know the limit of my life. I am vital because I know the exact worth of each second. I determine my destiny and this makes me what I am. I don't give these things up to the damn doctors. Can't you see that, young man?"

I started to speak to him when something darted just out of my field of vision back under the staircase to the upper deck. Brenner turned, too. Back by the doorstop a brown savannah sparrow huddled in the shadow.

The bird was small as a baby's fist. She sat squat, head buried into her wings: black eyes darting.

"What the hell?" Mr. Brenner said softly as he bent and picked her up.

"What do you think?" he asked me. "Think she ran into a window or something?" He held the little sparrow cupped in his fleshy hands, his fat cigar still cradled between his fingers. The bird was trying to disappear through a stone-like stillness.

"She probably flew to the ship when we were anchored in Sitka. She's used to marshes and the grassy beach fringe," I offered.

"My gosh, her heart is beating so fast. Do you think it's hurt? Broken wing or something?"

I was about to answer when the bird flew from his hands in a feathery storm around the deck, looping frantically toward the portholes. With each pull toward the deck rail the sparrow would catch the rush of wind from the ship's progress and veer back toward the sheltered deck. After several of these parries she landed again, in the lee of the stairwell, eerily still and silent.

"Let's just leave her," I suggested to Mr. Brenner and put my hand on the handle of the door to the Great Circle Lounge, where I could hear the band tearing into a Tommy Dorsey number.

"Nonsense," Brenner said with certainty. "She wants to go home." And he picked up the sparrow and heaved her across the rail.

The sparrow fell, stonelike for a moment, and then spasmed into flight. I followed her wing beats for a few seconds as she flew out past our stern wake and into the darkness heading east.

Brenner watched the little brown bird disappear. We said nothing and then he started to shake with the cold. His skin seemed pale and he clutched his arms around his shoulders. For the first time on the voyage he looked his age, and just briefly perhaps afraid. When he realized I was staring at him he jammed the cigar back into his mouth, then walked back into the lounge. I stayed out on deck listening to the laughter and the steel drums. I suddenly felt my age, too. After a while, I went inside to bed.

In the morning, the hull of the ship rattled and clunked through ice. Chunks of ice, from drink-sized cubes to frozen blocks the size of buses, scattered on the calm surface of the bay as if they were floating debris. There was a thin layer of clouds high in the sky and the water appeared an opaque milky white. The day felt cold, colder even than the temperature. Cold to the bone. Everything here was rock and ice and newly scrubbed land. The glacier itself was a crumbling bluff of ice extending a mile and a half along its face. From the ship you could feel its cold, like a freezer door left open. The massive bulk of the glacier ran away into the distance, leaving only the smoothed stone ridges on both sides of the bay. High on the hillside a few scrubby willows grew so that there was the slightest haze of green on these rocks. Nowhere else in this scoured and crumbling landscape was there any color.

Paul and the older man I assumed was his father walked toward the fantail to have a close look at the ice. Todd was there taking pictures and chatting to his shipmates. They stood shoulders hunched and bouncing on the balls of their feet. Puffs of vapor came from their mouths as they laughed. Todd was wearing his gray cardigan sweater over his shoulders and he had one of the light blue blankets the crew was handing out to passengers, one edge of it tucked into the back neck of his shirt. This seemed to keep the blanket in place. He wore earmuffs. These he got from God knows where.

I came up to him as he was explaining about calving. "Incredibly massive, these can be, whole towers, buttresses of ice . . ." he enthused to Paul and his father as I came closer. Just as I reached them, Todd pointed to a section of ice as large as a townhouse that gave way from the face of the glacier and slumped into the bay. A moment later the sound came to us as a grinding crack and then a sizzle. A wave rolled through the oily-looking slush near the glacier and came on under our hull and the *Westward* bobbed slightly.

Todd hurriedly took a picture of what had happened just moments before. Paul smiled and offered to take Todd's picture with the glacier in the background but Todd then insisted on taking a group shot with all of us in the frame. This led me to standing awkwardly next to the old man and Paul as Todd fiddled and fussed with his camera on the backs of two chairs put together. "He seems quite knowledgeable about glaciers," the old man told me.

"Yeah, but he doesn't know squat about his camera," I

said out of the side of my mouth. The old man looked up at me, a little distressed, as if I might not realize how Todd was "different" and that I might be being a little hard on him. Todd can oftentimes bring out surprising gentleness in other people.

"I'm his roommate," I told him, and the old man only said, "Ah!" as if that were all that needed to be said.

There was activity on the boat deck above us as the crew seemed to be preparing to launch a lifeboat. This caused some stir among the passengers. Paul and Todd went off to have a closer look. The old man stayed leaning against the rail. He stuck his hand out to me as we both watched Paul and Todd walk away.

"I'm Harold Standard," the old man said. "My son and I are cruising together." He nodded in Paul's direction.

Today, Paul seemed even paler, if that were possible. His skeletal frame seemed evident even under the bulky clothes he wore, if only because of the thin lines his shoulders cut into the jacket.

The old man mumbled something.

"I beg your pardon," I said.

"Oh," Mr. Standard said, "nothing. I was just muttering to myself." He could not take his eyes off his son. "I just remember Yeats said something like 'To people who have seen ghosts, human flesh seems so substantial.'"

From far away the glacier creaked and groaned, sending a shudder into the air. A little gray bird landed in the ship's rigging, looking like a toy trumpet.

"It's AIDS, you know," Mr. Standard said, and I said nothing. "He got it from a blood transfusion."

"Really?" I said. "That's tough. I mean . . . that's too bad."

The ship turned away from the bluff of ice and came to a stop. The captain lowered the boat with several crewmen and a Filipino man with a white tunic and a chef's hat on. The crewmen stuck their long oars into the opaque water and rowed toward the bow of the ship. They looked tiny. Their efforts against the oars hardly seemed to trouble the water. I noticed that I was starting to shiver. The man in the chef's hat was talking to the seamen, pointing to a huge blue chunk of ice. The crew bent into their oars and soon they were alongside it. The cook patted the tiny berg, examining it as if it were a used car. Then, after some consideration, he drove several bolts into its side and screwed them in tight.

The davits used for hauling the boats on board were used for bringing the ice on deck. The davits swiveled and allowed the ice to be placed on the edge of the fantail where others on the kitchen crew rushed to ease its landing on the deck. They had placed a round stand under the ice, and they were able to slide it on the deck around to the center of the fantail.

In shape and color the berg looked like an uncut diamond. In the milky white sunlight it almost appeared to glow blue. Hoses were attached to the stand and were run over to the scuppers on the side of the ship. Todd and Paul stood staring up at the great monument of ice.

"I can't . . ." Mr. Standard blurted out.

"I'm sorry?" I said, not sure I had heard him.

"No, I'm sorry. I'm just talking to myself." Mr. Standard hugged his arms around himself. He, too, was shivering. "I was just thinking, I can't help him. I don't know how much suffering another person can bear." He did not take his eyes off his son.

"I suppose you have to take their word for it," I offered lamely.

"That wasn't true," he said.

"Yeah, you might be right. I didn't mean to meddle," I said, embarrassed.

"No. Not that. I meant it's not true about the blood transfusion," Mr. Standard said, his cheeks slick with tears.

"That's all right." I put my hand awkwardly on his shoulder. "None of that matters now, I suppose."

The doors from the kitchen opened wide and the man in the chef's hat appeared with a mallet and a table full of chisels. The chef barked orders to his assistants. Assistants began drying and positioning the block of ice for carving; my shipmates began to gather. Mr. Standard mumbled something that I took as an apology and he walked away into the crowd of gawkers.

Isaac Brenner walked out on the fantail. There was no cigar and there was a quavering uncertainty to his step. He had a blanket draped over his shoulders. He looked as if he had aged a decade overnight. He came slowly over to me.

"Mr. Brenner!" I called out. "How are you this morning? Everything okay?"

Brenner was looking distractedly around at the crowd.

"Huh? Yes. Yes. Just a little off my game this morning . . ." His voice trailed off. "Have you seen that young man Paul?" Then he looked up to me and his face drained of blood.

I pointed down to the fantail and Brenner waved distractedly and shambled off.

◙ ◙ ◙

Jane Marie walked on the deck above the fantail and, looking down, saw me and waved. In a moment, she was standing next to me.

"Hello, sailor," she said and gave my arm a squeeze. She was warm and I could taste the life in her breath.

"Hey, beautiful," I said somewhat absently. I was watching Paul and Todd walking slowly around the block of ice and I couldn't stop shivering. Jane Marie put her arm around my waist.

"We really need to talk." She said it in a tone that worried me.

"Listen," I said, without looking at her, "I know we should talk but I just don't want to hear bad news right now. I've caught a bad chill."

Jane Marie took my face in her hands and turned it toward hers.

"Let's go warm up, then," she said, her dark eyes scanning my face, probing, looking for clues. "I can help." She touched my cut.

"Cecil," she said, softly and with a tone of tired resignation, "I'm tired of organizing games." And she paused as the face of the glacier cracked and groaned and the silver bird in the rigging flew away. "I want you to love me again."

I've known Jane Marie from when I was a kid growing up in Juneau. I had a crush on her when the Beatles first appeared on Ed Sullivan. Some of the best things in the modern era have occurred since I've started loving her. She was always smarter than me, always more mature and in all things I assumed she really knew the truth about me, but tolerated my friendship anyway. This is what I always thought love was: A tolerance. But maybe I had been wrong.

Jane Marie gave me a kiss. Her lips were warm and her grip on my neck was urgent. As she pulled away from me, her tongue flicked inside my lips and against my tongue. I could smell the soap in her hair and I could feel her muscles running down her back as she stepped into me for warmth.

"Cecil," she whispered into my ear, "this boat is too crowded. There is too much unhappiness here. Let's go someplace?" She nestled her mouth into the crook of my neck. "Please," she said.

We walked hand in hand down the passageways toward our room. As we rounded the stairs to Acapulco Deck, I smelled the strong scent of marijuana drifting down the hall. Jane Marie wrinkled her nose. Ahead, Todd was using his key in the lock on our room. Jane Marie and I stopped and looked around and noticed that the door to 800 was ajar. We walked up to it and knocked lightly, then looked in.

There were four young men in the room passing around a joint of Rastafarian proportions. Paul was there, flopped down on the made-up bunk. All four smiled up at us in the doorway, waving and motioning us to come in. One sucked on the spliff and a plume of sweet-smelling smoke came toward us. One of the other young men had an IV bag hanging from the bunk above and the other was propped on pillows next to him. The two on the bunk were completely bald. Their pale and inscrutable expressions were made more so by the lack of eyebrows.

"Don't be scared," the one with the closed eyes

murmured. "We won't hurt you." And they all broke into a languid laughter.

"No . . ." I said and started to back out. "Sorry to disturb you." And we walked back out into the hall.

Toddy was reading in his bunk so we kept walking down the hall. Down at this depth of the ship we could hear the ice grinding against the outside of the hull as the ship maneuvered even closer to the glacier. It was a low-pitched grinding shudder that I could feel through the bottoms of my feet.

Jane Marie pulled me to a stop and kissed me, touching the side of my face with her hands, and then she placed my hand lightly against her breast.

"I know someplace," she said and pulled me up one flight and down a short hall I hadn't been in. In the interior of the ship was one of the tiny laundry rooms provided for the passengers. There were three coin-operated washers and three dryers. With some unplugging and moving around I was able to block the door that led into the room.

Just as I finished pushing a dryer in front of the door, I turned to Jane Marie, who kissed me with an urgency that knocked me back against a washing machine. Her hair was a tangle around her face. We took sharp quick kisses as if we were both eating the same apple between us. We fumbled with my belt and the buttons of her pants. Her mouth and tongue felt slick on mine.

Someone had been drying a load of their vacation clothes. There were slacks and Hawaiian shirts. Panties and boxer shorts, blue towels and matching washcloths. All the fabric was hot and dry and I quickly piled everything on top of the two washers that were rumbling through their cycles. Jane Marie pulled off her sweater and her pants, then she pulled off my clothes.

Of course it was strange. The warm laundry scattered and fell on the floor. But I placed a towel under it all and we didn't feel the coolness of metal. She sat on the washer and I kissed her breasts and her lips. I worked down the linty sweetness of her whole body. I licked her and stroked her thighs as she arched her back into my face. Then she grabbed my hair, pulling me up to her.

One of the Hawaiian shirts had metal snaps which burned into my back, but not enough to distract from the warmth of her hands and her belly. She kissed me and said my name over and over. The spin cycle kicked in and she eased on top of me. I closed my eyes to keep from laughing. She piled clothes across my chest and I felt the grip of her body all around mine until we both shuddered with a warmth that drove away the chill.

Later, we folded some of the clothes and put some others back through the wash. We ate together that night and even made banana splits at the midnight dessert buffet. We danced and talked about all the passengers we had met and I told her about Cyril, Mr. Worthington, and Martha the angel girl.

I was grateful for it all, every second of happiness we had enjoyed, particularly the next morning when I learned that Paul was dead and the ship's doctor had turned up missing.

10

Coming Through Icy Strait

I was first aware that the whole silly adventure was starting to unravel when the alarm bells on the *Westward* starting clanging at six-ten in the morning the following day. The ship's engines were blaring through the floor and I could feel the ship lean into a steep turn. I heard the sound of urgent voices over hand-held radios as people padded quickly up and down the halls: Keys rattling on belts, buckles being clipped.

I poked my head out of my door and saw a crowd of men in ship uniforms standing around the door of the clinic. I dressed quickly and joined them.

The Panamanian first mate was standing in a crisp uniform with a clipboard in his hand. Three men, their credentials pinned to the pockets of their uniforms, blocked the way to the door. I tried to muscle through them but was grabbed and forced back against the door.

"I'm part of the Moonlight Bay team," I bluffed, but their grips relaxed just long enough for me to ease past them to the first mate.

The Mate looked irritated with me. He was listening to the two people talking by the examining table. The Mate held his hand distractedly out by my chest, more in an effort to make me be still rather than to throw me out. I was still, for the two men talking caught my attention immediately.

The saxophone player was talking to a sobbing Mr. Standard. The sax player wore a maroon jogging suit. He had a microcassette tape recorder in his right hand and was kneeling near Mr. Standard.

"Tell me where I can find the doctor, then," he said softly and with some comfort. Mr. Standard stared straight ahead. Tears ran down his face.

"He wasn't ready. It wasn't time," he said over and over.

"I know that, Harold." The sax player's voice was soothing. "I know that, and believe me we'll be looking into that, but right now we need to find the doctor. Tell me about what happened to the doctor, Harold. It will be much easier if you do."

"Where's Paul?" I asked the Mate and all eyes turned to me and the hands came from behind to throw me out. "Let's go," I heard from behind my right shoulder.

"Wait!" The sax player stood up and walked toward me.

"Come with me." The sax player spoke with some strong authority that everyone seemed to recognize, for as soon as he said those words the hands released me and the first mate stepped aside.

The two of us walked into a tiny office that had been a typing room for the clinic. The sax player went in first and after I walked inside he motioned for me to close the door. The sax player sat on the desk in front of me, his right hand on the typewriter and his feet resting on the only chair. I was not offered a seat and that made sense for there was nowhere else to sit down.

"My name is David Werdheimer from San Francisco," the sax player said and he nodded. Then he stood up to check the lock on the door.

In the world of professional private investigators there are only a handful of stars and there was only one who had kept hold of the lasting respect of the trade. The others had fallen away to become celebrity whores or high-profile "security analysts." A couple had become well-known thugs for their millionaire movie star clients. But the one who was legend among the working defense bar and professional investigators was David Werdheimer, from San Francisco, California, who was professionally known as "Word."

Word was famous mostly through gossip and misinformation. Stories about him circulated like the latest bad-taste joke. He had worked for mafia dons and cabinet members. There were investigative journalists who would have offered a year's pay just to know the list of his clients who hadn't been indicted. I stood there looking at this sax player and I scanned my memory. I could not come up with a mental picture of the famous "Word." There was none. He took pride in never being photographed under his own identity.

"You and I are in the same profession, Mr. Younger," Mr. Werdheimer said generously. "I was hired by the ship's company . . . by Empire Shipping . . . out of Singapore. Apparently they felt that the Great Circle Cruise Lines was not particularly forthcoming about the 'Moonlight Bay' situation."

He paused and stared at me as if expecting me to speak.

Then he added, "When they got word of Circle's own investigation, Empire decided they had better do one of their own."

"I'm honored," I said, trying to give my voice a special tone of tough-guy irony. "Where's Paul?"

"Paul's no longer any of your concern," Word said.

"I'll just be leaving then," I said, pulling against the door where Word had blocked it with his foot.

"Now don't get excited, Cecil." Word watched me closely. I noticed he was still wearing a saxophone strap around his neck. His voice was smooth and calm. "I was just going to ask you if you knew where the doctor was."

"I don't know, but I suppose I had better find out." I fought against my anger, afraid, I suppose, that it would come out whiny rather than fierce. I worked the knob on the door that Word kept me from opening.

Then he smirked and fiddled with his neck strap. "Whoa there, cowboy. Don't go running off half-cocked."

I turned and grabbed him by the thumb and bent it back until it straightened his arm. Then I put my forearm down hard against his elbow, forcing him down until his face was on the desk. I spoke slowly and clearly.

"Two things . . ." I said through clenched teeth. "I am not a cowboy." Word did not struggle, but his free hand moved to reach something in his jacket pocket as I slowly let the pressure relax on his arm. "And number two," I continued, "you are a very bad saxophone player."

For some reason I thought these were important points to make. I released him. Word gave a long sigh. He seemed unconcerned about the physical violence that had just passed between us. He straightened up. He adjusted his coat and held his pocket stun gun to my face. Then he worked the mechanism, sending a nasty spark arcing across the contact points. Word shook his head and put his hand lightly on my shoulder. "I never seem to have this thing when I need it," Word muttered as I backed out of the room.

In the hallway outside of the clinic Jane Marie was looking at a chart with the first mate. She was pointing with a pencil in one hand and had a tide book in the other. The Mate was listening intently. I tried to walk quickly past them, but she reached out and took my arm.

"Cecil, you've been ashore in this area before. Remember that time we were photographing that group of killer whales and you hit that rock?"

Word stood behind her, his hands in his pockets. "Yes. I remember," I said, trying to pull away.

"The captain may want to put a boat over and they've asked for our help. What do you think?"

I stood staring at Word and the door of the room I had just come out of. I was still thinking about the skull-numbing voltage that he wanted to put through my skin.

"Listen. I'll be right back. I've got to talk to someone."

She looked at me quizzically but did not ask her next question.

"Really. I'll be right back," I said as I walked away from them.

"We will load the boat from the Capri Deck. Port side," the first mate called after me, and when I turned I saw him block Word from following me.

"We'll wait for you," Jane Marie called as I turned the corner into Freetown.

There were clanging pipes and the engine throb swelled as I walked down the iron catwalk to the next lower landing where I half-remembered Mr. Worthington's quarters were. I wanted to see Paul and I suspected there was at least one person who had access to the place where he was most likely being stored.

"I don't know, sir," Mr. Worthington said as he unbent himself from the crawl space he was occupying between a boiler and the thin shelf above a fetid and oily bilge. "Cyril? No. I haven't seen Cyril since I came on shift. I'll find out, though." It amazed me how purely black Mr. Worthington was. He was almost completely covered in soot and the white jumpsuit showed white only in the creases. He wiped his hands on a towel-sized rag that hung from his back pocket, then he walked over to a pillar where there was a greasy phone. He punched a few numbers and then spoke in French, yelling to be understood over the din of the engine. I pulled my collar away from my neck, allowing only the heat to pour down against my skin.

Mr. Worthington hung up and yelled to me. "Cyril is on his break now. You wait here."

I nodded. "Where are we?" I yelled.

Mr. Worthington looked quizzical and shook his head. "We're at a stop. Holding a position some four and a half hours out of Skagway. I don't know more than that. They're just chiming in engine orders to hold us against the tide."

A vibration shuddered through the ship as the shaft for the propellers turned and the engine throbbed in the heart of the steel ship.

"Something strange is happening. This is for sure," Mr. Worthington said and he studied my face with the expression of a man who knew somehow that I was part of the trouble but wasn't going to ask. "Here, then." He nodded over my shoulder as we heard footsteps clattering on the catwalk.

Cyril was wearing his white boat coveralls and an orange float coat. He had a thin stocking cap pulled over his ears. "They got me on deck, sir. I cannot stay long."

I asked to see the body of the boy who had died the night before and Cyril made a pained expression. "Why I do this for you?" he yelped out at me. "Big trouble. Plenty of big trouble. Why I do this thing for you now?" Sweat was starting to bead on his forehead. I didn't want to argue with him. I held up my injured hand and pointed to it.

"I keep my secrets, Cyril. I need to see the boy's body. It is important. Nothing bad will happen to you. If anything happens I'll take all the blame. You know I will."

He shook his head and looked over to Mr. Worthington, who wiped his hands and nodded up to Cyril as if giving him permission.

"Okay then." Cyril turned and walked away. "Just hurry now. They'll be asking about me and I don't want them looking."

We made our way through the crew's dining hall. It was early morning but men were lounging around a TV having just come off their shift. The kitchen sizzled with the smell of pork cooking. The air was crowded with the cigarette smoke and the smell of men's sweat and the food they were about to eat. Cyril led me to a narrow hall behind the crew mess and there was a small room and a thick metal door with massive hinges.

"This the cooler then." He nodded and unclipped the ring of keys from one of his belt loops. "I stay here. Two minutes. If someone come I'm going to lock the door and tell them the key is lost. I chase them away but you be on your own. I will unlock you if I can but if you take too long I leave you there. Are we clear on this? Longer than two minutes I lock you in there with him."

I nodded my head and Cyril undid the padlock on the cooler.

There was only one bare bulb inside the cooler. There were waxed cartons of produce on stainless steel racks around the three walls. The space had the chilled smell of garden greens. Cramped in the middle of the space was a stretcher with a green rubber bag on it. I undid the bag and saw the dark hair of Mr. Standard's son.

I unzipped the bag its full length. The boy looked lost and out of place there. He looked collapsed and forgotten like an abandoned tent, caved in by the snow. He wore no clothes. The flesh of the dead is like river clay. Hard but still forgiving. You can press in a soft arm and see the impression your own warm and lurid finger can leave. Not that there was much flesh here. Paul's arms were reed thin. On the inside of each arm were multiple bruises and old needle sticks. But there was nothing obviously fresh or out of place. None of the needle marks seemed any more recent or different than the rest. I ran my fingers through his hair, looking for scars or cuts. I rolled him over and looked at what seemed to be the massive bruising but was only the blood pooling in the flaccid flesh of the dead boy's remains.

I was running out of time and I knew it. I tried to open his mouth but was unable to. I pulled back one of his eyelids and as I did the eye caught mine in the light of that one bare bulb and I shivered. The one eye stayed open and I heard Cyril's keys jangling and then the scratching on the door. I pushed my shoulder hard and forced my way out.

"He's all zipped up then?" Cyril whispered to me urgently.

"I'm not quite done. I haven't found it yet."

Cyril looked at me with an exasperated expression as if to be saying, "Stupid white people! How did I get involved in this?" But he didn't; he shoved me back toward the naked boy in the cooler.

"Ten seconds then. You go look at his feet." Cyril made the imaginary hypodermic gesture he had used before: Thumb pushing up between his two fingers. "Carefully, man. The feet, but you don't know it from me now."

I was back inside and Paul's one eye was still open as if expecting me. I unfolded one of the stiff legs and looked carefully at the foot, scaly white and clean. I pulled the toes apart and there between the largest toe and the next was a needle stick. There was a very thin crust of blood around it.

I straightened Paul as best I could and zipped the bag up quickly. When I stepped out of the cooler Cyril was gone.

I was given a jacket when I arrived at the boat station. Jane Marie stood with the captain and the first mate. She had my red rubber boots under her arms and set them down on the floor for me to take. Both the Mate and Jane Marie were in full boat gear. Jane Marie had her rain gear over the float coat and she had her binoculars slung around her neck. The captain was in uniform and he nodded to me as I zipped up my jacket. Cyril stood in front of the open door. He did not acknowledge me as I walked past.

"Good," the captain said and looked between Jane Marie and myself. "We have our native guides." He cleared his throat and spoke in a more official tone. "I am not sure what we are dealing with here just now. I have contacted the local Coast Guard. The pilot is on the bridge and is in charge of the ship. Mr. Calbran, the ship's first officer, will be in charge of this boat crew. We are at stop currently." He paused and looked out past Cyril through the open hatchway that led to the tender landing. He was thinking about what more to say. "One of our ship's personnel is missing," he finally said brusquely and with no outward sign of sentiment. "There is some reason to believe that he may have gone overboard in this area just as we were leaving Cross Sound and beginning to make our transit through Icy Strait. The ship was close to the southern shore and it is possible a person may have survived. If my information is accurate, our crewman went into the water an hour and a half ago. There is only a slight chance of survival if he remained in the water but because of the closeness of the shore I feel it necessary to check the near shore area." The captain was remarkably abrupt for a man of so practiced an authority. He turned to his first officer and looked up at him as he gave his final instructions.

"We of course, will be searching this ship and developing other information and, as that comes in, we will keep you informed by radio. We have not yet requested the Coast Guard to begin their search until we have developed the rest of the reliable information that can narrow our search."

Here the captain turned to Jane Marie and me and said in a slightly more personal tone, "There is no sense in

sending out helicopters from Sitka if there never really was
a man in the water, if you know what I mean."

We both nodded our heads that we knew what he
meant. Cyril and the Mate turned and walked down the
gangway to the tender. The captain shook Jane Marie's
hand and then mine.

"Be careful." He smiled down at me with his glittering eyes. "One accident is more than enough." Then he
walked away toward the elevator which stood open and
waiting for him.

Jane Marie turned to me and folded the collar of my coat
out. "Don't ask questions in front of Mr. Calbran, Cecil. I'll
tell you what I heard later. Just don't give anything out in
front of the Mate because I don't think we can really trust
him." She bent and kissed me. "You smell funny. Where
have you been?" She wrinkled her nose at me.

"I just need to do my laundry again," I told her and
she blushed as she went down the hanging stairs on the
outside of the ship.

It was a gray day on a flat green-gray sea. The ship lay
in a narrow inlet along the edge of a rain forest's shore
just around the corner from the open coast. There was a
swell running through the inlet and the outer rocks were
breaking white. Cyril stood at the helm of the little boat
and another seaman was busily pumping up a small three-
person raft. The plastic oars banged around under the row
of seats in the tender as if they were children's toys.

Both Jane Marie and the Mate scanned the near shore
with their binoculars.

"Look for birds," Jane Marie said over the engine noise.
"They'll be looking for a meal." The Mate took down his
glasses and made a sour face.

"It's true," Jane Marie shrugged.

"Was there any life ring or buoy deployed?" I asked.

The Mate scanned the shore and spoke slowly and deliberately. "In one version of the story there was no life ring thrown. In a later version, there was a ring thrown and there is a ring missing from its position. That is all I can tell you."

The Mate stood next to Cyril and pointed to the shore. "It looks like we can come in just to the west of that point and put them ashore at that gravel beach. You see?" The Mate looked at Cyril and then pointed to the shore and to the chart propped in front of the wheel. Cyril looked at the chart and then said only, "Yes, sir." He never looked at either Jane Marie or me.

The clouds were low in the sky and the light was streaking up the edges of those clouds in the southeast. The coast of the island showed ragged treelines against the sky: Spruce and hemlock forests that had stood sentinel over this coast for centuries.

The first Russian explorers had put boats ashore near this very spot. Their crews who had survived unbelievable hardships in the crossings watched their shipmates paddle through the fog into one of these unknown inlets. Those first boats had never returned and no trace of the Russian sailors has ever been found. The Tlingits had called those first explorers, "the people who came from the foot of the clouds." The Europeans were so strange and ghostly white I'm sure they were killed at first out of pure curiosity, the way collectors from the natural history museums later would kill specimens of unknown birds.

Eagles were perched in the trees back from the crescent gravel beach. Their white heads shone like new golf balls hanging in the branches. The water was smooth here and the beach was deep enough to carry a lot of water for the tender, but there was no fathometer on board so the Mate kept well off the beach and away from the gray-green rocks that were showing through the garlands of kelp.

The little raft was flopped over the side and the Mate pointed to the shore. "You can walk from here to that last point to the west then?"

Cyril had a long coil of rope in his hands. The end was tied to the raft so he could retrieve the raft back to the tender. He was looking at me but I knew better than to answer. Jane Marie had the expertise and experience. "Yes," she said loudly to grab back the Mate's attention. "We will cover this shoreline and meet you back here. You will give us a radio?"

"That will not be necessary." The Mate said it disdainfully as he motioned for us to go over the side. "You will not need a radio. You need to walk this shore. We will meet you back here in three hours in any case. If we should be coming early you will hear one long voice of the ship's whistle then. Understood?" He held Jane Marie's elbow as she sat in the doorway of the tender as she began to lower herself into the tiny raft. She reached back and grabbed her small day pack.

"We need a radio," I said with as much authority as I thought I could get away with.

"There is no radio," the Mate said firmly.

Cyril looked at me and shook his head silently. I couldn't interpret the specifics of his expression but I knew we would be getting no radio. I lowered myself into the trembly little rubber raft.

As we paddled to shore, Jane Marie spoke. "I've got

my own gear, Cecil. I have some survival packs, and a can of bear spray. As long as we don't do anything dumb we should be all right."

"Why am I not reassured?" I said as we stood on the beach watching Cyril pulling the empty little raft back to the tender.

The waves heaved long gravelly sighs up and down the beach. Each wave turned over little stones. As the tender left the cove, a calmness rushed in, numbing my ears and chest.

Gulls called in their broken two-toned voices and one of the eagles lumbered into the air, the empty spruce bough it had perched on bobbing up and down in its absence. Standing on this rocky beach my inner ear seemed to keep swaying to the rocking of a hull. I followed Jane Marie up the beach, our feet chomping into the gravel like shovel heads.

The beaches were littered with drift logs, spruce and hemlock mostly, that had escaped the floating rafts pulled by tugs to the mills. Each of the logs was worn smooth and free of bark. They piled parallel to the shore, in uneven rows, one tucked under the other and some crossed like pick-up sticks in a heap. Looking to the south we could see three coves, each progressively more rocky and steep. The last had just a few logs, splintered by the force of the ocean swells against a vertical cliff.

We could hear the swells booming on the outside and this played counterpoint to the whisper of the waves in our quiet cove. Another eagle took to the air and headed south briefly, then circled back to land on another branch already occupied. Jane Marie and I sat on a slick spruce log. We watched as the two large birds bickered.

Jane Marie was digging through her pack. "They never called the Coast Guard, Cecil. Mr. Standard found his son dead. Early this morning. He went to Dr. Edwards and when the doctor refused to give him any direct information about Paul's death there was a fight. Apparently the fight moved out to one of the decks and the doctor went overboard. The ship's crew, the captain and the first mate want to cover this up. I heard them talking about it. They haven't called the Coast Guard at all, Cecil. They don't want us talking on the radio because they don't want anyone to overhear."

"Do you think the doctor really went overboard?" I asked her.

She took a very old candy bar out of her pack and broke it in two. The wrapper had once been dark brown but was now rubbed tan with the lettering indistinguishable.

"Oh I have no idea, really." She handed me my piece of chocolate as she unwrapped her own. "I just know they wanted us off that boat. My impression is they don't really think we'll find anything and they can take care of everything nicely while we are off the ship."

"You know that weird saxophone player?" I asked and broke a piece of the crumbly chocolate with my teeth.

Jane Marie looked down at her lap, thinking. "Saxophone player? You mean the guy in Margie & the Navigators, the one with—"

"He's a spook," I interrupted. "He owns a fancy private investigative firm in San Francisco. I bet he makes a thousand bucks a day."

"Get out of town!" Jane Marie sat up straight. She looked thoughtful. "A thousand dollars . . . but he is such a bad sax player," she said to herself. "I thought he was trying to pick me up. He did ask a lot of questions about you. You know, I told him you were an investigator. He seemed so nice I just couldn't lie to him. I'm sorry." She pulled a long black strand of hair away from her eyes. "Did I screw things up?"

"Naw," I said and I held her hand. "I took care of that."

We decided to work our way to the south just to stretch our legs. We would let them put whatever they had to back in the closets on board the *Westward*. We climbed over the first windrow of logs and down to the barnacle-covered rocks and worked our way toward the outer beach.

This part of the coast gets more than one hundred inches of rain a year. Shadow is never very far off and today the clouds spread evenly with the daylight across the sky. It may have been sixty degrees by the time the sun finally tore away from the southern ridge line. The air was damp with the dual flavors of rain and salt water.

The tide was going out and with each moment more of the beach was exposed. There was no great rush, for the longer we waited the easier the walking would be. Deer tracks nibbled the sand and disappeared into tall grass under the forest canopy. There were river otter tracks and the faint etchings of gulls' feet on the tiny patches of wet sand that lay between the slick gray rocks. Some of the fallen trees were stripped clean, with thin roots bleached almost white in the air. Jane Marie walked low on the beach and scanned ahead with her binoculars and I clambered around in the piles of drift near the shore.

Between the logs I found bleach bottles and gas cans, hundreds of plastic floats from fishing nets. There were oil filter boxes and plastic hard hats. Tangled around one chunk of what looked like red cedar was a great mass of yellow buoy rope. There were red bag buoys and deflated yellow ones. Dried sea urchin shells as delicate as eggs wedged in the logs. The husks of tiny crabs and bits of shells. I saw metal gas cans and a single tennis shoe. A hockey glove and three small plastic bathtub toys: a red beaver, a green frog, and a yellow duck. The toys sat in the grass back behind the sand as if they were in conference. I slipped and stumbled over the logs. I found more floats and plastic bottle cartons, rusted aerosol cans and even several Japanese lightbulbs. There were orphan flip-flops and disposable butane lighters. Lumber bent to fit the hull of a broken ship. Pieces off the transom of a fiberglass skiff. Twisted bits of cable wrapped around a six-foot piece of Styrofoam float. Some logs had chains and staples; some had traces of bark still attached. I found a Bible. The ink on the pages had mostly worn away, but what writing was left mostly looked to be Japanese. Behind a long yellow cedar beam I picked up a plastic baby doll with one leg missing and the stuffing gone from her ripped torso. I climbed down over a massive spruce log and I saw a bearded man's head: porcelain-slick skin and spiky curls of wet hair. I shook my head in disbelief as if I could shake the image into focus. The man was dressed in torn blue pajamas. He was tucked into a fetal position. When I yelled at him, he did not move.

1 1

The Bear

There are some problems which are not possible to solve. Considering these problems is like sucking on a pebble, and expecting it to dissolve like hard candy.

I thought of this as I looked down at the body of the doctor curled like a child in a nest of sticks. There was a ship's life ring near his head. He had apparently lived for some moments after making it to shore. Near his feet was a tiny patch of sand that showed the ripple of impressions his toes had made as he shivered himself to death. In death, his lips were curled above the gums; two of his teeth were broken off and I noticed chips of broken tooth on top of the sand to the left of his head. An adult eagle perched in a spruce just above Dr. Edwards and me in the beach fringe. Its call caused me to shudder and cross my arms.

Jane Marie clambered up the logs from the lower beach. She sucked her breath in as she saw the corpse. With only a slight hesitation she jumped down and touched his face.

"What should we do, Cecil?" Her voice was trembling.

"He's very cold. His heart is not beating." With some effort she pulled the doctor's hand away from his face and above his head. The arm stayed suspended there stiffly for a moment, then slowly eased to the sand.

"He's very dead," I said as I jumped down beside them. The doctor had been dead a short time but his joints were beginning to stiffen. Ravens gathered in the bushes under the eagle's perch. The ravens chattered and growled to each other, agitated by this new presence on their beach. Another eagle settled on a perch above.

Dozens of tiny crabs had attached themselves to the skin on the doctor's face and neck. Sand flies worked in and out of his nostrils. His eyes were closed, yet his countenance did not seem restful. It appeared that he had unbuttoned his pajama tops and had tried to slip out of them. Hypothermia victims in the last stages often feel a burning heat as the last of their reserves run out. He had a crust of blood in and around his right ear, this perhaps from his fall from the ship, but I couldn't say for certain.

"We can't leave him here uncovered, Cecil," Jane Marie said to me without taking her eyes off of the corpse. Some crabs scuttled away through the sand and others pulled themselves up into his hair.

"Okay. Let's get him up off the beach anyway," I said and we began the chore of lugging him across the slick logs to the damp mossy ground just under the trees.

Dead people are hard to carry. Their weight shifts all over, seeming to pour itself out of your grip. It's as if the dead are refusing to be carried another foot. But with a minimum of fumbling and shin knocking we lugged Dr. Edwards above the high tide line into the shady beach fringe.

Jane Marie got him settled beside a grassy hummock and we both found ourselves wiping our hands together in a nervous gesture. Jane Marie sniffed at her fingertips, hunting, I suppose, for the smell of death.

I watched her for a moment and in an odd, out-of-body sensation felt how lucky I was to be with her just then. In this terrible situation we were troubled but not panicked. There was no sense that we were about to rush off into one of those frantic domino-effect rescue attempts that usually come to grief for us. Her dark eyes were steady and her breathing was calm. Every moment with the corpse reminded us that we were alive. This had a calming, if not numbing, effect.

I reached out and rubbed the back of my hand across her cheek. She curled into my hand and closed her eyes for a moment. When she opened them again she snapped to attention, looking out beyond the trees.

"My God, Cecil! They're leaving us!"

Her arm jerked up and pointed out to the inlet where the *Westward* was under way, moving slowly to the west with all the tender boats on board.

We ran to the beach and waved our arms and yelled. Of course, this was foolish. Only a few people stood on the back decks of the *Westward* and they were tiny specks to our naked eye. Jane Marie scanned the ship with her binoculars and saw some crewmen talking on the lower stern and a steward serving morning coffee on the fantail to a group of people huddled in their warm jackets and smoking cigarettes. No one was looking in our direction.

"They can't just be planning to leave us," she said angrily.

"I don't know. You were the one who said they didn't want us messing with this business."

"Oh I know, but Cecil, they couldn't just leave us here. I mean really. That would be kidnapping or something, wouldn't it?"

"No. I don't know. Murder, maybe." I started walking back to the trees.

Jane Marie said nothing for a moment. Eagles and gulls wheeled above us in silent entangling circles. Then she called out after me, "Don't say those things!"

It was perhaps sixty degrees. It wasn't raining at the moment but there was no guarantee about that. The temperature would drop into the low fifties in the evening. Our clothes were dry for the moment. We were warm. Looking through all of our supplies from my pockets and Jane Marie's day pack we had four plastic garbage bags; a pressurized can of caustic peppers, used theoretically to discourage a charging bear; a whistle; two pocket knives, mine and hers; a packet of waxed matches; a butane lighter; four balls of pitch and some pieces of waxed milk carton for a fire starter; six pieces of gum; two candy bars; a pair of binoculars; a bird identification book; some brochures for day trips in Skagway that had been jammed in my pants pocket; a quarter of a roll of toilet paper; and the keys to our stateroom.

We were on the northern shore of Yakobi Island. Realistically, we were a few miles from the town of Pelican, to the southeast, and Elfin Cove, to the northeast. Just over the hump of the island were three cabins in the tight anchorage of Greentop where a community of old bachelor fishermen had homesteaded in the fifties. But the towns were inaccessible because of the inlet between

Yakobi and Chichagof islands. Greentop was a possibility we would have to consider, although overland travel is difficult in the best of circumstances, and sitting abandoned on a beach with the body of a man who had presumably been murdered struck me as being a long way from the best of circumstances. Clearly, it would be better to build a fire and hunker down in our garbage bags and wait to see who came by in their boat. This was a busy stretch of water. With any luck we could attract some attention.

We spent most of the morning and early afternoon beachcombing and building a tiny shelter of drift lumber back into the mossy bank under the trees, about fifty yards from the body. Using strips of netting we untangled from the driftwood, we were able to tie wood together. We dug out the side of the hill and jammed planks of various lengths onto a frame. More netting went on top of the planks and then moss on top of that. We had a four-foot-by-six-foot hobbit hole by three in the afternoon.

About one o'clock one skiff went by and although we waved our float coats we were unseen. Most of the boat operators would be watching the rocks coming up and choosing their course for the outside passage. As the evening wore on Jane Marie gathered edible seaweed and intertidal animals for our supper. I found a small stick of red cedar back in under the trees, which seemed light and relatively dry, and was sitting down to whittle shavings to start a fire when she came back with her raincoat full of dinner: Gumboot chitons and sea slugs curled in a bed of black seaweed. They moved slowly and laboriously, twisting in the air like swollen tongues. She had also gathered some smaller mussels, chitons and one small abalone. She was beaming.

"Yummy," I said with as much enthusiasm as I could muster.

"Cecil," she said, sitting down breathlessly and pushing her hair out of her eyes with the back of her wrists. Her hands were coated with wet sand. "This is a great beach. There is loads and loads of food here. I mean, I don't think I've seen anyplace quite so productive. We need to just try a tiny piece of each thing and wait a while. I don't think we need to worry about red tide but, jeez, the way things are going I guess we should be careful." She looked at me, smiling, then leaned over and kissed me. As she leaned back her eyes darkened.

"How's the doc . . . I mean, you know, the body?" she stumbled.

"I covered him up with some wood and a piece of old roofing I found. I don't think the birds are getting to him."

She frowned. "I guess it doesn't really matter all that much now, huh?" She drew on the ground with her finger.

"No. But I think we should take good care of him. The body is the best evidence to figuring out what happened to him." I kept shaving long slivers of the fragrant wood.

"Sounds to me like Mr. Standard threw him overboard." She kept tracing something in the moss.

"That could be true," I replied. "But, why the life ring then? Do you kill somebody and then throw him a ring? I don't know."

"Well," she said smartly and dusted off her hand. "We'll take good care of him and flag down one of these boats soon enough. Right now I'm hungry. I found an old shovel head back down the beach. I'll go get it. I'll cook us up some real food."

"You know, I don't think I've seen you eat much all the

time you were on the trip," I commented to her as she stood up.

"No." Her voice dropped as if she'd been reminded of something sad. "No. I haven't been eating all that much. I don't know . . ." She brushed her hair back again, looking down and shaking her head. She stood without saying anything, with her brow wrinkled as if she were about to speak, but then the mood passed and she stood straight and alert as if coming out of a dream. "But I'm hungry tonight. Listen, honey, you want to cut a little piece of that mussel and rub it on your lips and gums. You know, if your lips tingle and get numb, then we will eat . . . I don't know . . . we'll eat the chocolate bars, I guess." Then she turned and walked briskly down the beach.

"Yes, honey," I murmured, laughing to myself.

As the afternoon wore on the bugs found us out. I started a nice smoky fire and made a kind of tall coatrack for my red float coat. It was just a "Y"-shaped stick that I could zip under the coat. I hoped to use it to wave at a passing boat. I could put it some six feet in the air and move the bright red coat back and forth in a larger, more noticeable arc. My gums did not grow numb when I rubbed the mussel against them so Jane Marie sliced and pounded the various sea slugs and intertidal creatures and steamed them up on the shovel head propped up on the edge of the fire.

The food tasted like the beach. Jane Marie had been right: There was plenty and it warmed me up. The long evening turned toward lavender twilight. The high clouds kept the rain at bay. There was a fresh breeze from the northeast and high streaky clouds began to move down from the northern interior. The forests of the islands across the sound lit up as the sun lowered to the west. Each tree seemed etched very clearly in light and shadow. The mountains sat squat and velvety, their robes folded out to the rocky shore. We sat enjoying it for only a short time, then went back to work gathering driftwood for our fire. We hoped to build a large enough fire to attract the attention of any skiff or ship that passed by. Our plan was to take turns tending the fire and keep a lookout for running lights going past on the water.

I was working down the beach alongside Jane Marie who was holding three small chunks of spruce in her arms when I saw strange fresh tracks in the sand to my left. I jumped up on a hemlock butt and saw two bare feet dragging along the sand in a jerking motion. They disappeared behind a rock outcropping.

When I turned the corner next to the rock outcropping, the brown bear had the doctor's body by the shoulder and was whipping it back and forth like a rag. The bear saw me and dropped the dead man as if it had been charged with a jolt of electricity. The bear stared toward me, sniffing, scanning, sniffing. Its great coffin-shaped nose swung back and forth in the damp air. I started to back away slowly. The bear lunged forward with a guttural howl I had never heard before. The sound was almost a bellow or a braying that came from a huge set of lungs. The bear snapped its jaws and this sound was like a cleaver snapping through meat.

"Hello, bear!" Jane Marie was standing next to me now. She was speaking loudly to the big animal. She took my hand and held it above our heads. She held her other hand up in the air. To the bear we may have looked like one very large creature.

"Hello, bear." Jane Marie called out again. "We are just poor stupid human beings. We are trying to get something to eat. Thank you for letting us use your beach. We mean you and your family no harm."

"Where's your bear spray?" I whispered frantically out of the side of my mouth.

"Hush," she whispered back to me.

The bear continued to sniff. It backed up and stood over the doctor's body. The black rind around its muzzle curled above the long yellow canine teeth. Its snout wrinkled: The leathery nose, wet and shiny, sucked in our scent.

Jane Marie continued speaking. "My friend was just saying that we mean you no harm. We could not hurt you if we wanted. We have no weapons. If you would like the body of this human being, of course you can have it. But I am just asking that you leave it for us so we can take it back to his family."

The bear lunged forward six feet in one jump, about a quarter of the distance to us. The tiny black eyes showed nothing, seeming lost in the giant head. But the head itself seemed small against the massive hump between the shoulders.

"But again . . ." Jane Marie cleared her throat. Her voice was quavering and unsteady but she kept it from breaking. "It is completely up to you." She took a step back. Hands still above our heads, we backed away steadily.

Seconds later our backs were against the stone outcropping. Ravens hopped on the rocks above us screaming, laughing and making their odd sounds like breaking stones. We could hear the bear snuffling and pitching at

the sand with its claws. We heard grunts and then the rip-
ping of thin cloth.

To our right was the edge of the trees. One large spruce
had dead limbs all the way to the mossy forest floor. There
was a crook high in the tree where a major limb had been
lost and overgrown some ages ago. The crook was thirty
feet in the air. I nodded to Jane Marie but saw that her eyes
were closed and both of her hands lay flat on her lower
belly as she stood stock-still, taking fast shallow breaths.
Then, there was another grunt and the shuffling sound
came louder, close to the edge of the rocks where we
stood. The ravens fell silent. Then they were gone.

"Let's climb a tree," I said as softly as I could.

"That would be fine," Jane Marie said with her eyes still
closed. "You got one picked out?"

"Yes," I said. "Follow me and we'll walk to it as fast as
you can. Don't look back and don't stop no matter what,"
I said and I didn't wait to discuss the matter. I pulled on
her hands and we set off, moving stiffly like race walkers
through the patch of sand and then awkwardly like children scrambling over the rows of drift logs.

The bear's bellow burned into my back like the heat
from a furnace. It was a deep ferocious bawling that
seemed to reach into my chest and push me to the ground.
I did not look back but nudged Jane Marie ahead of me as
we ran the last two yards to the tree.

I have no memory of climbing the spruce tree. I simply remember sitting in its crook some thirty feet in the
air watching the brown bear tear at the sand below and
shake its big head back and forth as if it had been stung in
the ear. Next to me, Jane Marie held my hand very tightly.
I remember I was light-headed and dizzy, feeling like I

might burst out crying or throw up, although I don't think I did either of those things.

As the minutes passed, the bear walked around our tree and then back over to the body in the sand. The bear charged the ravens who sat on the corpse's torn shoulder. They fluttered just a few feet away, making a mocking and disrespectful sound.

Finally, I asked Jane Marie, "Why did you talk to the bear that way?"

She shrugged her shoulders and hugged the spruce trunk. "Alfred Tom's grandma told me to talk that way. She said be respectful and tell the truth. She also said try not to lose your own dignity. Bears don't like that, apparently." Her hands were trembling as she squeezed my fingers. "I thought it was worth a try," she added.

Alfred Tom's grandma was a Tlingit woman who lived down the block from us. She gave us herring eggs in the spring and Jane Marie helped her put up jelly in the late summer. She was a good Christian woman, active in the Russian Orthodox church, but apparently she knew a lot about bears.

Eventually, the long evening gave way to darkness and a light rain began to fall. We stayed in the tree for hours. A skiff came by close in to the beach. I think they'd seen the smoke from our fire but no matter how much we yelled or waved from the cover of the tree, nothing we did attracted their attention.

The bear snuffled through our camp, ate the last of our dinner, then ate the candy bars, paper and all. The bear found the pressurized can of bear spray and pushed it around with its nose. The can had spent many months in Jane Marie's pack rubbing against bag lunches and

innumerable candy bars. The scent of food must have
been thick on the six-inch aluminum cylinder. The bear
took it in its teeth and broke the safety mechanism. Jane
Marie and I watched and grimaced in expectation. When
the trigger was pulled on an aerosol spray of caustic pepper designed to bring a charging omnivore to its knees,
a cloud of eye-stinging, vomit-inducing spray would be
released. This may have been of more abstract interest to
us if it weren't for the fact that the bear kept nosing the
canister closer to our perch.

But on this evening the bear's luck held better than
ours and after sniffling, licking, and gently chewing on the
canister, the bear, who I was certain was a large old boar,
simply spit it out, then shambled off into the woods.

We waited half an hour up in the tree. The canister
was beneath us and finally I climbed down and retrieved
it. After twenty minutes more we saw the running lights
of what looked to be a large fishing boat coming in from
the outside waters. Our fire had burned down to coals
that were promising to be extinguished by the soft rain
and I decided to go back to our camp and see if we could
rebuild it in time to catch the attention of the boat.

I built up the fire but the boat went on by. I could hear
the diesel engine and the chatter of a marine radio on the
back deck. If there had been any call out for us, any orga-
nized search, boats would have been notified by the Coast
Guard. There would be helicopters in the air, but instead
there was the drone of a single boat and its running lights
disappearing in the rain.

Jane Marie climbed down from the tree about another
half hour after I had. She dared not move toward where
the bear had apparently left the doctor's body but she did

bring another armload of wood to our fire. The flames moved up to eye level as the last sounds of the boat wake washed weakly up on the shore. Jane Marie stood in bright flickering relief from the fire.

"The tides come way up, Cecil. If the doctor's body is down the beach we'll lose it for sure."

"I think we may have lost it already." I poked a small dry stick under the flaming pyramid of logs.

"I'm going to go look" was all she said and she walked away from the fire.

I grabbed the pepper spray and pulled a stick from the fire to try and light my way after her.

The light was weak and mostly distracting as we rounded the black rock outcropping where the bear had been. We heard only the water on the sand, a light patter of rain falling on wet driftwood, the distant fire popping. I pushed the smoking ember of the stick into the sand so my eyes could adjust to the darkness.

There was a pit in the sand with only some bits of fabric on the edges. The bear's tracks had been rounded smooth by the rain so they appeared as dinner-plate-sized depressions in the wet sand. There were parallel lines where the doctor's heels had dragged across the ground. These lines moved up the beach and disappeared into the rocks. There was a bright splash of blood on a yellow cedar tree and just beyond that was a chunk of meat the size of a fist. When I picked it up I felt one side was raw and wet with blood while the other was smooth skin covered with black curly hair.

We curled up in our shelter for the rest of the night. The firelight flared at the mouth of our hut across the slick wet rocks. We curled with our arms around each other, our faces in darkness, our boots and pant legs lit. All around us in the darkness the trees whooshed and moaned, the small waves scrambled up the rocks, and drops of rain pattered on the walls. Once, I jerked my head up, catching myself in sleep, and I heard the shuffling of paws in sand and the close breath from a massive set of lungs.

12

Skagway

I thought I stayed awake all night, as the fire burned down and the sky began to lighten. It might have been so, but I also believed that this night both Jane Marie and I had turned into bears. We were curled against each other's thick brown fur deep in a burrow. Snow had piled around the mouth of our cave and our warm breath had crystallized on the roof. Outside a great storm was clattering, blowing pieces of my house back in Sitka around and around like the twister in *The Wizard of Oz,* but in our burrow we were warm and safe. Our breath was sour with mice and skunk cabbage, dead salmon, and seaweed. Our hides were thick and knotted with burrs and tiny flecks of fish bone. I curled in deeper toward Jane Marie's body and when something kicked at the sole of my foot I lunged forward with my fists clenched.

Toddy stood in the ashes of our fire. He was kneeling down, peering in. He looked vaguely startled but stood his ground.

"Excuse me, Cecil. I don't mean to disturb you, but

I was concerned that you might have succumbed to the effects of hypothermia." He said this very carefully.

I rubbed my eyes and shook my head, trying to shake the sleep out of my brain.

"No. No. We're fine, Todd. Listen, I'm sorry we . . . you know . . . didn't let you know we were going to be gone for a while. I hope you didn't worry."

"Actually, I wasn't all that concerned," Todd said and he reached out and shook my hand as if we were meeting for a business lunch. He was wearing his nice traveling coat and his low-cut leather shoes. He pumped my hand and went on, "No, in fact I wasn't aware that you were off the ship. I just assumed you were enjoying one of the many entertainment options that seem to be offered on the *West-ward*." There was not a trace of irony in Todd's voice. This is one of the most unnerving things about Todd: Irony and sarcasm are unknown to him.

Jane Marie crawled toward us on her knees, squinting into the clear morning light. Sonny Walters walked up behind Todd.

"You're all right then?" he said. It sounded like an accusation.

Sonny was wearing a snappy blue windbreaker and his spotless leather Top-Siders. He had a ball cap on and for some reason he reminded me of an actor playing one of the Apollo astronauts.

"You missed me. I can tell, Sonny," I told him.

Sonny Walters grunted as if the idea of this was too absurd to even consider.

"Listen, you two," Sonny said as he took off his ball cap and patted his hair. "First, I've got to say that neither I nor Great Circle Cruise Lines had anything to do with leaving you here on this beach overnight. I was not told of this situation until late last night. I was told by the first officer that you were searching for evidence. They would tell me nothing more. I don't know what is going on." Sonny's voice was building in pitch. "Several of my passengers are extremely agitated. The medical staff apparently has shut down the clinic. We've got rumors galore and apparently Dr. Edwards has been disciplined or is sick himself. And frankly, I don't know what in the Sam Hill is going on!" His voice reached a peak. "I've got shore excursions happening right now, and a gold rush revue supposed to take place in two hours, and I'm out here looking for you two." He glared at Jane Marie and me as if we were tardy for school. "Just what in the hell kind of evidence were you looking for?"

I took a deep breath. I was thinking about how to launch into the explanation when we heard a voice yell down the beach.

As we came around a tall pile of drift logs on the beach where the sand lay below the tide line, I could make out the words, "Hey! Hey! You go on! Get out of here, you son of a bitch!" It was a man's voice, deep and very agitated.

There on the sand sat a helicopter with its rotors stopped and the engine turbine whining down. The pilot had one foot on the rubber pontoon and the other inside the aircraft. And he was frantic. "You see that son of a bitch? You *see* him?" He was pointing up to the woods. But the rest of us were looking down at the sand some six feet from the chopper. We all stopped and stared stupidly at the scene.

The doctor's body was naked. He was bent with his head under his chest, as if he were a rag doll thrown down stairs. The flesh across his shoulders and his abdomen was punctured. Several chunks of flesh were missing; a bone protruded from the forearm. The pilot's eyes were wide and he appeared to be hyperventilating.

"That son of a bitch just carried it out of the woods and threw it down! He just *threw* it down here! He's still up there in the trees. Get in! Get in *now!* I'm getting this damn thing in the air."

"Oh my God in heaven," Sonny said as he began to choke. Todd was about to ask a question, but I put my hand on his shoulder and pointed.

The bear stood above us, a dark muscular outline in the shadows of the trees. This animal seemed as big as a compact car, and it made me shiver to see him hop lightly onto a gray drift log on the beach fringe. He seemed to shimmer with the same power that had lit the mountains the night before. Every inch of him rippled with energy held in reserve. He did not move. He did not sniff or scan the air in front of him. He appeared to be staring directly at Jane Marie.

"You go on, motherfucker!" The pilot's voice was gaining intensity and starting to crack. "Go on, get the fuck away from here!" He was fumbling under his seat where I could see a leather holster for a large handgun.

"Stop it." Jane Marie said it loudly, but without shouting. "Stop it now." She turned and burned her eyes into the pilot and repeated herself to make sure he knew she was talking to him.

"Stop it. Just get the poor man loaded and I will get our things." Then she turned to me. "I'll get everything, Cecil. I think we need to get all our stuff out of here. Don't let him use that gun. And try to get him to clean up his language."

We piled the doctor into a narrow cargo space behind the rear seat of the helicopter. Todd looked at me with questions in his eyes but he was not distressed. Sonny, on the other hand, was distressed. He couldn't bring himself to touch the corpse. He kept covering his mouth with his hand and watching the woods where the bear stood motionless, watching as Jane Marie walked away. When she was out of sight, the bear disappeared.

Todd, Sonny, and I piled into the backseat and fumbled for the seat belts. The pilot put on his headset and began pumping on the levers. The whine began to build and the rotor blades started turning slowly.

"I'm not going to fuck around here with this woo-woo, nature bullshit!" the pilot yelled above the engine noise. "If she's not here by the time we're ready, I'm not waiting around."

I patted him on the shoulder and spoke with as much fake confidence as I could muster. "Everything is going to be fine. Give her a couple of seconds."

Helicopters always feel unreasonably flimsy when I sit in them. The body of this one began to shake as the rotors gained speed, and the blades began to hum. The bear appeared back on the log near the beach fringe. The limbs of the trees blew in a wild frenzy. The bear's fur flattened in swirls like windblown wheat. The pilot began to pull back on the stick. I reached over across his shoulder and gripped his forearm as hard as I could. His whole body was shaking. With my other hand I lifted up his earpiece. I spoke as calmly as I could straight into his ear. "If you leave her here, I'll crash this bird. I am dead serious. It's not worth it. Just a few more seconds and I'll get out and get her."

The pilot didn't relax. But he did ease the engine back down.

Jane Marie came running. She held her rain gear and her day pack bundled like a baby in her arms. The pilot opened up the passenger door. Jane Marie threw in her gear and stood on the pontoon. "Just one more thing. Only a second," she yelled and jumped back out. The pilot yelled after her: For a minute I thought he was going to cry. I pressed my hand back on his shoulder.

Jane Marie walked up the beach, ducking her head far away from the swirling rotors. She walked straight toward the bear. She squatted down, holding her dark hair away from her face. Occasionally, she gestured toward the bear. She was speaking and shaking her head. Then she leaned over slightly. She spread her hands, palms up, and stayed that way for a moment.

Then she ran back to the helicopter.

We were in the air even before she had her seat belt on. The walls of the chopper vibrated and the engines complained and we pulled straight off the beach in the thin plastic-and-aluminum bubble as if we were in a carnival ride.

"Thanks," Jane Marie said to the pilot, who had a sour expression and pretended not to hear her. "I just had to take care of that one last thing," she added and then let it go. The pilot began talking on his radio as he scowled at Jane Marie. She sat back in the seat, took a deep breath, then took her binoculars out and looked out to see what we had been missing out on the water.

I can barely tolerate flying in planes. The fear that grips me is one that reason cannot answer. With most of the fears I encounter, if I talk through the reality of the situation I can see reality is much more secure than my imagination. I can talk through relationships or fear of bears, but this does not work with flying: Particularly in a helicopter, for the truth is much weirder and more dangerous than even my imagination could devise. The truth was we were encased in a flimsy plastic cage hung some twelve hundred feet above the earth. None of the reality comforted me, not the lift under the cutting edge of the rotors, not the flammable nature of the fuel that would spill over our clothes once the tanks ruptured, not the seat belt holding me inside the thin cage as the flames flickered just over my shoulder. Some people say I worry too much, but I consider myself a realist.

I closed my eyes and tried to dream of angels. A woman's face and her strong arms lifting me above the steep-sided fjord. But for some reason, I kept thinking of that soft-eyed dog in Sitka holding the dead chicken in his mouth. I thought of the feathers that can't fly and the ice sculpture on the fantail of the boat; maybe they had carved dead chickens out of ice. Sitting in that clattering deathtrap I couldn't gain purchase on the image of an angel, no matter how hard I tried.

The helicopter fluttered up and down into the strong headwind coming down Lynn Canal. I opened my eyes as we passed the town of Haines and wished we could have set down there. I opened my eyes again as the pilot throttled back and the helicopter banked to the left in a strange push-pull motion of slowing down in the air to land. The *Westward* was moored to one of the two docks in the tiny city of Skagway. There were two other ships in port. Hundreds of people loitered on a field as a narrow-gauge train

backed close to the side of the ship nearest the dock.
Three other helicopters sat near a giant "H" in the field,
their rotors turning. Next to the helipad stood both an
ambulance and a police car.

We came down to them in a shudder of dust. The
cop turned his back to us and held on to his hat. Across
the field I could see the captain and the first officer of the
Westward walking briskly in our direction.

The airship put down with a bump and the turbines
whined lower and lower as the pilot slowed the rotors.
The cop took a step forward and opened the door for
Jane Marie.

I hopped out on the other side and was intercepted by
the captain.

"I am certainly glad to see you are all right," he yelled
over the turbine as he grabbed me by the biceps and led
me out from under the rotor.

"We found your ship's medical officer," I told him.

"So I understand." The captain's eyes locked on mine
and his bushy eyebrows furrowed. He did not blink and for
a moment he did not say a thing.

"We were informed by the pilot," he said finally. "It will
be a relief to Dr. Edwards's family that you were able to
locate his remains."

"Why did you leave us on the beach?" I said as calmly
as possible.

The captain looked genuinely puzzled. "He should have
told you." He gestured to Sonny Walters, who had climbed
out of the helicopter before Todd could do so. "He insisted
that we not upset our passengers. We are, after all, in the
vacation business." He smiled at me ruefully.

The ambulance attendants unloaded the doctor's

corpse. Sonny Walters was speaking angrily to the ship's first officer and Todd took a picture of the helicopter. The cop was talking to Jane Marie and as he did she brushed the tangled hair from her eyes. The young cop nodded and wrote in his notebook.

I turned to the captain. "I have quite a story to tell the cops," I said and I tried to match his gaze. "It has to do with murder and with a cover-up. It has to do with your lack of concern for US authority and with tampering with evidence."

The captain smiled again. "I think it would be a mistake for you to tell this story, Mr. Younger. For I myself have a rather interesting story of murder and tampering with evidence. In fact, I have been advised that here in Alaska it is a felony to tamper with a corpse."

Jane Marie began walking away with the cop and the attendant slammed the back door of the ambulance. The rotors of the helicopter had stopped turning.

"The doctor's body was mauled by a bear," I told the captain. "That will be easy to prove. There are plenty of witnesses and the physical evidence will be conclusive."

The captain nodded to his first officer as we walked toward the *Westward*. The first officer cut short his discussion with Sonny Walters with a chopping motion of his right hand and then he turned and walked toward us. "Of course, of course. But then we have other bodies to be concerned with now, don't we?" the captain said without looking at me.

I was not to be interviewed by the Skagway police. I'm not sure whose arrangement this was but as far as I was concerned this was a plus. I was a long way from actually wanting to go on record with what had been happening on board the *Westward*. The first officer walked over to me and took a firm hold of my biceps. I was clearly being taken aboard. I tried to jerk away from the first officer's grip but was unable to.

"Please," the captain said gently. "There are passengers watching us. If you will cooperate with us for just a bit longer, Mr. Younger, I believe we can reach a satisfactory agreement." The captain patted me on the shoulder and I stepped up onto the aluminum gangway leading into the belly of the ship.

I was met by David Werdheimer, who smiled like a hairdresser at his movie-star client. The Captain passed me off to him saying only, "Please. Make him comfortable. Get him something to eat." Word nodded.

Food was brought to a small room just off the crew mess. There was a metal table and two black plastic ashtrays screwed into the top. There was a tape machine and three worn decks of cards piled next to a wire rack holding salt, pepper, soy sauce and some vile-looking green condiment with seeds and fleshy peppers suspended in it.

Word was a handsome man but his features were strangely equine. He stood next to the door and let the steward in carrying a shrimp salad and a thick steak sandwich. Then Word moved to sit across from me at the table. He stirred four spoons of sugar into his iced tea.

"Cecil, you are kind of a scamp, you know that?" He didn't look at me and I didn't say anything in return.

We sat in silence and I dipped a fleshy shrimp into the cocktail sauce. Word continued stirring his tea and said nothing. I suppose he figured me for a talker. So he'd made a vague, half-joking accusation and was waiting for me to spill my guts so he could like me again. Either he was really slick or he was just an ordinary flatfoot wannabe who didn't know what else to say.

"Could you hand me one of those crackers, please?" I asked, pointing with my salad fork to one of a pile of wrapped saltines next to the salt and pepper by his elbow.

"Cecil, how did you get access to Paul's body?" David Werdheimer said as he moved the basket of crackers closer.

I looked up at him, genuinely puzzled. "What are you talking about?" I picked up the sharp steak knife to cut into my sandwich.

"Come on now, Cecil," Word said. "We're in some real shit here. We got the cops outside. We don't have a doctor. We can't turn Paul's body over to them. Hell, we can't even let his father see the body. We're running out of explanations."

"I wish I could help you," I shrugged.

Word leaned over and took the steak knife out of my hand. He held it lightly by the tip.

"I really don't want to do this, Cecil. I mean, it is sloppy and frankly kind of, I don't know, complicated, but I'm going to turn you over for killing Paul."

I stopped chewing. "What are you talking about?"

"Cecil, I'm serious. You are in deep trouble, man. I can help you if you'd let me." Word's voice was soft and cloying, kind of like his sax playing.

"I don't know what the fuck you mean." My heart was pounding because I knew he was right. I was out of my depth and a long way from home.

"I'll show you." Word motioned me toward the door.

He had a key for the cooler. He snapped the light

on and unzipped the bag. He jerked down the rubber
fabric and immediately I saw how big my problem was:
Paul's throat had been deeply cut with a serrated knife.
The light inside the cooler glared down on the muscu-
lature in his neck. Sliced blood vessels curled out and
crusted dark red on the ends; the trachea was laid open,
bone-white and slippery-looking.

"This is bullshit," I said, gulping in my breath. "I saw this
body yesterday and that cut was not there. Hell, they will
be able to tell this was done postmortem."

Word came in behind me. Then he closed the door
softly.

"I'm glad you're starting to talk about this, Cecil." He
reached into his jacket pocket and fumbled for something
and I knew he had turned on his microcassette recorder.

"So you admit you were in this cooler tampering with
Paul Standard's body. But to what purpose, Cecil? I
mean—why you'd do it?"

I shook my head. I took two deep breaths and zipped
up the bag. I was not going to go on record confessing to a
murder I didn't commit. I started to walk toward the door.

Word blocked my way. He had dropped my steak knife
into a plastic bag. Now he dangled it in front of my eyes.
"Cecil, I know you did this. I know you cut up Paul's body.
If you give me enough time, I'll figure out how you threw
the doctor over the side."

"You really figure that?" I asked him.

Word shook his head sadly and he spoke slowly in an
effort to make himself clearly understood. "Cecil . . . what I
really think is always subject to change." And he stared up at
me with a genuine ferocity. "But I *know* that I can make you
take the fall for this and it will fuck you up for a good long

while. You're right—in the end they won't tag you for the murders, but that will take a while. I don't think the Skagway police department is very sophisticated in their forensic analysis. We've got you. We've got this knife. And we've got one of the crew members who let you into the cooler."

Suddenly, I felt relieved. He was fishing. He wouldn't have bothered with the theater of the steak knife if he really had a solid witness. He wanted the crewman's name and he was betting I was going to give it to him.

"Who talked?" I said slowly, letting my shoulders slump as if I had been beaten.

"This game's over for you, Cecil. He talked, he's giving you up. I'm telling you the crew down here in Freetown doesn't give a shit about your white ass. Give up the other one and I'm in the position to get you off this boat without any more questions. Give him up and you go home. Keep your mouth shut and this will be over." Word put his hand on my shoulder in his best Father Flanagan pose. I reached up and put both my hands on his shoulders for support. I took deep breaths building to sobs. I moved in close to Word and whispered into his face.

"Where is Mr. Standard, Paul's father?" I asked softly.

Word smiled broadly, shaking his head in deep sympathy for me. "Don't worry about other people's problems, Cecil. Mr. Standard is fine. In fact, he's upgraded. I think he understands the situation much better than you." His voice was melted butter.

"You've really taught me a lot, Mr. Werdheimer. Thank you." I gripped the shoulders of his jacket. "You've taught me that a detective can be decisive and powerful. I can see now why your clients pay you as much money as they do."

Word smiled sympathetically, nodding at the irrevocable

truth of what I was saying. Then I broke his nose by slamming my forehead into his face. Blood spattered over my neck and shoulders and the green rubber bag covering Paul Standard. I spun him around into the door and he clattered down, spilling boxes of vegetables across the dirty tile floor. I stepped out of the cooler and placed the padlock back into the outer hasp, clicked it shut, and walked to the dark metal stairwell.

I heard only a vague commotion behind me in the stairwell and then nothing at all as I stepped out of Freetown and onto the Acapulco Deck. The gray-green carpet and walls seemed to smother out all of my concerns. I quickly took a corner and grabbed the door of the elevator just as it was about to close. The two ladies standing there were dressed in halter tops and had silk jockey hats on but I didn't ask them why.

The Horizon Deck was awash in silver and gray. On the starboard, windows looked out to the mountains: Gray stone and blue sky, the calm green water lathered by the wind. A single gull struggled upwind. I walked toward the inside port cabins. If I were going to be "upgraded" in order to keep me happy and away from the police I would expect one of these cabins.

Four doors were spaced across the width of the upper deck. I was poised to knock on the first one I came to when the starboard door opened and a steward came out, pulling a sturdy food cart. The cart was covered with a white tablecloth and had one large covered food dish and an ice bucket with an open bottle of white wine resting inside it. The steward looked at me and I fumbled in my pocket as if looking for a key. Then the steward said, "Thank you, sir"

to a person inside the stateroom and dropped something
into his pocket. The door closed and before the steward
rolled the cart to the elevator he checked to make sure the
door he had just come through was locked.

I mumbled something about having forgotten something down in the bar and started to walk away. When
the steward rolled around the corner I walked quickly
to the starboard door, knocked softly, and said, "Mr.
Standard?"

Mr. Standard's eyes were bloodshot and his thinning
gray hair stuck out in wild spikes from his head. He had
not shaved. When he opened the door he looked puzzled
and ran his hand through his hair.

"I'm sorry but no one's here. It's just me, I mean," he
said and he stepped away from the door back into the
sunny stateroom.

"Do you remember me, Mr. Standard? I'm Cecil
Younger. I spoke to you the other day back at the Hubbard Glacier?"

Mr. Standard paused and I could tell he was trying to
think back a lifetime, his dead son's lifetime, yet it had
only been two days. He furrowed his brow and pulled at
his hair absently.

"Yes. Of course. Come in." And he gestured into the
room.

I entered a sitting room that had an oak table for six
and a leather couch near the wet bar. There was a globe in
a wooden stand next to a bookshelf and near the window
was an antique brass telescope with a heavy counterbalanc-
ing arm. Forward and to the starboard were floor-to-ceiling
windows. I paused to look up the valley where the miners
of the Klondike had once struggled up the pass.

"I'm sorry to hear about Paul," I said as I walked to the couch. Mr. Standard sat on the opposite end. He sat with his shoulders hunched and his hands down between his knees.

"I was expecting it, of course," he said and then he said nothing more. Far up the valley we heard a train whistle echo off the mountain walls. Helicopters came and went like dragonflies.

"He had said he would see me in the morning. Paul said he would see me in the morning. I knew what he wanted to do . . . But I wasn't ready . . . I don't think Paul was ready either but . . . I don't know." Mr. Standard's voice quavered. He opened his mouth and he tried to speak, but nothing came out. Then he started to cry.

There was a pile of papers on the table in front of us. Sobbing, Mr. Standard leaned forward and grabbed them and held them up to show me.

"That doctor gave me these. That morning he gave me these. Legal papers. He had them right there in his room. They are papers Paul signed absolving the doctor of any problems for his treatment that might result in his own death. These papers are very explicit. Paul wrote that the doctor could administer any medications in dosages that the doctor felt reasonable, even if they resulted in death."

I cleared my throat. "Mr. Standard, I'm sorry but right now we have to think about you, not Paul or the doctor. I think you are in serious trouble."

Mr. Standard drew in his breath and wiped away tears with the flat of his hand. "I am in trouble, aren't I?"

He looked at me beseechingly, then he drew a breath as if he were about to start the story of his life. I interrupted him.

"Listen, Mr. Standard, there's no time. We're both in trouble. Please tell me what you remember about the night Dr. Edwards went overboard."

Standard made a gesture with his hands as if he were erasing a terrible vision in front of him. He shook his head. "I was drinking that night with some of the people from the travel club, friends of Paul's. They were telling stories and laughing. We were drinking wine. I think some of them had been taking drugs. I don't know. It was late. I had gone to bed. I remember one of them came in and told me Paul was dead. The doctor had pronounced him dead a couple of hours earlier. I was furious. I told you, Paul was going to see me tomorrow. We were talking through things. We hadn't done that, you know. We hadn't talked about his life. The people he loved. We were talking through all that. So I went to Paul's room. The door was locked. I went to the clinic and no one was there. I finally got a crew person to tell me where the doctor's cabin was. The doctor was in his cabin. He apologized and he showed me the papers. Then I started shouting. I guess the walls are thin because he told me we had to go somewhere else. So we stepped out on the deck, the crew deck, where they tie the lines and have the hoists and anchor winch."

Mr. Standard squeezed his eyes shut. He held his hands out in front of him as if he were groping along a hallway in the dark.

"He was sorry, the doctor said. He said he could feel my pain, for Christ's sakes." Mr. Standard shook his head bitterly and went on. "But the doctor said there were many considerations, insurance costs, something about the needs of his other patients. He said it was what Paul wanted. He kept talking about the papers Paul had signed and what Paul had wanted and I kept getting more and more angry . . ." Tears were running down Mr. Standard's unshaven cheeks. "I realize now I was furious because I wanted to talk about *my* feelings. I knew my son was dying. I knew he was leaving me. I was furious, and that damn doctor kept talking about Paul's feelings, as if I had never considered my own son's feelings." His shoulders moved with his sobs. I waited.

"I was all twisted up in my own feelings. Of course I wanted my son to die with dignity. Of course I wanted him to be free of pain. I just didn't . . ."

Mr. Standard paused. He gathered himself, then went on. "I shook the doctor by the shoulders. I screamed at him. I remember pushing him against the rail. I did want to kill him, I will admit that. He hit me. He pushed me down. I remember falling and rolling on the deck and I remember standing backup and being alone. He was in the water. I saw him waving his arm up in the air. I remember throwing the life ring over the side. I called out for help."

"Did help come?" I asked.

"There was someone there immediately. A black crewman. I don't know his name. He was Caribbean. He sat me down and he went away. Then the ship's officers came and the alarms sounded. It seemed to take a long time but frankly I don't remember how long it took."

"Did anyone else see this happen? See the doctor go over?" I asked him.

Mr. Standard started to speak. Then he snapped his mouth shut. "No." There was a pause. "No. There was no one else."

"What are the ship's officers telling you now?" I asked and gestured around his cabin.

"They say they want to handle it internally. They say they will do everything they can to avoid turning me over to the authorities here in Alaska. I told them I wanted to talk to the police but they said I would be charged with the doctor's murder. They told me to stay in this cabin. I don't know. I don't know." He buried his head in his hands.

The door to the cabin opened and the same steward who had taken the cart out came back into the room. He bowed slightly at the waist and said to me, "Excuse, sir. But there is someone who wants a word with you." He gestured to the door behind him. "Forgive me, Mr. Standard," the steward said and then waited for me to stand and follow him.

Cyril stood in the hall. He had on civilian clothes, a lightweight jacket and new athletic shoes. He was holding his knife in his hand.

"Please, sir. What are we doing now?" He unfolded the knife. "You need to come with me then." And he turned me around holding my right elbow and putting the blade of the knife just under my ribs.

13

The Capital City

I could feel the knife slicing through the fabric of my shirt as Cyril pushed the button for the elevator. Like a dope I watched the letters above the door lighting up in turn. I listened to the rattling hydraulics inside the shaft. I saw lights rise up around the edges of the metal door and the clunk of the elevator car coming to a stop. Cyril pressed the knife harder and pushed me toward the opening door.

"Cecil! There you are! Oh thank goodness. I've been looking for you everywhere!"

Rosalind was standing inside the elevator. She was wearing a white chiffon scoop-necked dress. Her curly hair was piled on top of her head like a carnival hat. She had a string of gumball-sized faux pearls around her throat. She waved gaily and I think she might have even blown a kiss over my shoulder and then pushed me out of the elevator. The knife was gone from my back.

"It's tonight!" She was jumping up and down. She put her hands on my waist. Cyril stood in the elevator and held his hand on the button, keeping the door open, waiting for me to step in.

"The seventies dance revue! I knew you hadn't forgotten. I found you a suit. It's perfect!"

I didn't say anything. Cyril waited. Rosalind stopped bouncing and she looked worried.

"You are going to be able to come, aren't you? I mean, if you can't . . . I understand, but I . . ."

"No, no, no." I smiled and waltzed her away from the door.

"That's okay," I called over Rosalind's shoulder to Cyril. "You don't have to wait." Cyril scowled at me as if I were threatening his life. "Really," I said in a cheerful voice. "I'll get the next one." The elevator door closed and Rosalind blew me another kiss.

"So you didn't connect up with anyone?" I asked her.

"Oh." She shrugged her shoulders. "I did. I did and you know him, too." She stared at me as if I were going to start guessing and when I didn't she rushed on. "But he can't come." She watched me expectantly. "But you can, right?"

"I was just thinking . . ." I said down into Rosalind's upraised face. "That I didn't . . . know what I was going to wear."

And I walked with her down the hall listening to the rattle and hum of the elevator dropping away with Cyril inside.

The *Westward* unmoored from Skagway in the afternoon. Passengers came back from the train trip to the mountain pass talking of the scenery and the history they had been passed along. I went to Rosalind's cabin and tried on the white suit she had borrowed from the ship's theatrical

company. It was tight in the shoulders and the bell bottoms hung well above the tops of my shoes making my
ankles look like strange white clappers. I tried to add up
all of the different people on the *Westward* who may have
been interested in my whereabouts and then I tried to
think of how best to avoid them. But I needed to see Jane
Marie and Todd, and when I mentioned this to Rosalind
she seemed pleased.

"Oh, they are going to be at our table for dinner. I've got
it all arranged." And she hopped up on one foot slightly.
Then she went off on a search for a red satin shirt, leaving
me alone in her cabin.

Rosalind's creative block seemed to have lifted in the past
few days because her notebook was full of sketches. On
top of her table she had a few finished paintings. They
were done with ink and oil paints, and she appeared to use
blood for some lettering just as the old iconographers had
done. She had created images of angels hovering above
mountains and the fjords. Sad angels with gold flocking
and blissful angels with vaguely East Indian features. All
the angels were reaching out beyond the edge of the
painting but there were no humans in the frame. I sat on
Rosalind's bed and studied the image she had titled "The
One Who Cannot Be Denied." The angel's robes were
textured green and flowing out behind its body. The wing
feathers were black, as was the skin. The eyes were brown
and widely set. I stared at the painting. The angel's expression showed some kind of compassion. But the image
was more human than I was comfortable with. There was
something irritatingly familiar about it as well.

The door opened and Rosalind came in holding a

shiny red shirt. She held it up to me. "Fabulous. Don't you think?" And I agreed.

Soon there was a knock on the door and Rosalind opened it a crack. She whispered with Jane Marie for a moment and then let her in.

Jane Marie was in her black dress. The night we'd spent together on the beach had been washed away. I set the angels aside and she sat next to me on Rosalind's bed.

"What's going on, Cecil? The police only asked me a few questions. They kept referring to the doctor's drinking out on deck and kept talking about the 'accident.' Nothing was said about Mr. Standard and nothing was said about you." Jane Marie looked at me as if I were a feverish child. "Sonny Walters kept the whole conversation to finding the doctor's body on the beach this morning. Sonny told me specifically they didn't want your name brought up at all."

"I think I'm a problem for them." I touched the flat of my hand to her cheek.

"And I don't know how many times they've asked me about your whereabouts since the ship left port. They are tearing the place up looking for you. I was lucky to get here." She kissed my hand.

"Where's Todd?" I asked her.

"They've got him up in some fancy stateroom on Horizon Deck. They said we could stay there. Todd's in heaven. He's taking pictures of every square inch of the room and is drinking every soda in the refrigerator. But I don't think they are going to let him out of that room."

"No. I don't think so," I said and ran my hand across the silky red fabric of tonight's shirt.

◙ ◙ ◙

Now the truth is I'm not a very good sneak. I'm too self-conscious to be very effective skulking around, and besides, if I were caught skulking anywhere on the ship I felt almost certain I would be feeling some steel slicing through my skin. So after weighing my options I decided we were bound for the bright lights of the Great Circle Lounge. Slitting my throat during the seventies dance revival would surely risk ruining someone's vacation.

At dinner we sat with Rosalind and a very funny couple from Pakistan. The man bought our wine and did bits from *Monty Python's Flying Circus*. Rosalind drank almost a bottle of white wine and laughed with her mouth wide open. Jane Marie and I drank soda water while our Pakistani host threatened to cut down the largest tree in the forest with a herring.

The waiters smiled at me deferentially as they brought my porterhouse steak. I noticed a thin black man step out of the kitchen and point to our table. Rosalind followed my eyes there. When she saw the thin black man pointing she reached under the table and squeezed my hand.

In the Great Circle Lounge the mirrored ball sprayed light into the room like a sprinkler. The Bee Gees wheedled and thumped as we lunged around the room twisting, pointing into the ceiling and thrusting our hips awkwardly to the beat. I was feeling liberated. I had finally made it to the party and was going native along with the rest of my shipmates: women in strange dresses, clumsy, bouncing and totally unself-conscious, men in tight suits, their guts spilling out over their belts. I knew with a force of certainty that these were my people.

I danced with Rosalind and Jane Marie. Sweating and laughing, we mugged and flirted, completely foolish and beautiful. Outside, water fell from the steep rock walls down into Lynn Canal. Seabirds flew back to their rooker-ies and the great warm-blooded mammals came up for air.

Werdheimer was there, too, wearing the most godawful gold chains and doing a kind of nonchalant tough-guy routine. His outfit was not helped by the pack of gauze bandaged across his nose or the cotton sticking out of his nostrils. He circled the room staying on the outside of the dancers, watching me. I stayed in the middle of the floor and Jane Marie danced past him as if he were part of the furniture.

The ship's plan was to party our way down Lynn Canal and to moor in Juneau so that we could dance out into the after-hours parties on the narrow streets of the city. In the morning we could shop.

I didn't have much of a plan. I was hoping Mr. Worthing-ton might be able to help me. I was not going to bump into Cyril on the dance floor so I needed a way to escape down into Freetown.

The dance judges were moving through the dance floor, tapping certain couples on their shoulders and asking them to sit down. I wheeled Rosalind in an old country dance move called the eggbeater and nearly dislocated my shoulder. Jane Marie spun away from me and took Word's hand and pulled him in close to her body. Peter Frampton was making his guitar talk in that interminable passage of his old hit song. Jane Marie held Word tight and stared into his eyes with a conviction that made me want to stick around and see what was coming next. Jane Marie danced so close that she had to move her thigh up between Word's legs. She pressed his head down into the warm cleft between her neck and shoulder and he pulled back, gently protecting his battered nose. Rosalind and I spun to the edge of the dance floor and out of the Great Circle Lounge.

In the stairwells of Freetown it was always the same time of day. The weather was of machines and work. Metal rattled and diesel and cigarette smoke clung to everything. We ran down the circular staircase. I held Rosalind's hand. I took her with me as a witness, still thinking it would be hard for any of the crew to murder a perfectly healthy paying customer. But I had to admit this hope was starting to dim the closer I got to the belly of the ship, where I hoped Mr. Worthington was working on his boilers.

"I know someone who can help," Rosalind said behind me. I did not answer and I did not turn. I wasn't sure just where I was going: I was just trying to remember the turns in the maze that would lead me to Mr. Worthington.

Voices called out somewhere above us and there were shouts. Shoes clattered on the metal of stairs. Metal banged on a pipe overhead. I heard a man's voice calling, "That way! There!" And I ducked as I heard that metallic footfall again and again.

I saw a metal door and grabbed the knob. The door opened and I pushed in, dragging Rosalind behind me.

It was Mr. Worthington's door, but he was clearly not there. His children peered at us from their tiny photographs. His sooty coveralls were piled in the corner and there was a damp towel smudged black hanging across the chair.

The voices rattled down the hall, men calling and breathing hard as they went past the door. Rosalind stood with her back pressed against the door. Her face was flushed and her hair had fallen in loose strands touching the soft skin of her shoulders.

"I'll be right back," she said breathlessly, and lunged out of the room before I could grab her. Then she was around the corner and was gone. I heard the men's voices double back and their footsteps coming toward me. I ducked back into Mr. Worthington's room.

The voices faded. I locked the door and sat on his bed. On the shelf on the wall was a small tape recorder and propped against it was a Bible. He had tapes, all neatly labeled, of his children reading different stories. On the one counter space was a stack of papers with information about the medical services offered at the Mayo Clinic. Under the bed was a red toolbox. On top of the box was a short saw with a squared-off blade and fine teeth, the type of saw I associated with finishing woodwork.

I checked the lock again and punched the button on the tape machine and lay down. For a few minutes I listened to the voice of a child reading the story of God commanding a worm to nibble the roots of the fig tree that was shading Jonah.

There was a knock on the door and I turned off the tape. I went to the door and could hear Rosalind whispering. I opened the door and she was smiling a beatific smile as if she had just stepped out of the hot sun.

"I found him, Cecil. I just know he can help you." And she pulled on the arm of the man standing next to her.

Cyril walked into the room.

"I don't know if you remember him, Cecil. This is Cyril. We . . . well, you know, we walked in on him and that awful woman early on in the trip. Cyril was worried that I might tell so he came to talk to me about it, and you know we . . .

we became friends." Rosalind was holding Cyril's hand and Cyril was smiling down at his shoes.

With his eyes cast down I suddenly knew something. Cyril was Rosalind's angel.

"Hey, Cyril," I said. "You befriend her to keep her from talking and you cut off a hand and serve it to me in an ice bucket. What's up with that?"

Cyril looked startled. "No, sir. I never did cut off any hand."

"What? You just found a dead girl's hand lying around?"

"No, sir," Cyril repeated and he walked toward me. "You make trouble for us down here. Why is that now?" The knife was back out and Rosalind stared at Cyril in disbelief. Cyril came closer.

"I never meant to cause trouble down here, Cyril," I told him and stood my ground. "I just assumed you had cut off that dead girl's hand to scare me."

"Is this what you are telling the police then?" I could see Cyril had not slept well the last few nights. His eyes were rimmed red and he was having a hard time keeping them open.

"I told the police nothing," I told him truthfully.

"He say if we just let everything calm down a little we be fine." Cyril was motioning toward the pictures on Mr. Worthington's wall. "No one going to miss a sheep doctor. No one left to care about that doctor now." He held his knife almost carelessly, as if he were waiting for a potato to arrive before cutting his steak.

"Did you slice that dead boy's throat, too?" I wanted the answer and I watched the knife.

"I swear to God, sir, I did not." Cyril folded up the knife and put it back in his pocket. He stepped back, closed his eyes tight, then rubbed them as if he had been holding off tears for several days. "Oh dear God," he mumbled. "I don't know how I got into this. I truly don't."

Rosalind stepped forward. She rubbed the back of his neck and he let out a low moan.

"You better take me to Mr. Worthington then," I told him.

"He's not here." Cyril's eyes were still shut. A fat tear formed on his ebony cheek. "He's getting ready to go ashore."

"I need to speak with him," I said as forcefully as I could to the crying man. Rosalind looked questioningly at me.

"We'll go then," Cyril said and he backed toward the door.

I was walking ahead of Cyril and Rosalind, and as I turned the corner of the narrow hallway I ran straight into David Werdheimer's chest.

He did not say anything. He did not jump out of the way, nor did he hesitate. He pulled his arm back and punched me in the throat. I dropped to my knees. My head felt as if it were filled with bees. I clutched my throat and tried to suck in a breath. I did not succeed. Word kicked me in the crotch and I lay down.

"I got very cold in that cooler, Cecil." Word was speaking calmly in almost a friendly tone. His voice had a nasal quality, so I think he was consciously trying to talk more from his diaphragm because of his injury. "It took them almost an hour to let me out," he added without a trace of anger as he pulled his foot back for another kick. I tried to scramble away from him, clawing the sides of the wall.

"Calm down now," Word said. The bandages were

falling loose from his face and when I looked up at him from the floor he looked like a kid going out for Halloween in a hurry.

"I was right, Cecil, you really are a scamp." Word leaned over me. "I can almost forgive you for breaking my nose, but I can't let you run around loose, because we've almost got a deal. Just a few more hours and everything is wrapped up." He stepped on my hand and put his full weight on it. There was a gentle pop as my thumb came out of its socket. Rosalind gasped.

Word looked up and saw Rosalind clutching onto Cyril's shoulder. Now, Word looked as if he were going to cry. "Not another sheep!" He shook his head and just pointed above his head as he snapped a directive to Cyril. "Get her out of here. Upgrade her. Horizon Deck. I don't care. I don't want to deal with her right now."

Cyril and Rosalind backed away. David Werdheimer started kicking me in the stomach and the head, falling into a workman's rhythm alternating blows.

When I woke up I was in a dumpster along the wharf in downtown Juneau. The bees in my head had spilled out onto the smelly walls above my bed. All I could see was a flurry of tropical fish darting about in the darkness and a split of light above me.

I elbowed my way out of the garbage and stood waist-high in the dumpster. It was raining gently. The *Westward* loomed above me. Its immense white hull was lit by the streetlights. A string of colored lamps swung in the fresh breeze between its stack and fantail. Marine signal flags fluttered. There was a raven standing flat-footed on the dock some ten feet from me. He called and bickered at me standing there in his garbage, hackles up, feathers ruffling with the wind.

"I'm sorry," I said lamely, and the raven waddled away like a barrister, to another, less occupied, dumpster.

Off to my left a very small Filipino man stood gesturing to me. "Come. Come," he said and he pulled his hands to his chest as if he were calling a puppy. "Come. I take you."

I crawled out of the garbage and as I did the pain in my chest flashed everything red and when I woke up again I was looking into the face of the Filipino man. "I cannot call 911. Police come and I go. You come with me. I take you. Come. Come." And he lifted my throbbing elbow, helping me to my feet.

We walked without speaking. No one seemed to notice us on these dark narrow streets. Downtown Juneau had been built as a mining town, with wooden streets and old boardinghouses. The ghosts were used to seeing men lumbering home supporting one another. But tonight, revelers from all over the world were drinking and shelling peanuts onto sawdust floors. Music spilled from every bar and wealthy retirees rushed past the Indian men sleeping near the covered transformers. Pretty Filipino girls were laughing and tripping in their high-heeled shoes. Dark men in new warm-up jackets nodded as their friends strolled by. Drunks looked for fights and lonely state workers looked for conversation. The fudge store and hamburger stand stayed open. Up and across from the old steam laundry the discotheque thumped out bowel-shaking dance tunes. Cars drove slow; men looked for women. Women hunched against their stares or laughed them off.

My guide took me to a small restaurant away from the din where there was a karaoke machine in the front with one fat young white girl who was flipping through the book and absently twirling the cordless microphone. There was a beaded curtain in the back of the room. My guide pointed. "Back there. Okay?" he said and I walked through.

There was an alcove off the kitchen with a large round table. Magazines were stacked in the center, next to three glass ashtrays. Mr. Worthington sat at the table with his back to the corner, his jet-black features resplendent over his dark blue suit and white shirt open at the neck.

"You look terrible, sir," he said and gestured at me to sit down.

Looking at me, he shook his head as if I were living proof of something he long suspected. "They believe in their authority. It makes them stupid sometimes." Then he threw a menu across the table to me. "You eat something then. I'll take care of it."

An older woman gave me a glass of water. I took a sip, swirled the lemon-water in my mouth, and spit it out. The water turned red. The woman brought me another glass of water and a dry cloth with some ice. She pantomimed that I was to use the cloth and the ice on my face.

I wrapped the cubes in the cloth and when I raised it to my head, was surprised by the new shape of my face.

"Mr. Worthington, I have been stupid in this," I said. "I've run into some trouble and I've come to you for help." I worked my tongue along each of my teeth, checking for gaps.

He smiled and for the first time I noticed a row of gold caps far back in his mouth.

"I sent for you, sir, because you have been very useful to me and I want to help." He leaned forward. "You are the detective then. Did you figure out your case, yes?" He did not look worried.

I was very tired and my head hurt more with each beat of my heart. I thought I had two seriously loose teeth. I was not going to dance with Mr. Worthington.

"Here is what I think . . ." I looked down at the white cloth in my hand and saw only a smudge of my own blood. "Cyril says he did not mutilate the bodies, and I suppose I believe him. You have a carpenter's saw in your toolbox and I doubt there is a stick of wood on this boat you'd be cutting with it."

Mr. Worthington kept smiling broadly. "This is so." He spread his massive hands on the shelf-paper tablecloth. His expression was starting to change as he watched my battered face and listened to my voice as I laid it out.

"Mr. Worthington, you knew about the doctor and the euthanasia groups."

He held up one hand to stop me.

"I am not a foolish man, Mr. Younger. I know the difference between what they call 'passive' and 'active.' This man, this . . . doctor was not just letting the sickness take its course. Neither was he treating their pain and letting the drugs beat the disease to the end. I am not a zealot, Mr. Younger. Nor do I blame the doctor's patients for what they want. I know of people's suffering when they leave this world and they are the blessed, you know, sir."

"But the doctor was working on a schedule, wasn't he?" I said and I shifted the position of the ice against my jaw. The older woman brought me some custard I had never asked for and I tasted it and kept talking.

"The patients on the *Westward* wanted to end their lives precisely at the moment when they finished their business.

They wanted to go out to sea and never come back. But some of them lost their resolve. They were ambivalent and maybe they didn't know what they wanted. But the doctor, he couldn't just let them all wait until the last days of the trip. He had to make things work so as not to draw attention to himself. Or the company."

The custard tasted wonderful. I mashed it around in my mouth with my tongue, not wanting to touch any of my teeth, then swallowed.

"Dr. Edwards was treating more and more of these patients. He found himself having to work them through during each cruise. If they all waited until the end, it could be a problem. They couldn't have six or seven 'natural' deaths at one time. That would bring questions."

Mr. Worthington smiled steadily at me. He spoke with confidence. "So they start pressuring the patients. They get them to go early. Then they can keep it manageable." Mr. Worthington was brought a plate of red beans and rice with a large plate of pork ribs.

"So you began to mutilate the bodies to draw attention to the deaths," I said.

Mr. Worthington stared down at his pork ribs. "You know that they would have to investigate a body with a hand cut off. The police anywhere in the world would think that strange, don't you think, sir? Sure, I did that. I couldn't talk to the police myself. I'd be off the boat for sure then."

We sat and ate in silence. Down in the streets I heard glass breaking on the sidewalk and some men shouting. I heard the tinkle of a woman's laugh.

Mr. Worthington continued, "I took that poor dead girl's hand in Ketchikan. I thought sure somebody ask questions. But they make her disappear. They fake her name and they burn her quick. So . . ." He shook his head.

"So you send the hand up to me in an ice bucket."

"Sure, crazy I know, but I figure this get your interest. You are the detective, after all." He chewed carefully on a rib. Then he picked at a tooth with the nail on his little finger. He made a soft sucking sound.

"Did you throw the doctor overboard?" I asked out of genuine curiosity.

"Naw." Mr. Worthington shook his head. "I came up just after. But ask yourself, man, who would be angry if the doctor was moving up the dying list too fast?"

I held the spoon of custard in front of my lips. I was trying to work through this problem when the beads behind me parted and the captain of the *Westward* and Sonny Walters walked in.

The captain gave a gesture so that we could stay seated even though neither Mr. Worthington nor I ever offered to stand. Sonny Walters looked as if he were living one of those horrible test-taking dreams where you are not prepared and can't believe how you got back into the class.

"Gentlemen," the captain said in a lighthearted voice. As he sat down he got a good look at my face and he grimaced. Then he turned angrily to Sonny.

"This is your fault, you know," the captain snapped.

"My fault! He's *my* guy, for crying out loud. It was your thug that did this to him," Sonny whined.

The captain waved away Sonny's voice as if it were a bad smell.

"So," he said and turned to Mr. Worthington. "I understand we have an understanding."

"This could be true," Mr. Worthington replied.

The captain placed a black athletic bag on the table. It rattled the flatware. "This is the wages due you up to this point. And for the rest of the season, which you do not have to work."

Mr. Worthington smiled but did not reach for the black bag. The captain cleared his throat and continued. "There is also the bonus we mentioned. All in US currency. We will have all of your gear delivered to the airport here in Juneau. We will provide you with a plane ticket to Miami. From there you will have to deal with the cash yourself in order to move it back to the islands."

Sonny Walters sat forward and stabbed his finger at Mr. Worthington. "In exchange for this you have to sign this contract agreeing to cooperate with both our companies' direction. You will talk to no police agencies, no journalists, no other parties in any potential suits. In other words—to no one. You are not to discuss any of the medical practices on the ship, including medications, diagnosis, or record keeping. You will not mention anything about falsifying death records or any subject relating to any deaths on board ship. Do you understand?"

Mr. Worthington nodded but did not look at Sonny. Undaunted, Sonny kept on. "You will be listed as an employee of the cruise line and will be held liable to all our personnel policies." Sonny reached inside his blue blazer and took out a stapled sheaf of papers. "And if you don't sign this or refuse to meet all the terms of our agreement, we will turn you over to the authorities in the US and we will seek extradition for the mutilation of the bodies and as a suspect in the murder of the ship's doctor."

"What about the poor doctor after I sign this?" Mr.

Worthington took the pen Sonny offered him and began reading the agreement.

"We believe the doctor's death to be accidental in nature. Alcohol involvement, no doubt. Perhaps a suicide attempt gone . . . right." The captain looked at me and his massive eyebrows arched over the merry gleam in his eyes.

Sonny Walters was getting impatient. "Just sign the damn agreement. It's a standard employee agreement. What . . . you want your lawyer to go over it?" His voice squeaked with sarcasm.

"Health insurance. I'm going to have it." Mr. Worthington slapped down the pen.

"No way." Sonny slapped his hand on the table. He looked nervously at the captain. "No darn way am I putting a low level seaman who will not even be really working for us on our company health plan."

"Then I'm sorry, Mr. Walters." And Mr. Worthington pushed the papers back. "I'm going to need insurance for my Martha to go to the Mayo Clinic in Minnesota. No point to this otherwise."

The captain scowled at Sonny and shook his head, then grabbed the agreement and drew a circle and wrote something in the margins. "Do it," the captain said and pushed the papers back in front of Sonny Walters, who hung his head and begrudgingly initialed the changes.

"Excuse me," I piped up. "But what about me and my party?" I asked, sweet as pie.

The captain did not even look at me as he spoke. "You've been upgraded. Horizon Deck. Full service." Then he scowled at Sonny Walters. "As for the rest of it, you have to deal with . . . your boss." He said those last two words as if he were spitting piss out of his mouth.

"Cool," I said and slapped Sonny on the back in a sign of filial loyalty. Sonny slumped down in his chair and sighed.

After Mr. Worthington signed the agreement, the captain and Sonny did not stay to watch him finish his meal, but left abruptly like men with things to do. I was not one of those men so I stayed with Mr. Worthington and we exchanged addresses. He offered me a place to stay on the Island if I ever visited and I said I just might. When I finally pulled myself up, I offered him my hand and he took it.

I hobbled down the street slowly. The noise of the street parties was abating. The few men left out on the sidewalk were mostly too drunk to be festive. The women out on the street would curl up and sleep there till morning. I could smell popcorn in the air and some spilled beer.

As I walked near a knife store I heard a voice in a darkened doorway.

"Hey! Did they take care of everything then?"

It was Isaac Brenner. He was not smoking his fat cigar but was standing with a windbreaker pulled up on his neck. The tips of his leather shoes just caught the light from the street. I stopped short and looked at him. I did not answer. My brain felt as battered as my body. Brenner looked back at me and did not try to hide from my stare.

"You know, you can live a long time with prostate cancer," he said finally.

14

Home

It took several weeks for Todd to get his pictures back. I think he took twenty-five rolls of film into the drugstore to get developed. He plans to pay the bill in monthly install-ments. After we got home we sat around our kitchen table looking at the prints which he had spread out in a heap. Many of the shots were blurred: Eagles as specks against green. The backs of whales looking like chocolate chips floating in the sea. But the majority of the pictures were blurry and botched group-shot attempts. Most contained a streaky Todd half in and half out of the picture, either coming or going. Todd told me this was exactly what he liked about the shots. He said he was a verb in all of his memories and I was never really sure what he meant by that.

I fingered through the pile and picked a clear picture of Mr. Brenner standing on the dock in Victoria just as we were about to disembark from the *Westward*. He held an unlit cigar between his fingers. He was not looking at the camera but over the shoulder of whoever was taking the photograph. He looked distracted, as if someone was coming for him.

Isaac Brenner never got upgraded. He did visit Jane Marie and Todd and me in our palatial suite as we sailed down the inside passage for the last three days of our voyage. He was anxious and acted like he wanted to talk but never could bring himself around to the topic. I never pried because I didn't really want to know. But by the way Brenner kept coming back to our suite I knew that he knew I had some knowledge of what really happened to Dr. Edwards that night out on the crew deck. Brenner had to know my knowledge of it.

On our last night out the Filipino kitchen crew was singing songs to all of the people eating in the dining room. They had a guitar. The social staff finally ran the last horse race in the Great Circle Lounge. I stayed in the suite and ordered a steak to be sent up. I was drinking bottled water with lemon twists and was reading a book of poetry from the ship's library. Everyone else was down at the horse races when Brenner came to the suite. He settled in on the leather couch and we stared out at the dark and unlit forests that the ship was passing.

Finally, he blurted, "I don't know how much you know about all this—" and I held my hand up.

"I don't know anything and I don't really want to know. I am not a priest or your lawyer. You can't hire me, because I'm working for the cruise line. So I can't promise you any confidentiality." Then I paused and added, "I don't mean to sound unfriendly. I'm just being square with you."

"Understood," Mr. Brenner said. Then, "Let's just say hypothetically . . ." and he stared out the window. The wake of the ship billowed the green water, curling perfect waves onto the rocky shore of the narrow passage. He didn't talk.

"Hypothetically," I said.

"Yes. You know, I'm not talking about anything that *actually* happened but just a *what if* sort of thing."

"Okay."

Brenner cleared his throat. "Let's just say I killed the son of a bitch."

"All right," I agreed and took a sip of water.

Brenner's eyes were burning into mine. "I was concerned about what was going on. I talked to him about the first girl. I talked to him and he just brushed me off. But on the day before Paul died, that day we were at the glacier, I talked to the doctor again. He told me that things were backing up. It looked like people were going to wait until the end of the trip and he couldn't let that happen. He was . . ."

"Watching out for the interests of his own organization. His own practice?" I offered.

Brenner snapped at me. "He was killing people, for God's sake."

"You were *asking* him to kill people," I interrupted. "All your club members . . . L'Inconnue," I said.

Brenner rocked back and sputtered, "Yes but he was killing them to suit the ship's schedule. Not ours. How can it be murder if we—if I—stopped him?"

I thought for a second. Down in the heart of the ship there was a faint rumble as the engines changed pitch. I remembered a lecture a lawyer had once given me about self-defense and I trotted it out for Brenner: "A person can use deadly force to meet deadly force, or to prevent certain other crimes. That's in the law." I tipped my glass

at him and added, "You have to have a reasonable expectation of imminent danger and you have to try to withdraw
from that danger, if possible, before you resort to deadly
force. So let's say you—hypothetically—saw a person about
to kill you. You could counter their deadly force right
then. But you couldn't wait and come back to it later, after
the threat of death was no longer imminent."

"What if . . ." Brenner took a sip of my water. He was
not looking at me now. "I mean what if someone . . . a
ship's doctor, say . . . was injecting people with potassium
chloride? Injecting it into their foot as they slept?" He was
struggling.

"Mr. Brenner, were you worried Edwards was going to
do this to *you*, without your permission?"

Brenner didn't speak. The ice in my glass cracked as it
melted.

"No."

"What then . . . ?"

"He was overstepping his authority."

"The authority Paul gave him."

Brenner didn't want to argue. He brushed the shoulder
of his jacket as if something had unexpectedly alighted on
him. He stood up suddenly and walked to the door of the
suite. Then he turned back.

"You know, there is an interesting story about that
L'Inconnue de la Seine. Of course I don't know if it's true
or not."

The trees passed in darkness on the banks of the narrow channel. There was just enough of the pale summer
daylight to let me make out the tangle of limbs. An eagle
sat atop a massive dead snag. Mr. Brenner kept on with
his story.

"Remember everyone was in love with her image, this death mask of the young girl drowned in the river. She had become the center of the cult. Well sir, someone wanted to know more about this girl, and so they went to the artist who had made the death mask." Mr. Brenner chewed on his unlit cigar. "Well, this reporter or whoever it was, heck I don't know, a Shamus maybe, goes to the artist's house and rings on the bell and who do you think answers?"

We passed abeam of the eagle and the giant bird lumbered into flight. I shrugged my shoulders and did not answer Mr. Brenner's question.

"Well, sir, it was the artist's wife, and it was also this girl, this beautiful face that everyone had believed was the poor dead girl dragged from the river."

I took another sip of water. "So the whole thing was a hoax?"

Brenner clamped his hand on the handle of the cabin door. "Oh hell, they argue about it until this very day. I don't know . . ." He stared absently out the window. "I just know I like that story better . . . but I guess that doesn't make it the truth."

He waved dismissively, as if he could brush the truth away like lint. Then he walked out the door.

Of course, now I'm back at home looking at the pictures and putting the whole thing together. I was half expecting the story to unravel when Mr. Standard found out about the mutilation to Paul's body. I thought I would be ducking calls from lawyers, investigators, and cops, but I never heard a peep. Apparently, Mr. Standard was convinced he would get tapped for the killing of the doctor if he made a peep. This, I'm sure, was exactly the way both the cruise line and the ship's company wanted to keep it.

Sonny Walters never even saw me off the ship in Victoria. There was a note under our suite door from the cruise line's legal department reminding me that I had been hired pursuant to an in-house investigation and was subject to the privilege of confidentiality. The privilege expressly residing with the company, which meant I was supposed to keep my mouth shut until I heard from them. This was fine by me.

Rosalind and Cyril met us on the docks of Victoria and we all took the bus downtown to have cappuccinos at a sidewalk cafe next to a tobacco shop. I had black coffee, actually, and Todd had a soda and a slice of carrot cake. Cyril seemed uncomfortable to be out in the open with some of the sheep. He winced whenever any of the crew walked anywhere near us. But he drank his espresso calmly, stirring the oily drink with great dignity. Rosalind was in a fine mood and seemed unconcerned with her impending deadline. When I asked about the angel book she waved me off and said only, "Oh. They don't really care." I was left to consider which "they" it was that didn't really care. When we parted at the airport we had kisses all around and promises to write. Rosalind did write, as it turned out. There was a letter almost a year later enclosed in a first-edition copy of her *Encyclopedia of Angels*.

But the week after I got back to Sitka, I actually received a letter from Word himself. I couldn't believe it. It was a simple letter thanking me for all of my help on the cruise and an apology for any of the minor difficulties that we had encountered on the *Westward*. I was most impressed by his stationery. It was very heavy felt bond with only his

name and address across the top in beautiful Monotype
Baskerville type. He enclosed one of his cards, which was
wheat-colored with deep engraving: *David Werdheimer*
and his San Francisco and New York addresses: No title,
no nothing. If you had to ask what he did you obviously
couldn't afford him. This guy was so good I could almost
brag about getting an ass-kicking from him. Almost.

At the heart of every death is an unknowable darkness. It
certainly was dark on the back deck of the crew's lookout
the night the doctor went over the side of the *Westward.* I
tried to bring some light to his death as the weeks rolled
by, but I realized this light was only my imagination, and
my imagination was telling me Isaac Brenner and Harold Standard together had chucked the doctor over the
rail that night. But exactly how, I wasn't sure. Certainly
Mr. Standard and the doctor were on the crew deck and
there had been an argument. Mr. Brenner could have
been watching from the passenger's fantail and he could
have come down the inside passage. Mr. Standard may have
knocked the doctor down and unconscious or the doctor may have hit his head going over the side. No one
reported anyone crying out, but then the music was loud.
   I believed Mr. Standard when he said he threw the life
ring. But he must have had some role in getting the doctor
up and over that railing. What goes through the minds of
two old men who are about to kill someone? Here again,
you'd like to make some sense of it. I'd like to imagine the
words of grief for the lost son or of fear for your crowding
and impending death. But truthfully I don't know. They
probably reacted out of some mutual confluence of fear.
They both might have lifted the doctor by the armpits and

helped him overboard. They heard the splash and the call of the birds and when he realized what he had done Mr. Standard sounded the alarm but Mr. Brenner just walked inside and went to the bar. And whether by agreement or happenstance it worked out well. If they both hinted to me, unofficially, they were solely to blame, then neither of them could be convicted as the sole killer of Dr. Edwards and each would be afraid to try and snitch on the other. It was much easier for the ship company to let the dead bury the dead and send the living on their way.

But of course I was guessing. All I knew for certain was that Grant McGowan, Paul, the pale girl, and the doctor were all dead. Some of them were ready for death. Some of them weren't. And maybe they were all ghosts right now, drifting in the shadows, screaming the truth into my ear.

But I knew that I couldn't hear them and I also knew I wasn't ready to die because I was going over the pictures from my cruise. I looked at another photograph of Todd streaking across the frame with all of the awkward laughing expressions in the background. I smiled and listened to the birds. There was a pile of chocolate cake sitting out on the handrail of my deck over the channel. Gulls and ravens worked the air. There were a few fat pigeons planted in the crowd of squabbling birds.

The cake had been a gift. I had answered the door that afternoon and found myself face-to-face with Grant McGowan's girlfriend Vicky. She was holding a cake pan covered with a blue-striped dishcloth. She didn't want to come up. She just nodded at the cake, then she shoved it into my hands. Vicky walked a few steps down the street and turned back. Her mousy hair was stringy. She was wearing canvas coveralls. She slapped her hands against the sides of her legs.

"Cecil, I just wanted to say that I didn't . . . I don't really hate you," she said at last.

"Thanks, Vicky," I mumbled. Her skin looked gray and there were dark circles under her eyes. I could tell it was almost unbearably hard for her to have come this far, but I pressed on anyway: "I appreciate that. You sure you don't want to come up and have a piece of this cake?"

She shook her head and tucked a strand of hair behind her ear. "Naw, Cecil. I gotta go. I'll just come back and get the pan." She turned down the street and called over her shoulder. "Or you can bring it down to the boat, when-ever . . ."

I got her to wait where she was and I ran upstairs. I brought down my old copy of *Going for Coffee,* an anthology of poetry about work from a Canadian publisher. The book was dog-eared and the paper cover was creased and leathery. Patrick Lane had even signed one of his poems on page 182. It was called "Just Living." I handed the book to Vicky and she looked at it as if I were offering her a bribe.

"This was Grant's," I lied.

"I never saw this on the boat."

"Oh, it was his," I said. "Grant was really into this stuff."

Vicky looked at me and silence fell like rain.

"Well. Thanks then," she said, then turned and walked toward the corner by the fish plant where the hum of the generators swallowed the sound of her steps.

The cake was not all that good. It was some kind of chocolate applesauce but there was an odd taste, as if there had been bearing grease in the bowl she had used to mix it in. But I ate two slices, with a cup of coffee and toasted the poets of Canada. Then I fed the rest to the birds.

Toddy had a picture of the bear on the beach. In the snapshot the bear looked like a small brown stump, but the head jutted out from the roots in a bearlike way. I leaned back in my chair and looked at Jane Marie. She was wearing her black silk shirt but still had her gym shorts on from her soccer game. She had her hand on my shoulder. She looked at the photo of the bear in my hand. I kissed her hand and asked, "Do you think that bear really understood what you were saying to him?"

She wrinkled her nose and kissed me on the cheek, then plopped down and started to unlace her cleats. "The words? No, I doubt it." Then she stared over at Todd, who was sorting through his photographs. "I suppose indifference is the most you should hope for from a brown bear." Then she turned back to me. "But I do think it never hurts to show respect."

She threw her cleats into the corner near the woodstove. She took a deep breath and told me she was going to have a baby.

My head turned to a block of ice. Of course it all made sense—the moods and the illnesses. Jane Marie laughed and told me about the pregnancy as an accomplished fact. She had known before we went on the cruise. I was the father and there was no doubt about that. She was going to be a mother. She kissed me again and said only, "Cecil, you probably aren't a very good detective but I think you'd make a passable father. You think about it, anyway." Then she went to take a shower.

I started to slip into a daydream about having a baby.

The damp waxy smell of their breath and that weird wobbly expression they have when you hold them for the first time. I was filled with a giddy kind of emptiness.

I could hear the shower running and Todd was humming to himself. "Did you know about this baby thing?" I asked him. He nodded emphatically, excited to demonstrate his superior intelligence.

"Actually, yes," he said and then paused, delighted in drawing the moment out. "I have been aware of the situation from the outset." He smiled. "Jane Marie confided in me when she was first certain of her situation, and she asked me for my opinion."

"And what did you tell her?" I looked down at my shoes.

"I told her you didn't seem to mind looking stupid. That, I thought, spoke well of your potential role as a father."

"That's quite an endorsement. Thank you," I said.

"Don't mention it," Todd said and went back to his pictures.

That next morning I had a job building a new fence around the chicken house. For as much fun as the cruise ship had been, they'd never offered to pay me any wages. I wrapped my sore hand in bandages and a leather glove, then packed a sandwich and a jug of tea, and walked out to the road.

It was a clear cool day at the end of summer, one that would have ordinarily made me melancholy. There was a steady light rain and a sharp edge to the cold air. High up in the mountains a light snow dusted the trees but there was blue sky out over the ocean. It was as if you could actually stand on the beach and watch summer leaving.

I started digging postholes in the soggy ground. The chickens ran around nervously and the dog with the blocky head and the sweet eyes watched me all day long, indifferent to what I was doing and what it might mean to his nightly raids. He watched me, panted and grinned: Happy, I thought, just to have some company.

Although my head was unthawing about the news of the baby I couldn't shake the fact of it from my mind. After I dug the fourth posthole I realized I wasn't worrying about the future. And by the time I drank my tea I had stopped worrying about anything at all. I had realized, finally, that no one really cared about this story of my life, whether it was tangled up like fishing line in the trees or not. No one cared about my failures or those corpses that haunted me from the dark, or if they did care they were tolerant enough not to let me know. And too, I knew, finally, that I didn't care either, and as I threw a shovelful of wet dirt on that rare morning, it felt as if I had just been counted as one of the blessed.

Author's Note

I have been on many ships that ply the tourist trade in Alaska. None of them are the *Westward*. There is no such ship and she has carried no such characters. This book is a product of my imagination. There are, however, some real people who haunt my writing career and I must extend my thanks to: Nita Couchman, Marylin Newman and Lisa Busch for their fine attention and blunt advice; Rob Allen and Kodi, the handsome and well behaved husky, for their service to the Island Institute and the cultural life of Alaska; my shipmates Jan and Finn; and Patrick Lane for "Just Living."

Finally to Paul Monette, writer and AIDS activist, who, in 1994, read one of my books while cruising Alaska and sent me a short encouraging note. It was a small act made powerful by the courage of Monette's work: I offer my thanks to his memory.

Continue reading for the next
Cecil Younger Investigation

Cold Water Burning

1

The storm had passed, Toddy was dead and I was clinging to the overturned hull of my yellow skiff. I pulled down the hood of my rubber survival suit and looked up to see gulls circling the tangled mess my life had become. There was no help, and there wouldn't be. Light dazzled on the tip of every gray-green wave, but there were no ships. I was wide awake in the empty sea wishing I could go back in time, back to the dock before I had pushed away, back to the unsolved homicide, back to the recurring nightmare of murder, gasoline and children screaming.

It could be argued that being a private investigator in a small Alaskan town is one of the worst career decisions a person with a high-school diploma can make. But there's lots of opportunity for free time. In that regard, the summer started off well. I had spent six wonderful days catching a few of the early king salmon, all thanks to the money I'd made working for a rich herring boat captain who had crushed some fool charter fisherman's face in a bar brawl. The case was my dream come true: a rich client with serious felony charges. The summer was looking up, but summers are short here. The skipper settled his case long before trial; I had spent most of his money on bait and boat repairs before September came around.

I would never have gone out into that storm willingly. The weather radio had been tracking two low-pressure systems on a collision course in the north Pacific. If the systems joined forces it would become the kind of storm that would crack the limbs off alder trees and churn the shoreline white. I still remember the feeling of those few days as the storm moved in: black clouds like bags of anvils rolling up over the horizon, and the trees along the beach standing motionless as if they were trying to hide from what was coming. I remember the expectation and the dread before the storm hit.

It was two days before the peak of the storm when Patricia Ewers walked into my office and asked me to find her husband Richard, who had gone missing with fifty thousand dollars of their money. Richard Ewers's case may have been my greatest success as a defense investigator. Three years ago he had stood trial on four counts of first-degree murder and one count of arson, and had been found not guilty.

He had been accused of killing two adults and two children on board a fish-buying scow, soaking the deck with gas, and setting the whole mess on fire as he escaped in a red tin skiff. This was Richard Ewers. My client.

A five-month murder trial is an ordeal that forges loyalties that only come out of combat. All the subtle conflicts boil down to "us" against "them." I thought of Patricia Ewers as an old army buddy. Captain of the "us," Patricia provided the strength and calm presence during the

wildest part of the ordeal. All through the halfhearted
police protection, the ugly phone calls and the report-
ers digging through her garbage, she never wavered in
her support of Richard. She and her parents had stood
by him; they had lost both their houses and their savings
accounts to legal fees. The not-guilty verdict was some
vindication, but nothing could pay them back for what
they had been through.

When I saw her walk up my stairs unannounced three
years later, I knew something more serious than a multiple
murder count had to be bothering Patricia Ewers.

"Cecil, he's gone. I think they killed him this time."

I put my hand on her back and moved her to my sag-
ging couch near the woodstove. "He took the money. In
cash. A large amount of cash," she said as she flopped
herself on the old couch. Dust rose up in a plume. "I told
him not to take it."

"What money?" I asked her as I offered her a towel to
dry her hair, for she had been caught in a rain squall walking to my house.

"The tabloids. They kept offering Richard money for his
story. I told him not to take it. We were through the worst
of it. We had made it through the trial and things were
beginning to calm down. But they kept offering more and
more money. He's had trouble finding work, you know; no
one would hire him in the fishing industry. Anyway, when
they finally offered a hundred thousand dollars for an article, book, and film rights, he told them he would take it."

"One hundred thousand dollars?"

"We had only gotten half of it. There was fifty on signing
the deal and the rest after he did the interviews. I know, we
shouldn't have taken it."

"I wasn't going to say that, Patricia. I was just wondering if they wanted my story."

"Have you been found not guilty of mass murder?" She said it sarcastically.

"No," I said, "but I'm close friends with some people who were. That should be worth a couple of grand at least."

"You can have it, Cecil. I mean, jeepers, we have no control over the story. They could print anything." She held her hands up as if framing the headline in the air. "Mygirl Murderer Beats the Rap." Then she buried her head in her hands.

I could understand her concern. Richard's story had everything for the tabloids: drama, sympathetic victims, terrific color photographs. It had everything except a killer behind bars.

The murders occurred in late August of 1995. The *Mygirl* had been anchored in Kalinin Bay just north of Sitka. It was just after dark, past midnight on that Alaskan summer evening, when a man got into a skiff and pulled away from a conflagration. He left behind the bodies of a father, a mother, their nine-year-old daughter, and a teen-aged boy who had been visiting the scow.

The parents, Charlie and Edna Sands, were each shot once through the chest before the fire started. Their daughter Tina had been clubbed over the head and almost surely died in the blaze while she was semiconscious. Albert Chevalier, the fourteen-year-old visitor, was shot repeatedly, in the arms and legs and once through the skull. His body was the most charred because the arsonist had doused the boy's body with gasoline before spreading the accelerant throughout the rest of the scow. The two

Sands boys escaped the fire. The boys told investigators they had heard a commotion up in their parents' quarters and just as they went to investigate, the scow burst into flame.

Across the bay, Albert Chevalier's brother Jonathan had seen the first signs of the fire, rushed over in his skiff, and pulled the Sands boys off the burning scow.

Later, in trial, Jonathan Chevalier swore he saw someone leave the *Mygirl* in one of the scow's three tin skiffs. According to Jonathan, whose little brother, Albert, died that night, the driver of the tin skiff "could have been" Richard Ewers.

I've been asked dozens of times if I thought Ewers was guilty of four killings, and I always say the same thing. "I don't know who killed those people." But the truth is I believed wholeheartedly in Richard's innocence. I just couldn't prove it.

Ewers was the only hired crewman on board the *Mygirl*. Richard had been hired by Charlie Sands off the docks in Ballard, Washington. He had worked the Alaskan fisheries and Charlie needed a seasoned hand to help bring the scow up the coastline. It seemed incontrovertible that seconds after this mysterious man who could have been Richard Ewers pulled away from the *Mygirl* in a skiff, the scow went up in a bonnet of flame. Most of the usable evidence was lost in the fire and almost everything else of forensic value was washed overboard as local fishermen battled the fire.

A day and a half later, heat and smoke shimmered off the charred remains of the beached scow. There was little in the *My girl's* hulk left to tell the story of the four murders. Because of that lack of evidence, a major crime

investigation was based only on fragmented witness state-
ments. All the investigators were left with was grief and a
collection of wispy memories.

Richard's memory was bad. Particularly bad when he
was first interviewed and he couldn't quite decide where
he had been or what part he had had to play in the fire.
Finally he confessed to stealing some money from Charlie
Sands's till that night and heading to town in the scow's
skiff. When he left the *Mygirl,* Richard said, everything was
quiet and everyone on board was sleeping soundly. This
was his final story and he stuck to it.

His clothes bore some trace elements of gasoline, but
he said he'd had to pour gas into his fuel tank from a
jerry jug. This was a reasonable story. But the fact that all
three skiffs from the scow were accounted for, plus his
guilty demeanor when questioned and the theft of the
money, made Richard the trooper investigators' only via-
ble suspect.

I liked Richard Ewers. I had sat with him through some
of the worst days of his life. I was with him when children
spat on him while walking to court, and when each day's
mail brought new death threats. I never saw him bristle
or clench his fist. In short, I never saw the kind of explosive personality it takes to commit these kinds of killings.
Or so I thought. As has been pointed out to me many
times, I don't have a large pool of people to compare
him to. How many mass murderers does anybody get a
chance to know?

"He took half of the tabloid money. He said he was
going to end this whole thing one way or the other," Patricia told me and started to cry. "He was coming up here.
Ketchikan first, then Sitka. It's been a week and I haven't

heard from him. He hasn't called. He always calls, Cecil. You know that. He always calls."

She looked up at me with pleading eyes as if my just acknowledging the truth of that would bring her husband back.

"He always calls," I repeated lamely. I had been getting dressed to go out the road on a job when she arrived. I looked at this woman who had done so much to calm everyone else during her husband's trial. Her hands were cupped around her nose and mouth and her collar was wet where tears soaked it.

"It's going to be okay," I said, and I winced at the insincerity of my voice. "What was he going to do with the money?" I asked, trying to cover for myself.

"He wouldn't tell me," she said, wiping her nose on her sleeve, as I reached for a napkin that was inexplicably resting on the banister. "All he would say was he was going to straighten some things out. He said not to worry about taking the money from the tabloids because we weren't going to keep it."

I sneaked a look at my watch. I had to get out the road. I had been offered a ride, but I had just missed it.

"Did he ever take large sums of money before?" I asked while putting on my coat.

"No, no, he didn't." She was breathing hard now, no longer weeping but on the verge. "I don't think he was being blackmailed, Cecil. I don't know why, but it seemed like he wanted to do something with the money. He didn't act angry, like he was being forced. He was acting relieved."

"Why do you think someone has killed him?" I asked her. She would not look at me.

"Oh . . . I don't know really. It's all this . . . mess." That was how Patricia had always referred to the trial, the charges, the accusations of multiple homicide and arson: *this mess.*

"It was worse after he got some of the money. New people were angry and the old people—you know, the families—are furious now. We had calls. Mostly Richard hung up. But more and more he would talk to them. People saying he deserved to be shot and burned along with his blood money. Cecil, you know how people are."

How people are. Every time I begin to think I know something about how people are, I find out I am wrong.

My stomach hurt as I watched her because I knew she was right. The list of people who had wanted Richard Ewers dead was extensive. What concerned me most was that some of those on the list were quite capable of making it happen.

"Cecil, I want you to find him. I want you to start right now. I want you to go out to see some of those people in the families. I want you to ask them point-blank what they've done to my husband." The families she was referring to were those of the victims, the Chevaliers and the Sandses. Her blue eyes brimmed with tears and she stared at me as if there was something I could do.

"I will, Patricia, but first I've got . . . I've got a job to do for a person." I backed away from her and put my work gloves in my coat pocket.

"Cecil, we've got to start on this now. I can pay you, for gosh sakes." She dug into her zippered jacket pocket and fanned out some twenty-dollar bills. "I want you to start now. Please."

I said nothing. I wasn't going to tell her who I was going

to work for, because I knew just saying his name would send her into a rage.

"Listen," I said as I fussed around with my work gloves and keys, "you can stay here. I'll ask a few questions around town and then I'll be back, okay? You just make yourself comfortable here. I'll be back tonight and then we'll get started looking for Richard."

Patricia stood up and without speaking walked down the stairs to the street. She slapped her money against the banister as she walked. "I can't believe you're making me go to the police," she hissed as she slammed my door. After she left I straightened a picture on the wall in an effort to assert the correctness of my actions.

I walked out into the street and smelled the storm sulking off the coast. It was still the early part of September and the fireweed in the ditches was frothing with its soon-to-be-airborne seeds. Dozens of humpback whales lolled on the surface out in Eastern Channel, and the hours of daylight were shrinking down to that intense window of opportunity that can drive a depressive to drink.

I walked along my street in this little island town wondering how I could tell Patricia Ewers that I was going to work for George Doggy, the police detective who had persecuted her family through the investigation and the trial. To Patricia Ewers, George Doggy was the author of her family's misery, the captain of "them."

A fishing boat eased in past the breakwater, probably looking for its berth before the storm hit. The sun had cleared the mountains of Baranof Island, lighting them like a bad religious painting. The flat water in the channel sent the light rippling lazily up the sides of the old wooden buildings on the waterfront. Gulls worked the air and a few eagles sat perched on the Forest Service building as I walked to the only traffic light in town, jaywalked across Halibut Point Road, and wandered backwards on the edge of the pavement with my thumb out.

I had stood next to Patricia Ewers three years ago when the jury foreman read the not-guilty verdict. We had hugged each other and cried while the rest of the world looked at us in scorn. For some reason as I walked down the road now I felt a strange certainty that Richard was dead, and I didn't want to be the one to find him. I think I was getting tired of murder.

Harrison Teller had been Richard's lawyer. Teller was confined to a wheelchair these days, yet he was still a formidable figure. Every gesture, every nuance in the courtroom was charged with an instinct for communicating his client's case to the jury. When a sniper's bullet had paralyzed him from the waist down on the banks of the Nenana River in Fairbanks, Teller recuperated for a year. Then he found a way to work his newly limited mobility into his law practice. He had said to me, "Younger, I would give anything to walk again, but this goddamn wheelchair makes for great theater in court."

Teller also would have been furious if he had known I was working for George Doggy. But I needed the money. I was a parent now. Of course that wouldn't have mattered to Teller. He had kids and he hadn't lost his belly for murder. I was getting soft and worn out. He had said as much to my face.

When our daughter finally pushed through the birth canal amid all the breathing and stifled screams, I got the impression she was traveling light: her fists were clenched, her tiny walnut face enraged at the world's intrusion into her life. She was as naked as grief or joy, and when the doctor laid her in Jane Marie's arms and she settled to her mother's breast, I felt that aching sadness I encounter when confronting great beauty. It's a sadness that says no matter what you do from that moment on, nothing will ever be the same. Maybe Teller had been right. Maybe I had lost my stomach for murder.

I was thinking about this when a sleek sedan with a rental company sticker on both bumpers wheeled by with country music thumping from behind the closed windows. Patricia Ewers was driving. She flicked her hair in my direction and pinched her cigarette tightly between her lips. I looked at her as she made the turn, and although she looked back at me, her stare was dead.

In a moment, the rental car was gone and only a puff of exhaust remained, the engine's breath hanging in place above the pavement. I stepped through it, then resumed walking backwards, thumb out.

I didn't blame her for hating me. It's been said that I'm not much of a private investigator, even though I had done good work for her husband. Teller and I had torn the state's evidence apart until there was nothing left. But we hadn't been able to put their life back together. Or find the real killer.

I'm a good PI for the real world. I can wear blinders and I'm as steady as a tractor. But the fact that I don't save the day by finding the truth is not all my fault. People don't really want to know the truth, no matter what they say. I meet most of my clients after they have been arrested for a crime. Guilty or innocent, they want the same thing: they want whatever bit of their innocence is left intact. They want me to re-create it for them. That's all Richard Ewers had wanted, and that's what Teller had paid me for.

I'd been walking ten minutes when a rusted Chevy truck pulled over twenty yards down the road and Gary Gouker heaved open the passenger-side door. Gary was my gym partner and I knew why he had stopped.

"C, man, where you been? Have you been to the gym? I kind of slacked off after you didn't show up those times, Cecil."

"I'm going to cut wood for Doggy," I said, as if that explained everything in my life.

"Cutting wood's good," Gary agreed. I jumped onto the bench seat, which sagged badly to the outside of the vehicle.

"I can't drive you out there. I've got a guy coming in with a job. He's been on me. I mean *on* me! Sent his kid to drag my ass out of the coffee shop. He's probably up at my shop right now. I'll drive you to the corner."

I looked through the cracked windshield. The corner was some hundred yards away.

"Yeah, good," I said and slammed the door. Gary was a machinist and a blues harmonica player. His father had been the mill manager here for years and Gary had worked there too, but that was long ago now. The mill was closed, his dad was dead, and Gary's real love was the blues harmonica.

"What d'ya think of getting Cary Bell up here for Alaska Day? If not him, I'm pretty sure I could get Paul deLay. What d'ya think?"

"Perfect," I said. "Get them both and promise to take them fishing. I'm sure two great blues players would give anything to play Sitka, Alaska."

That was all the conversation we had because we were at the corner already.

Gary let me off and drove away quickly with a wave. There was a three-legged dog sniffing the stop sign by the funeral home and when he peed on it I noticed that he swung around so he didn't have to worry about lifting a leg. "Convenient," I thought, and stuck out my thumb. Only five miles to go.

I hadn't thought of the *Mygirl* killings since our daughter had been born three months ago. I hadn't had many coherent thoughts since I saw her push her way out into the light. She had been blood-slick and angry. We had decided to name her Blossom and despite my smile in the hospital room I had hated the birth experience with all the screaming and the blood. It reminded me of a bar fight without the drugs and the music. When the nurse started to hand my daughter to me, my first reaction was to shy away, thinking that this creature who had just bullied her way out of my lover's stomach must be some sort of enraged snapping turtle. I wasn't sure her name fit her.

The three-legged dog sniffed my leg. He was some kind of lab-husky-terrier beast, friendly, and I was sure he had an empty bladder. I thought of Blossom and wondered if we would get another dog for our house. My roommate Todd had a Staffordshire terrier named Wendell who seemed fine, but many of our friends were almost hysterical with anxiety over having Wendell around the baby and had tried to convince us to take Wendell out into the woods for a long dirt nap. I've noticed that we parents can justify almost anything in the name of protecting our children. Anything, including executing other people's dogs, or even their children if necessary. I had sided with the Staffordshire terrier. "How soft is that?" I wanted to ask Mr. Harrison Teller, with his belly for murder.

Bob Rose stopped in his coughing VW van. He was off to Sandy Beach to check the surfbreak. He told me Nels, Mark, and Steve were going to meet him there because a swell was running from the storm. The break "should really be working," he said. Bob had curly red hair and wire-rimmed glasses. He was wearing a thick wet suit pulled off his shoulders as he drove, and although he seemed interested in the surf, he wasn't stoked. When we got to the beach, none of his friends were there and the waves looked puny. Bob didn't seem to mind. He took a thermos out from under the seat and watched the waves intently as he poured himself a cup of cocoa. "Wait for the tide a bit," he said to himself, and I got the idea that this ritual of watching and waiting was as much part of the surf scene as actually getting wet.

I got out of the van and saw Jude and his sister Rachel standing by the rail watching the sun come up and pointing out the eagles to a woman standing between them. Jude waved me over and introduced me to his mother. Jude is a lawyer and has helped me out over the years, so it paid for me to be civil. Jude is handsome and funny and fairly successful, but in spite of all that he's a decent guy.

"This is my mother, Jammikins," he said, and I looked at him evenly because I never really know when Jude is joking. When I shook the woman's hand she smiled pleasantly and didn't appear to be laughing, so I said nothing about her name.

"Cecil is a detective," Rachel said brightly.

Jammikins looked at me with some vague tourist-like interest. "Really?" she said as she scanned my clothes: torn wool jacket, dirty purple scarf, and tattered canvas pants. I looked more like a Siberian street urchin than I did James Bond.

"I'm cutting wood today," I explained, then shook hands all around and walked out to the road hoping to get a longer ride to my job, but there were fewer cars coming this far out. I was past the big grocery store, and the liquor store at the far end of the road had shut down years before. If a ferry was coming in there was hope, but I couldn't remember the ferry schedule. Once again I stuck out my thumb, thinking that, like prayer, it couldn't hurt.

Teller thought I'd lost my belly for murder because I had stopped drinking, and had turned away from the intense comradeship forged in ugly murder trials. Teller liked to drink. Drinking with his investigator was the one form of comradeship he could tolerate.

But I had stopped tolerating it. The drinking and the lawyerly comradeship that had always been as thin as stone soup. Trial lawyers love their investigators the way bird hunters love their dogs: their affection is heartfelt and intense at the moment, but it's understood the hunter will eventually get another dog.

I remember when I stopped drinking. I remember the moment but not the exact place. I was in a bathtub in a strange hotel room. It was a tiny plastic tub with a thick ring of gray-green soap scum. The bath water was cement gray and cold. The skin on my feet was soft as a sea anemone's. I held the barrel of a revolver in my mouth and propped my elbows on the islands of my knees. I remember how the front sight rattled against my teeth, how the gun oil tasted metallic on my tongue and slicked my lips.

I pulled back the hammer, then eased it down. I stepped out of the tub and toweled off. I knew I wanted a drink but I also knew I wasn't going to drink anymore. I don't know why. "Some haystacks have no needles," William Stafford wrote somewhere, and maybe he's right.

Only three cars had passed. None stopped. I looked up the hillside and noticed I was near Sean and Kevin Sands's trailer. I thought about calling George Doggy and telling him I was still on my way. And I *should* stop and talk to the Sandses. For one thing, I could get Patricia Ewers off my conscience. And for another, in the last few months I had tried to befriend the younger Sands brother, Sean, and had promised I would drop by but I hadn't yet. Sean's brother Kevin didn't like surprises of the "just dropping by" variety, but I now could use the excuse of needing to use their phone to justify my visit. If I walked quickly, I could manage to get to Doggy's in twenty minutes or so, even if I didn't get a ride.

Doggy would understand. Besides being a retired police detective, George Doggy was an old family friend who had offered to pay me to help him put up firewood for the year. George was the retired head of the Alaska State Troopers. He had been a hunting companion of my father's and a confidant to several governors all the way back to territorial days. Doggy was a man who had lived the Alaskan life before jet service and during the era of steamships and dog teams. He had run things, and would come into service if a commissioner or governor asked nicely.

Doggy had been shot several times in his duties, once

while working a case I had gotten him mixed up in, and more than any person in my life he was invested in shaping me up. I have to say that he had grown more relaxed in his semiretirement and had taken on the kind of philosophical laissez-faire that some people can accommodate if they've outlived most of the people they ever loved, which meant George's lectures were getting shorter and the war stories longer. At least Doggy was talking to me. Harrison Teller had dropped out of sight after Richard Ewers's trial ended.

In the last six months Doggy had grown noticeably more irritable. He appeared more distracted; he would sometimes pause a long time to find a word and would snap at anyone who tried to supply it. I think he was getting to be an old man, and it bothered him.

Doggy has suggested that I was trying to take Sean, the younger Sands brother, under my wing solely out of the guilt I felt for what I had done to free his family's murderer. That's not entirely true. I had always liked Kevin Sands as an alternative suspect during the Ewers trial. He had the profile, repressed hostility and explosive temper. He had a history of violent arguments, some with his own father. Unfortunately for my theory Kevin also had two alibi witnesses: his brother Sean and Jonathan Chevalier. Sean swore consistently that when the shooting started on the *Mygirl* Kevin had thrown him down on the floor and hidden him under the bunk until Jonathan Chevalier broke through the door and got them out of the fire. Jonathan backed this story up. Teller could possibly have sold Kevin as a murderer to the jury but could never have broken down his two witnesses who had both lost family members themselves and were unshakable in their testimony.

But I had always looked for something in Kevin, something that might tell me more about who had done the
shooting on the scow. That . . . and my concern for his
little brother made me stay close to the both of them.
Even before the murders on the *Mygirl,* the Sands brothers were seriously troubled young people. But afterwards
they consistently got into trouble and needed legal help.
I had worked their cases for free. But it's true I couldn't
shake the image of the dead bodies in the burned-out
scow. Kevin Sands was so hardened I suspected I wouldn't
glean any new information from him. But Sean was different. If Richard Ewers wasn't the killer and Sean knew it, I
suspected he would someday have to let it slip. That was
part of the reason I wanted to help him. That, and the fact
that I wanted some tiny new bit of information that might
change the plotline of my own nightmares.

George Doggy had tried to warn me off helping Sean
Sands. "Forget about it, Cecil. That boy's damaged too
bad. He'll do life in prison on the installment plan," Doggy
had told me.

Sean Sands was twelve and Kevin was twenty-one that
September, and by that time I had worked for Kevin's lawyers on at least ten different cases. Kevin had been tough
even before the murder of his family. As a juvenile, Kevin
had lit fires, broken into schools, and been accused of
killing pets. Now he bullied people for money and, I was
told, expedited various criminal activities. As far as I knew,
he had avoided the more obvious forms of vice like drinking and drugs. I figured Kevin liked the buzz he got from
being in the atmosphere of violence.

Someone once told me that because God did not abide
in time the way human beings had to, He could prevent

suffering that had occurred in the past. I stopped and fished a pebble out of my shoe and watched a raven watching me from a wire. I wondered if it were possible for God to prevent the pain the Sands brothers had felt in their lives.

If God could relieve suffering in the past, why wouldn't He do it for the Sands brothers? Maybe they had to be more deserving. Certainly Kevin hadn't made it easy. At every juncture in his life he seemed to lead with sullen rage. He was keen with attention, as if his hungry eyes could suck up light. His little brother, Sean, was a dreamy boy. He had been held back a grade in school, so I think he felt awkward and too big, but he could show sensitivity. He had become a fat kid who liked camping, and his eyes held some sadness and empathy that couldn't be detected in his brother's.

I looked out toward the bay and beyond to the Gulf of Alaska. Up the hill the daylight had spread through the forest. The sun seemed to illuminate each needle of every hemlock and spruce tree. To the west, the breeze freshened and the black clouds edged a little closer. I was struck by a feeling that I urgently wanted to remember this moment all my life, but at the time I had no idea why.

I had decided to see if there was anything I could do for Sean because I knew I hadn't really helped Kevin by assisting him in his criminal cases. In his last case, Kevin had slashed a young fisherman's forehead with a hunting knife so deeply that the flap of skin hung down over the fisherman's eyes. Even when the stunned fisherman held up the flap of skin, the flow of blood blinded him so he had to be led by hand up the harbor ramp to the waiting ambulance.

Kevin was thin and blond, with strange, vacant good

looks. When I talked to Kevin in jail and asked him why he had slashed the man, he shrugged his shoulders and said, "I don't know. He just kind of pissed me off." He was wearing a green prison jumpsuit, and his doughy white face was as vexed as if he were waiting for the ferry.

As a defense investigator I am supposed to fill out my client's experience for the court. I am supposed to find all the complex mitigating factors that will help explain actions that might otherwise seem bizarre. But as far as I could tell, there really was no more to the story with Kevin. It really was as easy as that: the fisherman had "kind of pissed him off," so he cut his face. Maybe all the empathy he had ever felt for anyone had been burned on board the *Mygirl* along with his parents and little sister.

The psychiatrist from Chicago who shrank Kevin the last time didn't want to give us a written report, which is always a little worrying for a defense team. The doctor spoke slowly over the phone so we could hear him through the static. "There are some clients you can easily describe as delusional. They are experiencing a reality which no one else does, which can be very dramatic and fairly straightforward to treat, but this doesn't describe Mr. Sands. There are others you can say have a particular type of personality disorder resulting in enhanced psychosexual impulse problems. These clients are overcome with repressed rage and are unable to control themselves—Ted Bundy, perhaps, or Gacy. This does not really apply to Mr. Sands either. Others could be said to have character disorders which cause them to have eccentric or unique moral values systems. They simply believe different things and are acting in accordance with those beliefs. Even that doesn't apply to Mr. Sands, although he is close. He has some . . .

humanity . . . let's call it—but it appears his ability to appreciate anyone else's suffering is . . . diminishing. This may
be partially due to the posttraumatic stress he has suffered
with the loss of his family, but that doesn't account for his
condition. He is close to his younger brother but apparently not to anyone else. He has impulse control problems,
which you might expect of a young man affected by his
kind of stress. He's defensive and guarded, but my greatest fear for this young man is that he will become . . ." and
the doctor paused as if he didn't really want to even say
the words. "My fear is that Kevin Sands has turned into
something very much like the person who stole his family
from him. He may be becoming what could only be called
. . ."—he coughed, then finished quickly—". . . a monster."

I thought of the inside of the scow as it had appeared in
my dreams—iron decks, slick with blood and quiet, thick
with gasoline fumes just as someone was striking a match.
The doctor continued, "A person of this sort is sane and,
in a sense, normal in most respects, but they like to cause
pain—death even—out of the merest bored interest. A
person like this will murder someone, will make them suffer, not out of some explosive rage, but out of some vague
interest stemming from boredom. This person kills other
humans the way you might eat one more doughnut, Mr.
Younger," and he paused, "even though you know you
shouldn't. This is my fear for Kevin Sands."

We got Kevin off on the assault charges. He had a plau-
sible self-defense claim, and we were lucky the victim
testified and Kevin never had to. There was no written
psychological report; the shrink stayed in Chicago and
never came near the courtroom. The lawyer's closing argument was a rambling flag-waver filled with non sequiturs

about the Constitution and the right to bear arms, even sharpened fishing knives, and the jury was unable to reach a verdict. After a lot of bluster and bluffing the DA finally dismissed. The fisherman with the cut face sat outside the courtroom after we all filed out. Kevin didn't acknowledge him sitting there. The fisherman shook his head and stared down at the floor. Kevin chuckled and blew him a kiss just as I pushed him into the waiting elevator.

The Sands boys had been the survivors in my most important murder case. Kevin Sands let me work on his cases even though he hated me, even though he knew I suspected him in the murder of his own parents, even though I had tried to befriend his younger brother, hoping that I might save him from becoming a monster, too. Kevin saw right through me but it didn't hurt my pride. I don't have much practice at doing good, so I hadn't developed that much of it—pride, that is. So little practice, in fact, that I had no words to reply to Patricia Ewers when she came to me again for help. In her eyes, just by talking to these boys, I was sleeping with the enemy. She might even consider me a suspect in the disappearance of her husband. I couldn't blame her.

I looked up at the trailer park where old cars lay near the ditches with their hoods open like dark mouths. Ravens picked apart the garbage bags piled near the firewood stacks. I suspected that Kevin was bullying or abusing Sean. I didn't even want to fully examine what I suspected, and as I stood there looking up at their trailer, I remember now that I felt a strange pain near my heart and some kind of pressure behind my eyes as if I might start crying. I wondered if, in the same way God could prevent things in the past, perhaps He could make someone experience future suffering. Maybe that was what I had been feeling ever since the Ewers verdict: suffering that sat inside me like a swallowed pin, inching closer and closer to my heart until finally I would not remember anything—the pin, the heart, or a fine, mild day before a storm came ashore.

When I looked out to sea the sun flared off a breaking wave, and when I looked back to the road the raven had tipped forward off the nearest corner of Kevin Sands's trailer house and landed right in front of me. The black bird cackled, then barked, and I shuddered as if ice had been dropped down my shirt.

Just then, Jane Marie pulled her old station wagon up next to me and honked the horn loud enough to save me from a bad case of the creeps.

"Hey, handsome, storm coming. I'd better give you a ride." She smiled, and I knew no matter how long I had to live, I was a lucky, lucky man.

Jane Marie was headed out the road to check out a potential garage sale. There were many new things I never thought we would need that were apparently necessities now.

"I saw in the paper they had baby clothes and a playpen. I know we don't need a playpen now, Cecil, but we will before long."

Blossom was in her carrier next to her mom, and I got into the backseat and warily fluffed up her downy hair.

"Can you drop me at Doggy's?" I said to Jane Marie while stroking our daughter's wildly flabby cheeks. Blossom raised her nose as she tried to get me in focus. She looked a little like Winston Churchill and I couldn't get over the feeling that she was going to snap at me.

"Sure," Jane Marie said, and she looked up in the rearview at me. "You okay, big guy?"

"I'm just thinking," I said, as we pulled away from the Sandses' trailer court and Blossom chewed on the callused tip of my finger. If I was struggling with my own attitudes, I knew for certain Jane Marie was tired of my life of crime.

George Doggy had bought a couple of adjacent lots at the end of a dead-end road near the boat repair yard. They must have cost a fortune, because both lots had nice waterfront houses. George lived in the smaller one nearer the bend in the cove, and he had converted the larger one into a bed-and-breakfast. Ever since Blossom had been born, Doggy had been offering to let me manage the B-and-B. He'd give us a place to live in a little cabin back behind the houses, and we could work cleaning and scheduling people in. I couldn't drive a car thanks to having had my license jerked during my drinking days, but I could certainly drive a boat to take visiting white men with thick necks out salmon fishing. I had passed on Doggy's offer repeatedly. Jane Marie made enough money to pay her expenses: the maintenance on her boat and the fuel to run it. She made enough money from her publications and selling photographs so that she could remain independent. She had never put pressure on me to earn more, even when we had been well short of money, and I loved her for that, but it had been dawning on me that we were running out of options on this island and maybe it was time for me to take Doggy up on his offer.

She stopped at the end of the road and pulled on the Subaru's hand brake. She turned and looked at me with concern. Jane Marie has black hair and sparkling dark eyes. She is truthfully prettier than any of the anorexic movie stars plying their trade today. If anything she most resembles Myrna Loy in the old Thin Man movies. Jane

Marie has the hooded eyes and crooked smile of the perfect drinking companion. She is so pretty that I often can't pay attention to what she's telling me.

"Cecil," she said softly, "have you looked at our checking account lately?"

"Huh?" I said. "No . . . no, I haven't."

Jane Marie leaned her forearms above Blossom's carrier so her face was right in front of mine. All I could see was her.

"You know what I like least about being a mother?"

"Is there a quiz on this later?"

"No," she snapped. "What I'm trying to tell you is, you know, I always liked our lives. I liked that you did what you loved, and not having a lot of money felt like freedom to me."

"But now?" I offered her the opening. I looked at her and felt that pin near my heart.

Jane Marie stroked the top of our daughter's head and looked into her tiny face. "Now, our life feels too much like poverty. I hate that feeling, Cecil. I do. But that's the truth."

I had two hundred-dollar bills from the herring fisherman's case that I still carried around in my pants just to feel flush walking around town. I fished them out of my pocket. Jane Marie bit her lip.

"Don't get me wrong, Cecil. You've been great. You're not drinking or whatever." She leaned over the seat and kissed me. I could taste waxy lip balm and the coffee on her tongue. "But maybe it's time for something else, something that pays a little better."

I handed her a hundred-dollar bill and she crumpled it in her hand. Then she shoved it back at me.

"Forget it, Cecil. I can't do this. I'm not going to start down this road. You've done enough."

"Janey, I haven't done jack shit. You do everything."

She kissed me again, harder this time so I felt the cat-like roughness of her tongue. "You're here. You quit drinking. You walk with me and swim with me. That's enough, Cecil. Heck, if I could pay you to be my companion I would."

Blossom squawked, and I opened the car door.

"Male escort. That might pay better than private eye work," I said and frizzed Blossom's hair one more time and she bobbled her head around accusingly.

Jane Marie rolled her eyes at me and locked the car door. The baby made some little barking sound. I swear that strange little girl was growling at me.

"Go cut some firewood." Jane Marie smiled, then blew me a kiss.

After she released the brake she called out through the window, "Hey, I almost forgot. Patricia Ewers called for you, must have been just after you left. There was a message on the machine. She sounded sad. Said she was going to make the calls herself and that she was sorry for walking out on you."

I waved as if it didn't matter. Truthfully, I didn't want to think about murder so soon after kissing this beautiful woman.

"She's back in town," I told Jane Marie. "She got mad I couldn't do something right away. It will be all right. I'll talk to her later," I said, as I jammed the crumpled hundred-dollar bill back into my pants pocket. I turned and saw George Doggy coming down the steps of his house putting on his leather work gloves.

"Bye, sweetie. Call me if you need a ride." Then she was

gone. The wheels of the station wagon kicked up a few fallen alder leaves. The weather was a swirl of possibilities, but all of them called for change.

So here is the question I was posing to myself as I got out of the car: How much of this did I really need to carry with me during the day? In a story, you expect that every single person will be part of the plot, but how does that happen? If your life is a story, a story you revise over and over again in your memory, how do you choose the themes? How do you choose the people? Richard Ewers was missing but Bob Rose was surfing Sandy Beach by now. Jude and Rachel were most likely taking their tourist mother for coffee. Gary was fabricating a part in his machine shop. Paul deLay was probably playing the blues in Portland, Oregon. And I had made it to work with the help of a beautiful woman in the company of her cranky and unexpected baby, Kevin Sands's parents were dead. George Doggy had lived a long and productive life. And all of these people were part of my story this morning. But what to make of that? Every investigation, whether a murder or a shoplifting, begins with a swirl of unimportant facts. The trick is not to throw any of them away too soon.

I kept going back to that raven on the roof of the Sandses' trailer. I couldn't shake the feeling that God was reaching back from the future and showing me a clue, that the raven was telling me, "Right now! Pay attention. Don't throw this one away." Of course, it could all have been a trick of memory, or maybe this shudder I felt was just the storm pushing in, foam-flecked and howling, indifferent to any story other than its own.

OTHER TITLES IN THE SOHO CRIME SERIES

Leighton Gage
(Brazil)
Blood of the Wicked
Buried Strangers
Dying Gasp
Every Bitter Thing
A Vine in the Blood
Perfect Hatred
The Ways of Evil Men

Michael Genelin
(Slovakia)
Siren of the Waters
Dark Dreams
The Magician's Accomplice
Requiem for a Gypsy

Timothy Hallinan
(Thailand)
The Fear Artist
For the Dead
The Hot Countries
Fools' River

(Los Angeles)
Crashed
Little Elvises
The Fame Thief
Herbie's Game
King Maybe
Fields Where They Lay

Karo Hämäläinen
(Finland)
Cruel Is the Night

Mette Ivie Harrison
(Mormon Utah)
The Bishop's Wife
His Right Hand
For Time and All Eternities

Mick Herron
(England)
Down Cemetery Road
The Last Voice You Hear
Reconstruction
Smoke and Whispers
Why We Die
Slow Horses
Dead Lions

Mick Herron cont.
Nobody Walks
Real Tigers
Spook Street
This Is What Happened
London Rules

**Lene Kaaberbøl &
Agnete Friis**
(Denmark)
The Boy in the Suitcase
Invisible Murder
Death of a Nightingale
The Considerate Killer

Heda Margolius Kovály
(1950s Prague)
Innocence

Martin Limón
(South Korea)
Jade Lady Burning
Slicky Boys
Buddha's Money
The Door to Bitterness
The Wandering Ghost
G.I. Bones
Mr. Kill
The Joy Brigade
Nightmare Range
The Iron Sickle
The Ville Rat
Ping-Pong Heart
The Nine-Tailed Fox

Ed Lin
(Taiwan)
Ghost Month
Incensed

Peter Lovesey
(England)
The Circle
The Headhunters
False Inspector Dew
Rough Cider
On the Edge
The Reaper

(Bath, England)
The Last Detective

Peter Lovesey cont.
Diamond Solitaire
The Summons
Bloodhounds
Upon a Dark Night
The Vault
Diamond Dust
The House Sitter
The Secret Hangman
Skeleton Hill
Stagestruck
Cop to Corpse
The Tooth Tattoo
The Stone Wife
*Down Among
the Dead Men*
Another One Goes Tonight
Beau Death

(London, England)
Wobble to Death
*The Detective Wore
Silk Drawers*
Abracadaver
Mad Hatter's Holiday
The Tick of Death
A Case of Spirits
Swing, Swing Together
Waxwork

Jassy Mackenzie
(South Africa)
Random Violence
Stolen Lives
The Fallen
Pale Horses
Bad Seeds

Sujata Massey
(1920s Bombay)
*The Widows of
Malabar Hill*

Francine Mathews
(Nantucket)
Death in the Off-Season
Death in Rough Water
Death in a Mood Indigo
Death in a Cold Hard Light
Death on Nantucket

Seichō Matsumoto
(Japan)
*Inspector Imanishi
Investigates*

Magdalen Nabb
(Italy)
*Death of an Englishman
Death of a Dutchman
Death in Springtime
Death in Autumn
The Marshal and
the Murderer
The Marshal and
the Madwoman
The Marshal's Own Case
The Marshal Makes
His Report
The Marshal
at the Villa Torrini
Property of Blood
Some Bitter Taste
The Innocent
Vita Nuova
The Monster of Florence*

Fuminori Nakamura
(Japan)
*The Thief
Evil and the Mask
Last Winter, We Parted
The Kingdom
The Boy in the Earth
Cult X*

Stuart Neville
(Northern Ireland)
*The Ghosts of Belfast
Collusion
Stolen Souls
The Final Silence
Those We Left Behind
So Say the Fallen*

(Dublin)
Ratlines

Rebecca Pawel
(1930s Spain)
*Death of a Nationalist
Law of Return
The Watcher in the Pine
The Summer Snow*

Kwei Quartey
(Ghana)
*Murder at Cape
Three Points
Gold of Our Fathers
Death by His Grace*

Qiu Xiaolong
(China)
*Death of a Red Heroine
A Loyal Character Dancer
When Red Is Black*

John Straley
(Sitka, Alaska)

*The Woman Who Married
a Bear
The Curious Eat Themselves
The Music of What Happens
Death and the Language of
Happiness
The Angels Will Not Care
Cold Water Burning
Baby's First Felony*

(Cold Storage, Alaska)
*The Big Both Ways
Cold Storage, Alaska*

Akimitsu Takagi
(Japan)
*The Tattoo Murder Case
Honeymoon to Nowhere
The Informer*

Helene Tursten
(Sweden)
*Detective Inspector Huss
The Torso
The Glass Devil
Night Rounds*

Helene Tursten cont.
*The Golden Calf
The Fire Dance
The Beige Man
The Treacherous Net
Who Watcheth
Protected by the Shadows*

**Janwillem van de
Wetering**
(Holland)
*Outsider in Amsterdam
Tumbleweed
The Corpse on the Dike
Death of a Hawker
The Japanese Corpse
The Blond Baboon
The Maine Massacre
The Mind-Murders
The Streetbird
The Rattle-Rat
Hard Rain
Just a Corpse at Twilight
Hollow-Eyed Angel
The Perfidious Parrot
The Sergeant's Cat:
Collected Stories*

Timothy Williams
(Guadeloupe)
*Another Sun
The Honest Folk
of Guadeloupe*

(Italy)
*Converging Parallels
The Puppeteer
Persona Non Grata
Black August
Big Italy
The Second Day
of the Renaissance*

Jacqueline Winspear
(1920s England)
*Maisie Dobbs
Birds of a Feather*